The Priest's Son

by Nicky Moxey

ISBN-13: 978-1-9997832-4-2

Nicky Moxey

To Wimer the Chaplain;
on whose oak stump I still go and lean
when I need to talk a problem out
with a good listener.

Chapter 1

PARLES-TU ANGLAIS?

The knot of wood was helping. Pretending it was an eye and having a staring contest with it made him feel less sick, and he'd discovered that the sticking-out splinter, exactly where the inner corner of the eye would be, was strong and sharp. The back of his hand was covered with small scars and fresh spots of blood where he'd hit it against the knot, over and over again; it seemed to help with the headache, a little.

The waggon jerked to a halt, driving a spike of pure white pain through Jean's head. He tried to lift himself to an elbow, to see where they were, just as the guard leaned over him, the fusty smell of unwashed wool adding to his nausea. The guard called over to the monk leaning on the open gate, first in French, then in this horrid English that made his head hurt even more,

"Delivery for Father Wimer?"

Jean struggled to sit up at the name, and frowned at the insult – he was not a package, he was a boy! He forced some of the sick pain away – were they here? It would be a miracle, after the weeks on the road, half of them with this awful headache getting worse and worse.

The monk gestured towards the whitewashed

buildings at the foot of the hill. It must be! For once he scarcely noticed the pain, as the guard clicked his tongue at the horses and the waggon moved on.

He looked ahead, desperate to catch a glimpse of this Wimer and try to work out how best to serve him, as his father had told him he must do. Again, the thought of his father made the tears rise, and he knuckled them away hard. He had to find a way to be useful, and showing up blubbing his eyes out wouldn't do at all.

He glared down at the priory, to take his mind off home. It was set like a pearl in a crescent of bright green grass, close-cropped by dots of white sheep, darker greens and browns from the woodland circling the meadow setting it all off in the early spring sunshine. The first building was clearly the church, only three bays long. The buildings behind, one tall and made of flint but most low and wooden, must be the monks' quarters and cloisters. Up the slope to the left might be the stables, with more roofs visible further up the path.

He had spent so long imagining this moment, and now he was nearly here. He shivered and tried to be still. His headache was coming back in waves.

They pulled up outside the church door and the guard asked for Wimer again.

Seeing two monks walking towards them from the depths of the church, Jean slid from the waggon seat and down, to greet his benefactor standing.

The jolt as his feet hit the ground made the pain in his head blossom. He grabbed at the waggon as his sight drew in to a tight, piercingly bright point. The pain was now a sound, ringing to drown out all earthly noises. His knees seemed to melt under him, and rough wood scraped along his arm as his grip gave way. He was granted a single instant of clear vision, of an elderly man in a monk's dark-brown habit reaching for him as the world tilted slowly sideways, then nothingness.

***

Some unmeasurable time later he opened his eyes to find blessed darkness. Even that small movement of his eyelids hurt, so he closed them again. The next time his eyes opened, it was daytime, and the elderly monk was leaning over him. Blink, and dark. Blink, light. Jean became mildly amused with the game, with that part of his mind which was aware. Light, dark. Once there was movement as someone carried him somewhere else. Each step pulled a small puff of pain from him, eyes firmly shut.

The new place brought more sensations. Once, he thought his mother smoothed his forehead, but when he opened his eyes a stranger looked back, and the sharp pang of that repeated loss forced him under again. Once he dreamed of his father's leave-taking, and the relived abandonment shocked him awake for a heartbeat or two before shame-filled sleep reclaimed him. Once, the face of an angel, blond and elfin, moved past.

It was this angel who persisted, the day when two eye-blinks brought the same image. Unused muscles tried to smile – which had the wrong effect; the vision called something and backed away. His eyes closed against his will, and when they opened again, she had gone.

The next time felt like a proper awakening. A ray of sunshine lit his blanket, falling through the smoke hole in the roof. It must be late – for a second, he thought to leap out of bed, before Father saw his laziness and disapproved. The tensing of muscles brought his headache banging back, as well as the memory of Father riding away to join the Crusade. He turned his face to the wall and slept again.

The strange woman was waiting for him when he opened his eyes again. She smiled and helped him to sit up a little so he could sip some broth. It smelled amazing... She said something to him, in English – then again in French! He was so surprised that some of the liquid went down the wrong way, and then by the time they'd finished dealing with his coughing and spluttering, he was too tired to talk – but he drifted back to sleep feeling much less alone.

Jean was sitting up in bed, idly listening to Goda's chatter, and gently carding some wool for her. She was using English. They'd worked out that her French was even worse than his English. When they were trying to say something in particular they got by in a mix of the two languages, with some arm-waving; but if she was just talking to him for company, she did it in English. Some of it was beginning to make a bit of sense, he thought, drowsily wondering if he had time for a nap before the midday meal. There were some very tempting smells wafting from the cook-pot... He rolled combs and wool away into their cloth and was sliding back under the blanket when someone knocked. A monk came straight in without waiting for an answer. Goda dropped her broom and curtseyed, then ran over and hugged him!

"My Lord! - " and the rest was in English, incomprehensible.

Jean threw off the blanket and tried to stand and make his own bow, to show respect to Goda's guest. He was stupidly wobbly, still, and it ended with the monk steadying him, one hand firmly gripping his upper arm.

"Whoa, lad – easy! You look about as steady on your feet as a newborn lamb! Can you stand?"

Goda said something, anxiously. It wasn't until she spoke that Jean realised – grace a Dieu! - that the monk had been speaking French. He opened his mouth then closed it again. If he said anything, he would cry. It had been so hard, trying to understand what was happening, and what people were saying to him. He swallowed hard and nodded instead. The monk lifted one eyebrow at him and eased him down anyway.

"Well, if you don't mind, I think I would like to sit down for a while. Can I share your pallet? Thank you. Here, you tuck this around you, no point in getting a chill..." and before Jean knew what was happening, he had been propped up in the corner, wrapped in the blanket, with the monk sitting cross-legged next to him. The man asked Goda for some tea, and she bustled off to fetch it.

"So, young man – I'm glad you've decided to stay in the land of the living! I wasn't looking forward to telling your father that the Lord had taken you before we'd got a chance to know each other. Welcome to Dodnash Priory! I'm Wimer. Your grandfather and I went to school together, when we were boys. About your age, in fact. I feel I have met you already, your grandfather often used to include news of you when we wrote to each other."

This was Wimer! Jean felt like he'd known this man forever. Certainly he'd been part of the stories his grandfather used to tell him before he died, of his time in England – but even the monk's face looked familiar. He'd seen that finely-drawn intelligence before, one eyebrow always ready to quirk upwards in sardonic humour. Now the face was lit with a broad, welcoming smile; but he'd seen it frowning, and dark. Of course! He was the monk who had been there so often when he opened his eyes! He remembered his manners.

"My Lord, I am honoured to meet you. My grandfather used to tell me so much about you!"

The smile turned into a grin.

"Hah! You must tell me his tales sometime, and I'll tell you which of them are true! I have some stories of my own! But, much as I loved your grandfather, your appearance was, shall we say, unlooked for. Do you know the details of the letter your father sent with you?"

The face was now frowning slightly, not in anger, Jean thought, but in concern.

"No, my Lord, only that he was going to ask you to look after me until he got back from the Crusades." he looked down and away. One bare foot sticking out of the blanket caught his attention.

"Since Maman and the baby died, that's all he's talked about."

A warm hand covered the foot.

"Well, you have a place with us, for as long as he's away. We'll get you settled at the Priory, and you can start school there. We have one or two other boys studying with us too."

Jean wrinkled his nose at the thought of school, and it turned into a yawn. Wimer chuckled.

"You curl up and get some sleep. Nothing like it, as a healer." He leaned over and marked Jean's forehead with the sign of a cross, then rose and went over to where Goda was straining tea. Jean could feel the mark as he drifted off, strange but comforting.

***

He moved politely to one side to let his elders out of church first. Everyone was busy chatting to one another, and in no hurry to go out into the rain; the knots of people kept forming and reforming in different groups, none of them very aware of a skinny boy. He got fed up with being squeezed against the wall and slid up towards the altar end where there was a little more space.

Father Wimer was still in his alb but had taken off his stole. As Jean watched, he knelt with it in his hands to pray; Jean turned round to give him some privacy.

He knew no-one at all in the crowd, which was at last beginning to move through the doors. One or two of the boys from school had been to the service with their parents, but they'd all gone now. He leaned against the wall, its coolness matching his mood, and sighed. It was going to be such a long, boring day, with no-one to talk to. The monks would all be doing whatever they did in the afternoons, when he was usually busy with chores; but on a Sunday, there was nothing for him to do, and no-one to do it with. He shut his eyes and tried not to think about endless sunny days in France, full of laughter and mock-fights with the boys from the village, the whole pack of them tumbling from one game to the next with not a care in the world.

The hand on his shoulder came as a shock. He turned to Wimer - now back in his black habit, alb and stole folded over one arm - who smiled at him.

"How are you doing, lad? Rainy Sundays can be a bit quiet around here... Do you have any plans for your free time?"

Jean shook his head, eyes down to hide his sadness. The last parishioner turned and waved farewell at Wimer, who lifted the arm with the alb in response.

"Excellent! I confess to hoping that you'd say that - I have a particular task laid on me this afternoon that will go much quicker with two pairs of hands, would you help?"

Jean nodded dumbly. *Anything would be better than sitting watching the rain...*

The Chapter House was a hive of industry when he popped his head around the door. Most of the monks were there, it seemed. Wimer saw him and waved, and he picked his way towards him, careful not to knock into the writing tables set up by the door to get the best light. Brother Lawrence was concentrating hard and barely glanced at him as he squeezed by, but Father Adam, who was just starting to paint something, looked up and smiled at him, as did many of the monks. There was a low buzz of conversation, making the room feel very cozy. He worked his way around people bent over mending, avoided Brother Michael's wildly turning spindle, rescued a ball of yarn that had got away from an elderly monk he didn't know, and finally reached Wimer's corner.

Wimer sat cross-legged on a mat with a most curious set of objects in front of him, stirring a pot full of liquid. He grinned up at Jean and patted the mat beside him.

"Welcome, lad - we're going to be doing something magical today, in the name of the Lord; are you ready?"

Jean sat down and stared at the heaps of strange things. There were little brown balls the size of his thumbnail, bright green crystals, a large jar of water, some flasks, and a bowl... he looked at Wimer, who laughed out loud at his expression. He leaned down and whispered,

"Don't tell anyone, but this is one of my favourite jobs! We're going to be making ink."

He sat up again and pointed at the brown balls.

"Any idea what these are? No? They're oak galls. We'll mix them with some of this green stuff and it'll make the blackest of black inks!" He laughed at Jean's expression.

Jean crossed his arms and hunched his shoulders. *He's playing a joke on me!*

Wimer smiled at him.

"No, truly, lad - you'll see! Here, your first job is to crush this down to powder. I've already been soaking some oak galls, and I'll cut some more up and start a new jar-full whilst you're doing that."

He handed Jean a pestle and mortar and sprinkled in a few of the green crystals. Jean moved the pestle round and round. It didn't seem to be doing much… then he got the hang of it and bashed it up and down. He was a bit overenthusiastic, and a little shower of the crystals escaped and had to be picked up one by one. Soon he had a fine, even powder. Wimer looked over.

"Yes, that's it - good job! Now, let's fasten some cloth over this bowl, loosely, so we can get rid of the solids … Here, pour this in, slowly."

He unstoppered a flask and handed it to Jean. "Slowly, mind, or it'll spill everywhere!"

The liquid in the flask was thick and brown, with bits of oak gall floating in it. Jean did the best he could, but there was a little ring of spillage around the bowl by the time he'd finished. Wimer took the cloth off the bowl and used it to wipe up the mess.

"Good boy! Now, for the magic. Are you ready? Take a big pinch of the green powder - that's it - and sprinkle it in the bowl. Here's a stick, stir like mad!"

The stuff in the bowl turned from thin mud to darkest black ink right in front of his eyes! He looked up at Wimer, who was grinning like mad, and matched his grin.

"That is magic!"

"Yes, isn't it fun, thank the Lord for pleasures such as these! One last step;" and Wimer took a little horn-tip full of a sweet-smelling gum and handed it to him. "Sprinkle another pinch of this in and stir again well; careful, it'll try and clump. This is gum arabic, it keeps the ink from splitting. Then we can strain it again into a clean flask, to make sure it's smooth as can be."

This time the straining went without incident. Wimer picked up the flask, ground its stopper in firmly, and handed it back.

"There we are; one flask of best oak gall ink, that'll sink into the parchment and stay dark forever; none of your nasty shoddy lamp-black stuff, that wipes off as soon as look at you. Here, go and give it to Brother Lawrence."

Jean carefully carried the flask through the obstacle course of monks putting their activities away in readiness for the evening meal. He reached Brother Lawrence unscathed and held out the ink.

"Excuse me, Brother - Father Wimer said that you need this."

Lawrence looked up from sanding his parchment and took it from him.

"Thank you, Jean, I do indeed. I saw you learning how to make it - it's good to know that you have skills the Priory needs. Now go and wash your hands."

Wow, That's got to be the nicest thing he's said to me! And I think I could make it again, on my own. His tummy rumbled, and he ran off to do as he was bid, humming to himself.

***

Edeva was in her favourite place in the whole world, and feeling slightly guilty about it. Now she was eleven, she was nearly of marriageable age, and young ladies who wished to marry well should not be climbing trees. Should not be *caught* climbing trees, she amended the thought, and grinned. The sunlight warmed her back, and she stretched upwards like a cat, leaning her chest against the branch in front of her. Everything was still winter-dun, but in the sunshine the dry grasses glowed, and the bushes beneath her were full of bird noise; the year had turned. She loved being tucked up here, on the old pine at the edge of the heath, hidden from view by the fragrant greenery but with the whole open expanse at her feet.

Ah, bother, there were those noisy boys from the Priory! She crossed her arms on the branch and waited for them to go away and give her back her uninterrupted view. No trees to climb in Orford, and far more chores - this visit to see Father Wimer was nearly over, they were leaving tomorrow and those horrid boys were spoiling her last day – GO AWAY! She wished them.

Instead, they left the path, and hunkered down behind a large gorse bush. They would be hidden if anyone came past. What were they doing? It must be something wrong. From her hide in the tree, she couldn't quite see properly.

Nasty old Maurice from Dodnash was in charge, as usual; he was waving his arms, clearly telling them what to do. The skinny new French boy, the one who had been so ill, who Grandmama had looked after, wasn't doing what he was told. Maurice gave him a huge push and knocked him over. The boy leapt up and thumped Maurice hard. Edeva cheered, very quietly. Maurice was a dreadful bully. He needed someone to stand up to him. The French boy might get pounded into potage though, he was much smaller.

They were fighting for real now. Maurice was swinging huge punches, but the other boy was ducking and weaving – all of the blows looked like they were missing. Good thing, thought Edeva, any of them might kill him… Suddenly, Maurice was on his backside, clutching his mouth. The skinny boy waited for a heartbeat or two, to see if he was going to get up, then spat on the ground and walked off.

Edeva watched him until he was out of sight. He looked very alone.

***

Jean tried to stretch a bit taller. He was half-running on tiptoes anyway, trying to keep the pain in his ear to a minimum. It wasn't working – the Prior was marching along, holding Jean, and Maurice beside him, out in front, trotting like ill-matched horses. Jean had no idea where they were going. He couldn't see, anyway, his head was turned to the side, to keep his earlobe pointed in the direction the Prior was heading. He just wished they'd get there, so the Prior would let go…

"Ah! There he is!" the Prior muttered, and turned his victims towards the stream.

Jean's stomach began to flutter. He had assumed that the Prior was dragging them off to some sort of punishment – but what kind of disciplinarian would be by the stream? The worry crystallised when the Prior bellowed:

"Wimer! Come here, I need you!"

Now Jean wished they'd never get there. He was beginning to like his father's old friend very much and wanted to keep Wimer's opinion of him high. It might be too late for that, though…

At last, the Prior stopped, and released his victims. Jean rubbed his ear. Maurice did the same, whilst glaring at Jean – he still had crusted blood in a line down his jaw. Wimer climbed up the stream bank. He looked like he'd been clearing shrub. His habit was tucked into his belt, so his lower legs were bare, and dripping; he had a dusty twig caught in his hair; and a little alarmingly, he was carrying a bill hook on a long pole, with a huge sharpened blade.

As he stood up and took in the group, one eyebrow shot up. He absent-mindedly swiped a hand over his head, dislodging the twig, put the bill hook down, and bowed.

"Yes, Father Prior?"

Jean tried to wake his mind up, so he could understand the wretched English. He got the first bit;

"Both these young idiots are your responsibility. Sort them out, or I will ban them from the Priory."

Wimer was clearly asking for details, but Jean had stopped listening. Besides, he knew what the Prior was going to say. What did he mean, both of them were Wimer's responsibility? And Oh! What would he do if the Prior did throw him out? He'd let his father down. He hated this stupid country, with its grating language, and ugly, bullying pigs like this Maurice. But his father... He had another thought. He had promised his mother on her deathbed that he would try to control his temper – and then, almost the first time he had been tested, he had lashed out. He had failed her too...

The Prior finished his speech by slapping both boys on the side of the head and walking off. The blow was so unexpected that it brought the tears to Jean's eyes. He turned his head and tried to blink them away.

Wimer's finger on his jaw brought his gaze back.

"Tell me what happened, please, Jean?"

"'Ee calls me sheet for brains, so I heet heem." Jean hung his head and waited for the axe to fall. Perhaps he could work his way back to Normandy on a ship, and on to home? But he didn't have a home there any more, not until Papa returned, the estate manager would just pack him off somewhere else...

The finger lifted his head again. Wimer was looking puzzled. He switched to French:

"When did you hit him? That blood is dry."

They both turned and looked at Maurice. He looked defensive.

"What?"

"We were on the heath." Jean explained. "We were going to play dice – I think Stupid there -" Wimer looked sideways at him; Jean sighed "- Maurice – wanted me to be the look-out, but I didn't want to. So he called me that rude name, we had a fight and I hit him, then walked away."

"Dice, eh? I bet the Prior didn't know that. But he said you were fighting in the cloister, that's why he's so upset?"

"Ah. When I got back, I went to sit on that bit of cloister wall where it's always sunny. Maurice arrived later, swore at me and said I should go back where I came from, and tried to kick me. I hooked his foot and dumped him on the floor. He bellowed like a castrated calf – which of course brought everyone running."

"Hmmm. I did something similar to a bully once." Jean blinked. Had Wimer just winked at him? The monk turned to Maurice, raised both eyebrows as high as they would go, and said

"Dice?"

Maurice, whose scowl had been darkening as they spoke, blushed. He opened his mouth, but Wimer went on – in English, so Jean stopped listening. Did that wink mean that Wimer could sort everything out? He realised that Wimer had said something to him.

"Pardon?"

Wimer frowned at him and said in English;

"Did you understand what I just said?"

Jean shook his head.

Wimer's frown deepened. He went on in French:

"I have been saying to Maurice that we will all go to his father's house. He can explain to him why he was teaching other boys to gamble; that alone might get him expelled from the Priory school if he was caught. You can apologise to William for maiming his eldest son."

Jean hung his head again. Butterflies were stirring in his stomach.

Wimer hadn't finished. He turned to Maurice, and asked, in French:

"How good is your French, boy?"

Maurice mangled an answer.

"I thought so. We will add a layer of punishment that might actually be useful. Jean, you may not speak to any child except Maurice for a week, and you must do so in English. He may only speak to you, and in French. You and I will work on your English together."

Wimer turned and said the same thing to Maurice in English. He and Jean glowered at each other. It was going to be a long week.

Chapter 2

MEET THE FAMILY

It began straight away. Wimer told Maurice to wash his face in the stream, in French; then pointed and mimed it for him when he didn't understand. When he was finished, they walked in single file along the valley path, so quietly that they could hear Cook shouting at someone in the kitchen from two fields away. When Jean asked where they were going, Wimer said "In English!", and he fell silent again. They turned up the Great Way when they reached it and walked uphill for a bit, then went east into the woods at a narrow path guarded by an enormous oak tree. Wimer patted it as he passed. The path soon led to a large clearing, with a good-sized house at the far end.

Wimer knocked on the door and waited. A little girl came to the doorway and smiled as soon as she saw Wimer. A young boy peeked from behind her, then wriggled past;

"Uncle! Pick me up!"

Jean stared at him in amazement. Was Wimer really the boy's uncle? Wimer tossed him in the air, caught him, and said something to him. He ran off along the clearing, shouting "Dad! Dad! Dad!"

Seeing Jean's look, Wimer smiled and explained,

"These are my grandniece and nephews. Their father is my nephew William; his brother, Hervey, has children too. I'm blessed with shared children, you among them! Ah, here he comes."

Jean would have known he was Maurice's father without being told. They had the same blocky, powerful build, sandy hair, and deep-set eyes. William arrived playing horsey with the boy on his back and set him down laughing.

"Uncle! Good to see you." He looked down at Maurice's face. It was beginning to look quite impressive, as his lip got puffier and angrier and the bruise started to show. He was dribbling a bit, too. William's laughter switched to a scowl, which made him look even more like his son.

"God's eye, boy – who hit you?"

Maurice waved at Jean and mumbled, "him…"

Wimer spoke quickly.

"This is the grandson of a friend. His name is Jean – he is something of an adopted son of mine, at least for the moment."

Adopted son! What a lovely thing to say! Jean caught a strange look on William's face. It might have been panic? It changed back to a scowl, as William frowned at Jean and said something incomprehensible.

"He don't speak English, Dad." Maurice wiped drool from his lip.

William turned the corners of his mouth up into what was probably meant to be a smile. His eyes were cold, and Jean glanced over his shoulder instinctively to look for a way out. William went on, in passable French;

"So, boy – was it a fair fight?" he made a show of looking Jean up and down. "Doesn't look like you've got the muscles for it. Still, you've managed to make your mark – he's lost a tooth, I see."

Jean could think of nothing to say. He kicked at the dirt a little and did what Wimer had told him to do; apologise.

"Sorry, Sir." He didn't sound all that apologetic, even to himself.

William snorted and opened his mouth to reply. Wimer intervened.

"I've discussed the merits of fighting with them both. You might want to ask Maurice here what they were doing when the fight broke out; the answer may surprise you."

William turned to glare at his son, beefy arms folded over his chest. "Well?"

Maurice sucked in air and rattled off; "We was just playing. There were four or five of us."

William and Wimer spoke together. "Playing at what?" "Tell the truth, boy!"

Jean glanced at Maurice. He was biting his little fingernail, hand clenched so tightly that the freckles stood out like flecks of mud. He puffed out a breath. All the fight seemed to go out of him with it.

"We were playing at dice," He told his shoe.

William grabbed him by the shirt and pulled him close to his face.

"You stupid little shit! Don't you realise that you could be thrown out of school for that? I'm paying good money for you to be taught how to read and figure!" He half pushed, half threw Maurice towards the house. "Get inside. I'll see to you shortly."

Wimer spoke. "I'm pretty sure the Prior doesn't know what they were up to, Nephew - but it does seem like it was Maurice's idea. You should be able to nip it in the bud. Right, well, we'll leave you to it; come along, Jean."

They had hardly got out of the clearing before the sound of blows started. Jean winced in sympathy with each one.

***

Maurice was still walking a little stiffly the next morning, which was a special service for St Ethelbert's feast day. Jean kept a wary eye on him as everyone milled around waiting for the doors of the church to open, staying at the opposite edge of the crowd - but William surprised him. He came from behind and gripped Jean's shoulder, pulling him round, then leant forward until their faces were level, a finger jabbing at him.

"Do you recall what the Holy Bible says about injury, boy? A tooth for a tooth?"

Jean looked into those unsmiling eyes and acted before his rising fear paralysed him. He bit William's thick finger as hard as he could, then twisted out of his grip as it lifted. William's jeer followed him as he sprinted away.

"Stay off my land, you vicious little runt, or I'll take my due from your mouth, and your hide!"

He put his head down and ran as fast as his legs

would go up the path to the fish ponds. He stopped, out of breath, beside the fish kitchen and looked around. No-one was in sight. The Priory bell wasn't ringing any more, so he was late for service - he might as well stay here for a bit... He went round the opposite side of the building from the path and settled back against the warm wood, closing his eyes against the sun's glare.

He woke with a start - someone was whistling, and coming nearer! He leaped to his feet in case it was William looking for him and sprinted round the corner to get away - and bounced off the generous bulk of the cook.

"Whoa there, lad - are you all right?"

Jean nodded and tried to move around him. The cook stepped to the left to let him past as Jean moved to the right, and they nearly bumped into each other again. Jean went to the left - the cook went to the right - and they both burst out laughing. The cook held his arms up and bowed low.

"Would you care to dance, lad? Or would you rather sit here in the last of the sun and share this pasty and jug of cider I just happen to have with me?"

So Jean found himself comfortably ensconced on the sheltered side of the fish kitchen again, clutching half a hot pasty, with the jug between him and the cook. They munched away in happy silence. Finally Cook burped, had a last swig of cider, and wiped his mouth with the back of his hand.

"Ah! That was good, even if I do say so myself, as shouldn't... ARE you all right, lad? You looked like you were running from the devil himself when we met. Who were you afraid I might be?"

Jean blurted "William" without stopping to think.

"William of Dodnash? Yes, a nasty piece of work, that one. A right thug - and clever with it, what's worse; how did a lad like you get on his wrong side?"

So Jean told him the whole story - stumbling a little over some of the words, but able to get the gist of it over. When he had finished, Cook thumped him on the arm companionably.

"Well, if you need a bolt-hole, he don't come into my kitchen. He and I had words ourselves a few years back, aye and a few blows too, and he don't get under my hair no more. Course, I might put you to chopping swede or the like, but you'd be safe with me - deal?"

Jean smiled and nodded vigorously. Cook smiled back, levered himself to his feet, and held out a hand to help Jean up.

"Come on then, I'll walk you back. And maybe I'll tell you how I got the better of Master William on the way."

***

Jean slid along the bridge railing a bit, to hunt out a solid patch of shade. Lovely though it was to have the sun warming his skin, the glare was hurting his eyes. The dappled shade by the side of the Great Way wasn't helping; the breeze was sending ripples of dark and light shadows over his face. He was getting that buzzy feeling that meant he was going to get sick again. It seemed to be a regular thing – every few weeks, he'd be hit by the headaches from Hell for a few days. The infirmary walls were old friends...

He wished Goda would hurry up. She should have been here ages ago! A thought occurred to him – why was he sent to welcome her, and not one of the other boys? He must be looking sick, as well as feeling it. Great. Why were the monks bothering with him, when he wasn't well enough to DO anything? He was fed up with being sent to the cloisters with some Latin verbs to learn, when everyone else was out working. Just a useless...

The sound of a covered waggon rattling over the brow of the hill brought him out of his fugue. The driver leapt to his feet and hauled on the brake. A half-familiar face looked through the curtain and nimbly climbed onto the bench to take the reins. Between them, the old lady and the driver wrestled the horses down the steep path, and brought them to a halt at the bridge, ready for the turn up to the Priory.

Jean stood up and said,

"Mistress Goda! Father Wimer bids you welcome, and says that he has arranged for you to have use of the house at Flatford Mill whilst you are here. He suggests you carry on along the main road to it and get settled, then visit him after prayers."

He would have bowed, but it didn't feel safe.

"Why, young Jean! How are you doing? My, you've grown!"

She called back into the waggon, "Edeva! Come and see who's here!"

"I'm well, Mistress." Jean lied. Goda handed the reins to the driver and climbed carefully down. She reached to cup his jaw in her hand and peered at him closely.

"You don't look well. Come into the light…"

Jean only got a glimpse of the delicate, lovely figure that peeked out through the curtain – his jaw was still firmly in Goda's grasp – but then she spoke, and he was sure.

"Still skinny as a beanpole, then!"

It was his angel! He thought he'd dreamed her! Goda was saying something to him. She gave his head a little shake, and he nearly swooned.

"Yes, I see you are. Are the headaches worse at night?"

He nodded.

"And go away, then come back weeks later?"

He nodded again.

She let go and nodded herself. He risked a glance – his angel had gone.

"Yes, I'm afraid you have the ague. It may keep coming back for years – but at least you didn't die of it; many do. You come to my lodgings tonight, I'll give you a potion that will ease the pain and let you sleep. In the meantime, you stay out of the sun, all right?"

She gave him a last pat on the cheek and climbed back up to the driver's bench. He lifted the reins and clicked the horses into a start. Jean watched until they were entirely out of sight, but no fair face looked out of the back.

***

Jean followed his healer's orders and climbed up the wooded slope until he came to a shady clearing. It had a splendid view, of part of the road and the field beyond, and a wide expanse of blue sky. He lay on his back, hands behind his head, and watched the clouds for a while. He might almost be back in France, before his world had changed forever... He shut his eyes and relaxed into the memory.

Something woke him. He sat up, feeling better for the rest, and tried to pinpoint it. The road was quiet, but someone had been busy in the field; a couple of lines of dark-brown furrows broke the pale stubble. They were a bit wobbly, and Jean spared a thought for the oxen. It must be hard for them, working on the steep slope.

They came in to view, and Jean frowned. They were quite young – which was not a problem in itself; but where was the man walking beside them, helping them to stay on line and pulling together? Surely the ploughman wasn't trying to guide them from his place at the plough? An untested pair of oxen could get into all kinds of trouble without a firm hand at their head.

Almost as he finished the thought, the up-slope ox went to one knee, banging against its companion on the way down. It skittered sideways, and there was a cry of pain from the man just out of view. Jean's imagination filled in an image of the plough being jerked out of the furrow, smashing into flesh.

He was on his feet and running before he realised he was going to help. He got to the bottom of the hill and deliberately slowed to a walk, controlling his breathing. By the time he got to the oxen he was projecting calmness and order. The downslope beast was still panicking, trying to wrench its way out of the yoke. Jean took its head rope, rubbed the hair between its horns, and sang to it softly, a nursery rhyme his mother used to sing to him. Slowly, the beast stopped rolling its eyes and calmed. The other was still on its knees, breathing heavily. It would be good to get them out of the yoke, but he was pretty sure he couldn't lift it on his own – nothing to be done about it.

He stepped away, and the beast on its feet calmly took a bite of grass. The other staggered up to copy it. Good, time to check on the ploughman. He stroked the flank of the ox and stepped clear of its back legs. The ploughman was just sitting up, clutching his belly. Jean stopped moving. It was Maurice! Well, the stupid idiot. He might have known it would be that bullish fool who thought he was man enough to be ploughman and trace man all in one. His anger moved him forward.

"You by-our-lady fool! You could have killed those beasts, working this hill alone! What in hell's name do you think you're playing at?"

He stopped yelling. Maurice was crying, pulling great, shuddering breaths in, his mouth twisted into a tight rose with each one. He spared an arm from hugging his stomach and ran an elbow over his eyes. He squinted up at Jean, his face blank.

"Are you hurt?" Maurice still didn't acknowledge him. Jean walked over and tried to pry his arm loose. Maurice rolled away, curled up into a ball, but at least his sobs sounded more normal. Jean patted him awkwardly on the shoulder. Now what? He couldn't leave him, either boy or beast might need more attention. He shrugged, and sat down beside Maurice, looking across the valley into Dodnash wood.

"You know, back home, the cows were my favourite animals. We had Normande cattle, beautiful creamy white, and speckled with black – I knew all their names. We had a pair called Roland and Oberon. They were our best plough team. I used to sit on Oberon's neck with a stick and believe that I was making them go in the right direction – my father's man walking beside had nothing to do with it, of course!" Jean sighed, and lost himself in the memory.

The sobs slowed, then stopped. Maurice uncurled.

"Would you help me?"

Jean turned and looked at him.

"Please? My father is always saying how useless I am. I wanted to do something to make him happy. Please say you will? You're so good with the oxen! We could get the field ploughed in no time. Please?"

"MAURICE!" the bellow was faint with distance, but had lost none of its menace.

"Mon Dieu! Your father – I must go." and Jean leapt to his feet and ran.

"Is that you, Frenchy? Get back here!"

He didn't stop until he was safe at the Priory, his head pounding.

***

William paused at the bottom of the hill, slightly before the path to the Priory split off from the main way. The stream was chuckling along in its bed beside him, but had he heard something else? Something high and piercing, dangerous mayhap? He shook his head at his own fancies. He'd put hard silver on there not being a faery queen up there on the hillside, whatever the village scolds said about there being a doorway to the other side at the spring. He pulled his knife up a little from its scabbard and touched the iron blade, just to be sure.

On an impulse he turned up beside the stream, rather than take the path. In a few strides he was safely hidden amongst the green. Not that he was terribly worried about any of the monks catching him off the path; he did have right on his side, with that little French idiot trespassing first. He grinned. He really had young Froggy on the run. Literally... That was a strange tale that Maurice was going on about, though, the boy singing the oxen calm. Perhaps it was a good job the frog had been around. He was proud of Maurice for taking the initiative with the ploughing, but it was definitely more than the boy could handle on his own. Pity he hadn't picked the field above, now that actually could do with being turned over, the lower was too claggy to plough for weeks yet. Well, he'd come out of it with no more than a bit of bruising and a tanned backside, he'd live and learn.

William looked to his left. Was it time yet to cut across Bridge Field and rejoin the path, so he could look innocent as he came up to the Priory? He wasn't sure. He wasn't in any hurry, anyway, it wouldn't matter if he had to backtrack. It was going to taste like bitter gall to humble himself to Prior Adam and beg for a loan. That was another thing – what had old Wimer been on about, saying the boy was his adopted son? William used a slim young birch to haul himself up a bank, and stood beside it looking down into a clear pool in the stream, thinking. He'd been counting on the old boy to pass on a legacy – the harvest had been so poor the last couple of years, he'd had to use all his savings for seed. He needed Wimer's money, by God's bollocks, he was on the edge! The old man still looked annoyingly hale, though. And had told him plain the last time he'd asked for money that there'd be no more loans. If he was going to get hold of enough salt to see them through the year, it was cap in hand to the Prior... Where did this French boy come in? Surely the pious old fool hadn't been dipping his wick where he shouldn't? Perhaps he should complain about the boy, get the little runt sent back where he came from, Wimer might even be thankful to get him out of sight...

His line of thought was interrupted by what was unmistakably song, coming from upstream. William very quietly backed away from the bank, and moved one soft foot at a time towards the music, careful not to rustle a leaf or step on a twig. The voice was female, and very pure. Thoughts of faerie intruded again. He was just about to give up the chase for prudence's sake when he saw her. She was kneeling on the far bank of the stream, golden hair cascading into the water, as human as he. She finished rinsing, and squeezed the water out – then to his astonishment, stood and shook her head round and round, sending water drops sparkling from the wheel of hair. She was well grown, her damp top clinging to her body in interesting ways.

His gaze fixed on her nipples, dark through her linen bodice. He swallowed. Since his Mary had died, bearing the babe that had soon followed her, he'd had no opportunity to admire a woman's body. She'd finished her dance with the water and was plaiting one side of her hair, face turned away. She turned her head towards him to plait the rest, and he realised he'd seen her before - the healer's daughter was her mother, what was her name? - yes, that was it, Goda's granddaughter, ummm - Ada? No, Edeva. Now he thought about it, hadn't he heard the girl's parents had died? The girl was ripe, no doubt about it. He frowned. Goda's husband had been Wimer's liege man when he was alive. It was very possible he was the girl's guardian. Everything came back to Old Man Wimer...

A plan began to form itself in his mind. It was high time he married again; Becky tried her best, but the place really needed a woman's hand, not a half-grown girl. Besides, in the blink of an eye she'd be ripe for marriage herself, and then where would he be? He did some swift figuring. This girl must be at least two or three years older than Becky, and nearly ripe for marriage. He needed to find out if Wimer was her guardian. Could he use the boy's trespass as a bargaining counter, threaten to go to the Prior if Wimer wouldn't agree to his suit? But he might not need to say anything about that at all. Why wouldn't Wimer agree? He was a good match, a man with land, and two sons to be custodians of it after him.

He straightened and squared his shoulders. Something startled the girl – he didn't think she'd seen him, but she had gathered her things and was gone in an instant. He stood a moment more, regretting the loss of the stolen view, then turned away himself to walk up the hill.

He'd come a little further than he'd meant, and was going to reach the Priory from the far side. He walked along the boundary between the wood and a field that had been newly cut from the trees. He paced it out, trying to estimate how much the assart tax would be, and whistled when he added it up. The crafty old Prior was planning on declaring it to the sheriff, wasn't he? The field was very well hidden from the path, and therefore from the sheriff's assessors – he was glad he'd come the long way, what an interesting piece of information he now had. He ran out of woodland and stepped carefully round some beehives to walk down to the path snaking up from the old Roman road, past the stables. He slipped into the church to give thanks to God for giving him this lever, then went to find the Prior.

Chapter 3

WILLIAM IS BROKE

"Master's pet!" Peter hissed at him as he pushed past. Jean could feel the frustration building inside him. *It's not my fault I can read Latin better than you!* He was sick of the nasty little comments when he did well in lessons. *I suppose I could stop answering the questions, or get a few wrong on purpose - but I need to keep showing the monks that I'm worth my food and lodging!*

He focused his eyes back on the scroll he'd been given to read as a reward for doing well at Latin translation. Peter had come second in the class... it was a history of Roman emperors, and it was a pretty boring treat. There were some good bits though... The next emperor was called Elagabalus. He said the name out loud, enjoying the way the syllables rolled in his mouth. Huh! He was only 14 when he came to power! He read on, wincing a bit at some of Elagabalus' nastier deeds. Some of the things he did were quite fun - one idea in particular...

Jean held his breath as Maurice headed for his favourite seat in the cloisters a few days later. Would he spot the new bit of cushioning underneath the cover? You had to sit quite heavily to make it work, but Maurice always flumped down hard... He burst out laughing as the pig's bladder made a great farting noise, and Maurice jumped up as though he'd been stung.

"What?! That wasn't me! Who did that? What are you giggling at, Frenchy, was it you?"

"Pooh! Stinky!" "Maurice, you pig!" Some of the other boys were fanning their hands in front of their faces, pretending to faint, and generally mucking around.

Maurice glared at them all, advancing towards Jean. "Did you have something to do with this, Frenchy? I'll pound you to sausage meat if you did!" Jean waved his hands at him, still grinning.

"No, wait! Look, let me show you."

He danced around Maurice and rescued the pig's bladder from the seat.

"Here! I got the idea from Latin class - an emperor invented it!"

He undid the leather tie at the neck and blew it up again. Maurice was still lumbering towards him, so he pulled the cord almost closed and squeezed the bladder between his palms, fast. The resulting fart actually echoed off the far wall of the cloister. Maurice stopped and began to grin too.

"Well, well, Frenchy - ain't you the living proof that book-learning's good for something after all! Give it here..."

By now the other boys had crowded round too, elbowing Jean to the outskirts of the crowd. Maurice was turning the bladder over and over. He scrunched the neck in his fist and blew, then did what Jean had done and squashed the bladder between his hands. Nothing much happened. Maurice looked around.

"Here, where's Frenchy gone - oy! How do I make it fart?"

Jean showed him how to twist the neck almost closed, so the air was forced out through the flap. Maurice grabbed it back and made it fart again and again and again. The whole herd of boys were laughing and demanding a turn, but Maurice held it out of their reach.

"Oh no, we don't want to break it! I've got just the right place to put this. Imagine the Prior's face when he sits on it after Grace this supper-time? Come on, let's set it up!"

The boys ran after him, laughing and making farting noises with their lips. Jean sank into the now-safe seat. *Oh dear Lord, what have I done! I only wanted to have a bit of fun with the others, and now Maurice is going to humiliate the Prior with it! It's all my fault!*

He stood up and took a couple of steps after them. *I should go to the Prior and warn him. Oh God, but if I do, Maurice will kill me! But if I don't, it will come out that it was my idea! The last time I was in this much trouble, the Prior said he'd ban me from the Priory! Please Lord, I can't let that happen, what can I do?*

He sat back down again and put his head in his hands. *I've got to think of something...*

He was still there when the bell for supper rang. *Should I run away? Where to? I have to go and face it.* He bit his lip and launched himself at the refectory, before he changed his mind. The Grace prayer seemed both terribly short, and to last forever. Finally the Prior finished and indicated they could sit down, brushing his habit smooth underneath his legs as he sat himself. Jean stayed standing, his eyes firmly shut against the horrible noise that was just about to happen. Only it didn't. When he peeked, the Prior was sitting perfectly happily. Jean plonked abruptly onto the bench, and without taking his eyes off the Prior, whispered to the boy next to him,

"What happened to the bladder? Did you put it on his seat?"

"Naw. Maurice burst it before we could, silly idiot."

The Prior turned and glared in their direction.

"Silence! Attend to the reading!"

Jean was hollow with relief. He felt sick with how close he'd come to risking his place here... The beginnings of a headache were starting up, and he pushed his plate away.

***

William balanced on the running-board for a few last instructions to Maurice.

"Have you got that farthing I gave you for the market fee? Good. Remember that you're to give it to the Sheriff's man, no other - and tell him your name clearly, don't mumble! And don't forget to stop as near to..."

"To St Stephen's as possible, so anyone walking up from the quay wanting hurdles and splints will see me first, but we'll still get the trade from the town. Yes, Father, you've told me so often I can't possibly forget!"

"Ay, well, be sure you do! I shall look for you there first. And keep a civil tongue in your head, damn you!" William hopped off the board and watched as Maurice turned the cart down Upper Brook Street. The boy had been sullen ever since he'd learnt about the wedding to Edeva. Worrying about a stepmother bossing him about, probably.

William shook his head and turned away to walk up to the Holy Trinity priory. Mayhap he was being too hard on the boy - he was old enough to remember his mother, and feel her loss. Young William's death at Christmastide might have brought it back, too. Perhaps he was just sad? Well, he'd better snap out of it, or have it beaten out of him! Nothing was going to spoil the wedding. Unless the Holy Trinity Prior, stuck-up Father Gilbert, wouldn't cooperate... no point in asking Father Adam for any more help, he was going to be late with the tithe for his Dodnash fields as it was. Again. Always money... Maybe a miracle would happen and Maurice would sell every scrap of wood at the market. He shut his eyes and sent up a brief prayer to Saint Isidore before taking a deep breath and knocking on the gate.

He ran out of words, and stood there feeling a fool, twisting his cap. It was impossible to see the Prior's expression clearly - he looked like he was smiling gently, but the light from the window behind him was full in William's face. It might be a scowl... William shifted from one foot to the other, and the Prior turned slowly to look at him.

"Have you finished?"

William nodded, dry-mouthed. It had been a mistake to come; the tight-arsed old fool was going to enjoy humiliating him, he'd go home with a flea in his ear, he'd have to call off the wedding, or worse, have a wedding feast with nothing but black bread and weak ale, he'd be the laughing-

The Prior's cool, light voice cut into his thoughts.

"I'm sure you realise that we don't make a habit of remitting the tithe. The Church has many mouths to feed. IF I allow it, it would only be a very temporary measure, you understand."

Now it was very definitely a scowl. William swallowed hard and nodded again.

"I am however minded to make you an offer." The Prior looked out of the window again and spoke into the sunlight. "I will defer the tithe you owe now, until Michelmas; so you must pay me two portions at that time. And in case you find difficulty in making that payment, I will take surety in the form of that field of yours along the Great Way in Bentley that is under plough. If you're turning it this early in the year, it must be good, light soil; you might even have time for two crops from it."

The Prior turned back and smiled pleasantly.

"What say you?"

William stared at him blankly. He hadn't put the plough to anything yet, what was he talking about? Then it hit him. He must mean those few scratchings that Maurice had made in the bottom field!

"Oh, no, Father, you don't understand - that's pure

clay, that field; you don't want that. My boy started ploughing it way too early, trying to impress me, I won't be able to get on it properly for a good month or two yet."

The Prior turned back to the window and sighed. William thought frantically.

"Uh... what if you took the meadow below it as surety? It's good grazing, and that's a permanent stream through it. I own a half share with my brother Hervey."

The Prior stood abruptly and stuck out his hand. William took it without thinking.

"Agreed! Good day to you, William of Dodnash. I pray your crop prospers."

William found himself the other side of the door. What had he done! In debt to Holy Trinity, for a wedding feast - it had better be a good year!

***

Edeva sat demurely on the stool, skirts neatly tucked around her, hands clasped in her lap. Her face was carefully turned to Father Wimer as he paced up and down in front of her. She was trying to listen to him, really she was – but what he was saying was fading in and out as her excitement mounted. His first few words had been enough to make her want to dance – although from behind him, they had caused Grandmama to drop a pot, which Edeva hadn't heard her cleaning up yet. Edeva allowed a bit more of what he was saying to sink in, to expand her bubble;

"-and he suggests, if you are willing, that the first

banns be read on the first Sunday after the Michaelmas service next year…"

Edeva added months up on her fingers and approved. A celebration in mid-November would brighten her least favourite time of the year; and she could beg the fine wool cloth that Grandmama was weaving for a new gown. It was a lovely deep shade of blue, it would set her hair off beautifully - and after all, she had helped pick the woad leaves to dye it with. That was the problem with getting married in winter, of course; there would be no flowers in her hair. On the other hand, with the harvest safely in, the feast would be good…

"- William and Maurice will remain his heirs, whether or not you bear any further children - "

Ah, there was the downside. Stinky old Maurice came along with the bargain! And his nonentity sister. Becky, that was her name. Little Will was quite sweet… They'd all have to obey her, as their stepmother, or she could whip them! What a lovely thought! But she would be gracious, of course; it wouldn't be easy for the children to accept that someone had taken the place of their mother. It would be wonderful to have a house of her own… She sat up a little straighter and practised behaving like a mature matron. Now she was nearly 12, it came quite easily; playing house had, after all, been her favourite game for as long as she could remember.

"- I will add a little marragiatum. Not much, mind, but enough that you'll have something of your own "

Edeva's control snapped, and she leapt up and hugged the old man.

"Oh, Father, you are so good to me! Thankyou! Thankyou for arranging all this for me – I'm so excited!" and she kissed him on the cheek and twirled.

"Oh, for heaven's sake, child!" Goda stepped forward and folded her into a hug. "He's not the husband I'd wish for you – with you almost the same age as his daughter, and him a hard man, always careful to get his due. You're so young – why don't you wait a while and see what other fish are in the sea?"

Edeva broke out of the hug and held her by both her shoulders. "No, Grandmama, my mind is made up - and besides, next year is forever away! When the time comes, I will take William of Dodnash as my husband, and be glad. Be happy for me?"

Her grandmother picked up the hem of her shawl, to wipe a tear away. Edeva wrapped her arms round her, and suffered a wet shoulder. It didn't matter. Nothing did! Soon she would be Mistress Edeva, with a house of her own!

Chapter 4

SHE LOVES ME / SHE LOVES ME NOT

Jean had been hearing a noise for a little while, grumbling along in the background. It might be raised voices; but as it wasn't him being yelled at, he was ignoring it. Suddenly it got a lot louder. It sounded like many people shouting - what on earth was going on? Was that Prior Adam yelling No? Jean became aware of the sacristy cupboard open behind him, the polished silverwork gleaming from the depths, and the pile still to do in front of him where he was sitting. Before he could think what to do, the West door was thrown open, and a rush of people darkened the entrance. Jean jammed the goblet and paten he had been rubbing with beeswax under the cupboard and stood up, still clutching his woollen cloth.

It was the Prior shouting – pushed through the door at last by a pair of rough-looking types in leather jerkins. Jean caught sight of a drawn sword and gasped. Not bandits, if they could afford good weapons! Whose men were they, and what was going on? Another soldier behind them looked in his direction and blustered past the Prior.

"Here it is, lads – all laid on display for us!"

He shoved Jean aside and started to pull the silverware from the cupboard and stuff it into his jerkin.

"Hi! You can't do that!" Jean's voice squeaked embarrassingly.

The soldier didn't even bother to look at him. Another soldier joined him, then the third, as Prior Adam gave up the fight, and pulled Jean aside.

"But Father! What's happening? Where are they taking our silver?"

"Shhh, lad, they're the Sheriff's men – apparently they have orders to take every piece of silver and gold they can find, to raise money for the King's war in France - a last big push, they say. Better we lose our silver, than our lives! You and I will just stay quiet here and stand witness; make sure they take what they have come for and go, with no other affront to the Church."

The Prior was a picture of stern serenity, arms tucked under his cloak. Jean was itching to ask questions, but one look at the Prior's face and the urge died. Finally the looting finished. A soldier came over to them and bowed mockingly to the Prior, then turned and grabbed Jean's jaw. The man's fingers were crushing into his cheekbones, but his voice was pleasant.

"Any more silver anywhere, son?"

Jean tried to shake his head, and rolled his eyes when the pressure grew. The man laughed, let him go, and sauntered outside. Jean and the Prior followed, Jean rubbing his face. One soldier was busy packing their silver into a mule's pannier. Jean winced as he ripped off the silver rim from a plain wooden cup and tossed the cup aside. The soldier had wandered over to the little knot of people who had gathered to watch. Edeva was there, Jean noticed, his eyes drawn to her as usual. The soldier said something to her, and she blushed and started to turn away. He grabbed her wrist, and she cried out. Without thought, Jean was running to her aid. A breath later and he was on his back, his chest burning. The soldier who had hurt him before was leaning over him, shaking his head.

"Scrappy young feller, aren't you! Didn't your Mam ever tell you to pick on people yer own size?" The soldier moved away, calling.

"Come on, you two, move out. We've got everything worth having here."

Jean managed to sit up. Edeva was nowhere to be seen… no, there she was, at the back, with her shawl over her head. She was all right. He went cold with relief. If anything had happened to her… The soldiers were almost at the ridge. He levered himself to his feet and hobbled towards her, but she was already walking away fast. He stood and watched until she was out of sight.

***

Three paces up; turn; three paces down. She loves me; she loves me not. She loves me; she loves me not. Jean had spent most of the morning hiding in the stables, trying to work out what he ought to do. Thinking, though, was impossible; he was either giddy with a joy so sweet that his stomach soared, or full of black hatred at his own stupidity. Of course she doesn't love me! She barely looks at me! Why should she... I love the colour of her hair, like bright corn, the way it curls round her wimple, how small and neat her hands are, and oh God her bosoms... He marched up and down again. The sturdy chestnut cob in the corner stall stuck his head over the partition to snort at him.

"Oh, I know, fellow, but please don't laugh at me. I can't help it..." He rubbed the horse's muzzle, reached for the curry brush, and went into the stall.

"She's such a wonderful person, you know, boy - oh, is that itchy there? Better? - but she doesn't even see me. I don't think she's said more than a handful of words to me since we were children. And I nearly died when I thought the soldiers had hurt her this morning."

He concentrated on a muddy spot on the horse's shoulder.

"Sorry, is that tickly? Stand still, there's a good fellow... Maybe that's part of the problem; I haven't said much to her either. Do you think that'd help? If I went and spoke to her? Treated her like a normal human being and had an actual conversation with her?" The horse snagged a mouthful of hay from the bag and munched. Jean ducked under his neck and moved to the other side.

"I don't know what we'd talk about, though. What DO women talk about? I suppose I could ask her and find out! I know it sounds ridiculous, but seeing her makes my whole day brighter. My whole week! Is that incredibly stupid?" The horse flicked its tail at him. "Do you think so? Move over a bit... If she said something like that to me, making her day better by seeing me, I'd just die with happiness. How does she know I like her, if I don't tell her?"

He finished with the brush and reached over the partition to hang it back up. "How's your water bucket, fellow? Good - and the hay? What do you reckon, should I go and talk to her? No, I haven't any apples, sorry." The horse gave his tunic one last sniff and nudged him to keep brushing.

"Hey, stop pushing! All right, all right, I'll go. I'll march right up to her, speak an actual sentence, and see what happens! Thank you for the encouragement!" He gave the soft muzzle one more pat and headed off in search of Edeva.

His luck was in, she was in the first place he looked, getting water from the well a little up the path from the fish ponds. He stood for a few seconds screened by the hawthorn hedge, drinking in the sight of her, as ever his chest tightening with wonder at the purity of her beauty. Then he shut his eyes, gulped a deep breath, and half-ran across to her before his courage went.

"H-hello!" he managed, his voice not TOO squeaky - and clenched his fists in frustration as a blush flooded his face.

She looked up in surprise, and swiped at a fly that had landed on her face.

"Hello, Frenchy! What are you doing here? - Hey, whilst you are here - crank the handle, would you? It's hard work in this heat!"

He took over, grateful for the chance to bury his face and concentrate on the rhythm of the work. She watched him for a while, then bounced round to lean against the well coping, looking up at him.

"Hey, Frenchy! Have you heard my news?"

Jean shook his head and stretched past her to grab the bucket handle and heave it out of the well mouth. Her perfume filled his nostrils, and he'd almost brushed against her arm… he could see the fine downy hairs on it. What would it be like to run his lips along them…

"I'm going to be married! Isn't that something? To William of Dodnash, next November!"

He dropped the bucket the last inch or two with a clang, and stared at her, aghast.

"I shall be Mistress Edeva to you! I can't wait!" She twirled a full circle, joyously.

He could feel his mouth was gaping stupidly. He didn't seem to be able to do anything about it.

She patted his cheek. "Thanks for helping with the water!", then grabbed the handle and sashayed up the path, the bucket in imminent danger of spilling with each step.

She called back to him, "Au 'voir, Frenchy! I hope you'll get married one day and be as happy as I am right now!" She waved.

He half lifted a hand in response, then sank down beside the well. His cheek still blazed from her touch. All the joy had drained from the world. There was a taste of ashes on his tongue.

***

There was a small puddle forming by Jean's left foot.

Every so often, a raindrop from the cloister thatch plinked into it, and a little spray of droplets dampened Jean's hose. He didn't care. He sat staring at the puddle, hugging his knee to his chest, each breath underlining how hollow he felt. Nothing would ever be in colour again. He would spend the rest of his life locked in shades of grey, seeing Edeva go past every day, the knife twisting in his heart. He could feel the tears welling up again, and bit down on his knee, unable to bear the shame of crying on top of everything else. A creeping cold in his foot as the puddle reached him was the last straw, and a fat, hot drop splashed down his leg - luckily on the far side from the monks.

" - didn't you, lad?" A friendly slap on the shoulder shocked him out of his self-preoccupation.

"P-pardon?" He looked up. Everyone was smiling at him.

Wimer, who was sitting next to him winding strips of linen into bandages, explained "Your bit of heroics! Even though it could have put you in the stocks, or worse!"

For a dizzy second Jean wondered how he knew about his encounter with Edeva - and WHY would that put him in the stocks? - then he realised that they must be talking about the soldiers. He smiled sheepishly and shook his head, taking advantage of the movement to wipe his eyes on his knee. He shifted his foot out of the puddle and looked around the cloister. The sky was still grey, but it had stopped raining. The monks had gone back to their conversation - all but Wimer, who as usual had missed nothing. The old man leaned on him to stand up, then held out his hand to help him up in his turn.

"Come on, son - lend me your shoulder, would you - I'm stiff from sitting too long, I need a bit of a leg-stretch; and the beehives need telling all about our eventful day."

They walked in silence, Wimer's arm a comforting weight through his, until they turned the corner and started across the dip at the back of the church, away from any possible listeners.

"So, lad - are you going to tell me why your face looks like a wet week? You won't really get into trouble, you know. The Prior's delighted with your quick thinking."

"I don't understand, Father - what do you mean?"

"Weren't you listening to a word we were saying, earlier?" Wimer looked more closely at him. "Is anything else wrong?"

Jean shook his head dumbly, then thought of something to ask to get Wimer talking instead. "Tell me why the soldiers were here again?"

"Wait until we get to the hives, then I won't have to tell it twice!" Jean smiled at the old monk in relief. *He's not going to push for an answer, thank the Lord. He's so comforting just to be with... has he shrunk? How strange! Maybe I've grown, I'm almost as tall as he is now...*

They got to the beehives tucked under the shelter of the alder grove, and Wimer filled the bees in on the doings of King Richard - how he'd been stupid enough to get caught on his way back from the Crusade, and quite how eyewateringly enormous his ransom was. How Wimer would have left him to rot, the country was doing fine without him, but that would mean that evil little toad John as King… Jean looked round once or twice, making sure there was no-one in hearing range, afraid that Wimer - ex-Sheriff or not - would be in trouble; but only the bees were listening. Wimer would up by explaining about the terrible thing the Queen had done - the old Queen, Eleanor, Jean realised - by sending soldiers out to steal all the gold and silver from every church in the land to pay for the King's ransom. And how this young man here had saved the most important pieces of silver, so that the Lord's table, in this church at least, would be properly dressed.

"There you go, son - that should give you a good report; now I'm going to check on the horses, you tell the bees all about whatever it is you're not telling me!" and with a fierce nod, the monk hobbled off. Jean watched him go, then did as he was bid - surprised at how much better it made him feel.

***

Someone must have moved the mounting block - Wimer was riding round in front of the stables looking forlorn. Jean ran to help him. Wimer had been spending more and more time in Ipswich, and it was obvious that the journeys were tiring him. Jean made a step out of linked hands and eased the old man to the ground.

"Ah, thanks, son. Would you carry my bags for me, I swear they get heavier as the day goes on?"

Wimer hauled the saddlebags off the horse with a

grunt and handed them over. Jean slung them over one shoulder and offered Wimer the other arm.

"Where have you been today, Father?"

"To see Earl Bigod's factor at the port. It occurred to me that my brother Hervey might well have used Bigod ships to send goods to France, and if I was very lucky, the factor might have a record of picking up a consignment of wool or parchment from him. Any sheep products must have come from the disputed meadow, Hervey had everything else under the plough. As it happens, the factor had an old waybill that called him by name - Hervey son of Aelfric of Dodnash - but it didn't list what he was shipping. Shame. It would have made my life so much simpler."

"The Prior of Holy Trinity is still insisting that the meadow is his, then?"

"Yes, he's quoting some agreement that William made with him last year before little Will died, but that meadow is mine, William has no right to it." Wimer paused as they neared the church.

"Take my bags to the cloisters, lad, would you? And bring me a beaker of small beer and my writing kit? I want to beg the Lord for a bit of guidance before I write some notes whilst the light is good."

Jean watched him go into the stillness of the church and noticed again how thin he was. *I'll ask the kitchen for some cheese for him as well as his drink. He could do with feeding up!*

He sat on a bench in the sun, guarding the cheese from the flies and waiting for Wimer. It was so good to be still and simply allow the sunshine to soak into his bones. *I do love it here... It feels so strange to think about leaving.* He watched an ant using a crack in the plaster to scale the heights of the wall. *I can remember being that tall. The walls have my measure.* For an instant he remembered another wall in the sunshine, his mother giggling with him as he stood on highest tippy-toe to have his mark drawn on his birth day, his father trying to be stern and make him stand up properly but laughing too. He resolutely pushed the image away. *Another wall lost to me. It seems to be my fate to be rootless, loveless, and homeless.* The gripe was back in the pit of his stomach.

"My boy, whatever is wrong? You look like the weight of the world is on your shoulders!"

Wimer eased himself down onto the edge of the bench, turning so he could continue to study Jean's face.

"Come on, out with it; no-one else here."

Jean shook his head, but gave in to the concern in Wimer's eyes.

"Oh, it's nothing, really. The Novice Master has refused to take me as a postulant, that's all. I'm trying to work out what I can do when I have to leave the Priory, I've no real skill to earn a living by."

"My dear boy! No-one is going to make you leave until you're eager to go out into the world. And besides, a good education is always worth having. People will always need a trustworthy man who can read, write, and figure."

Wimer regarded him steadily, then suddenly reached out a hand to turn his chin sideways.

"Good heavens! Hairs! You've grown in a blink, boy,

it seems only yesterday you came here. I will have to give thought to what provision I can make for you, what's happening with your father's estate is still very unclear." He sighed. "The latest news from Outremer is inconclusive, I'm afraid; I have had one report stating that your father has been dead for many years, and another claiming to have seen him only a few months ago. You may need my services as a lawyer yourself, to establish your right to inherit." He shook his head and glared at Jean.

"But what's this about postulancy? This is the first I've heard about you wanting to be a man of the cloth."

"Don't you see, Father? This place is my home. All I've learned of God, of belonging somewhere, I've learned here. It doesn't really matter if my father is alive or dead, I haven't seen him for years and years, and even when I was in France, he could barely stand to look at me once Mama died, he said I looked far too much like her. I belong here now, and I want to stay here for the rest of my life!" *As close to Edeva as I can...*

Wimer shook his head again, absent-mindedly picked up the chunk of cheese, and waved it for emphasis.

"But you are terribly young, Jean! Your whole life is ahead of you; why would you want to lock yourself up in here? Mmmm this is good. And besides, if your father is dead, you're his heir; you will have worldly responsibilities, and possibly a fair amount of wealth." He nibbled the cheese again. "Perhaps we should send you away somewhere to learn how to manage it."

Jean leaped to his feet, shaking his head. "I don't WANT to have money! The Church can have it all! I want to stay here forever. All that I've had of care, of teaching, of love itself, has been here!"

He sat down again, head in his hands, and muttered into his chest

"I nearly unmanned myself when the Novice Master wouldn't accept me as a postulant. I want it so much...

"Well, I must say that I'm still surprised. I just didn't think you had a vocation." The last of the cheese vanished, and Wimer washed it down with a big gulp of ale. "Ah! That was good. Deo gratia... But you shouldn't take Brother Lawrence's refusal too much to heart yet, lad. He has to refuse you three times, you know; the Order requires it, to let you prove that you really want it. You don't need to be down in the dumps unless he refuses you a fourth time. Now stop looking at me like a poleaxed steer and go and do something useful, like asking God for a sign that you really do have a vocation. I have work to do. Shoo!"

Jean stared at him for a moment longer, then leaped to his feet and over the low cloister wall almost in one movement. He might be able to stay here after all! *Please God!*, he remembered to add.

***

It felt like her head was full to bursting - in a good way! There was just so much to do before the wedding, even if it was nearly a whole year and a half away! Edeva stopped sewing for a moment to admire the neat row of stitches in the linen nightshirt she was making for William. It was going to be such FUN to be her own mistress! Not having anyone remind her of jobs undone, or tell her what she was doing wrong, or to complain if she took even a MINUTE for herself...

"Edeva! You haven't been listening to a word I've been saying, have you!"

Edeva flushed. It was very true - she'd lost interest somewhere around the second sentence...

"I'm sorry, Grandmama - I'm so distracted at the moment. Please could you tell me again?" She smiled up at her grandmother, expecting to see her raising her eyes to heaven in mock despair - instead, she was nearly crying!

"Oh Grandmama, please don't be upset! I'll only be a hop and a skip away from the Priory, you know I will; you can visit whenever you're here, and maybe I can come and visit you in Orford sometimes?" She jumped up and hugged her grandmother.

"Ow! Careful of that needle, child! Please - just sit and listen to me for a minute. I really shouldn't be telling you this at all, the Church would call me out as a witch if they knew, but only the Lord knows if I will live to see you wed next year - please, whilst there's no-one around!"

Interest piqued now, Edeva sat, sewing unheeded in her lap. Grandmama stared solemnly at her for so long that Edeva began to wriggle. *What? What's wrong? What have I done now?* Finally she began to speak.

"Pennyroyal. Do you know its uses?"

Edeva frowned. *Huh? A medicine lesson, now?* "The leaves? No. Not really, Grandmama. Can you make a tea from them? Or a poultice? What property do they have?"

Goda glanced at the shut door, then back to her.

"Do you want babies, Edeva?"

Edeva shrugged. "I haven't really thought about it. I suppose they'll come when God wills it."

"Do you remember William's first wife, Ann? - pretty little thing, she was. I was the midwife for all her births, you know. Those babies were huge. The girl, not so bad; but even so, Ann tore and bled badly. Then William got her with child so quickly she could scarce have recovered; and the same again with the third child. I told William he should wait until the babe was weaned - but that doesn't seem to be in his nature. So she carried that third babe when she was still pale and listless from the birth of the second child. And she grew so huge - I knew it was going to be a difficult birth."

She stopped and ran her hands over her face, fingers wiping away tears under her eyes. Edeva closed her mouth and shivered. *And she died giving birth to William junior, I know... What a waste of two lives, since he died - when - a couple of years ago?* She pulled her thoughts away from such gloomy things and back to the present.

"But Grandmama, what has this got to do with pennyroyal? Is it good to stop bleeding after a birth?"

"No, lass." She was frowning at Edeva again. "It's for getting rid of an unwanted baby before it grows."

Edeva must have looked as puzzled as she felt.

"In the womb. If you drink a tea made from the herb - dried or fresh, it doesn't matter - the baby will never plant in the womb. But you have to be careful; if you've missed more than three monthlies, it's too late. Do you understand? If you miss two monthlies, you can take the tea and there will be no baby. Take it too late into a pregnancy and both you and the baby might die."

Edeva put her hand up to cover her mouth. She felt sick...

"I generally only tell girls about the tea if they need it - like poor Ann; sometimes they refuse to listen. The Church preaches that it's a mortal sin. Well, I think that forcing an ill wife to bed too soon is the sin, and sometimes a woman has to protect herself..."

My eyes must be as wide as an owl's...

"Oh for heaven's sake, child, don't look so gormless! I wouldn't tell you at all, except that I can't stand the thought of William killing another young girl - you! - because he can't control his appetites, and he sets big babies. I'm not going to be around forever; you need to know about it now, just in case. Right. Well, I'm glad we had this little chat." With a speed belying her age she stood, grabbed her shawl from the peg, and slammed the door behind her.

Edeva looked down at her lap and slowly picked up her sewing. It took a while for her thoughts to settle, her needle moving at a snail's pace. *A mortal sin! How could Grandmama do it? And she said she'd told many girls! But I suppose the sin is theirs for making the tea? Knowing about it isn't a sin itself, is it?* She thought about that for a bit longer. Finally she shook herself and started to stitch at her usual speed.

"Ow ow ow!" She put her finger in her mouth. "That hurts!"

An image of a baby tearing its way out of her body appeared unbidden. She shuddered. *Dear Lord, that must be agony! I don't think I want William's children, if birthing them is like that!*

She inspected the linen. *Oh blast it!* She sucked the cloth hard, but the blood had gone into the weave, it would need a soak. She gave up, and stared into the distance, very carefully tucking the information about the pennyroyal tea away. *I'm sure it's not a sin unless I actually drink it... I hope.*

Chapter 5

WIMER IN COURT

Lawrence knocked on the Prior's door and settled himself for a wait. Hopefully not too long - the new novice-brother from St Osyth's was due for another reading lesson. How they thought it was right to accept his vows when he didn't have the brains to read the simplest Divine text...

The Prior's door opened suddenly. Opening his own door! Really! Lawrence thought, then remembered his manners and bowed. The Prior had already turned and was speaking over his shoulder.

"I'm sorry to keep you waiting, Brother - please come in. Can I pour you some beer? Lawrence pursed his lips again. I do wish he'd pay heed to ceremony more. How can I teach the proper awe of his office when the man pours his own beer?

"Come in, come in, sit down. Tell me how things are going?"

Lawrence glanced round at the mess. There was two choices of visitor seating; a stool with an unstable pile of scrolls on it, and a chair with the Priory cat curled asleep on the cushion. He lifted his skirts and flapped them at the cat, which opened one baleful eye and then poured itself off the chair and underneath Prior Adam's work desk. Lawrence gave one more flap to get rid of as much cat hair as possible and sat down. The Prior turned around from the ale table with a cup in each hand and passed him one.

"How's the new novice getting on? I was chatting to him the other day, he was sweeping the cloister, and seemed to be truly offering the service to God."

Lawrence took a sip of ale to cover his annoyance. *Honestly, the man bounces around poking his nose into everything...*

"He's doing well enough at the more menial tasks. My major concern is with his intellectual ability. He can scarcely read, and his Latin is appalling."

The Prior perched on the corner of the desk, looking thoughtful.

"Shame I can't lend you Wimer as a tutor, but he's needed to sort out this land dispute with Holy Trinity. How about Brother Augustus, he's not a bad scholar?"

Lawrence shook his head.

"Thank you, Father, I've been giving him a little tutoring myself, and my perception is that - unless he improves drastically - we ought to consider the lay brother route for him, rather than allow him to take the novice's vows; I'm not at all sure he has what it takes up here." He waved a hand at his head.

"But with your permission; that wasn't the matter I wanted to discuss with you, today at least. It's actually young Jean. He has asked me, very formally and properly, to become a postulant - three times now. I shall have to give him a final answer if he asks again, and I'm not at all sure what it should be."

Having relieved himself of the burden, he leaned back against the wall as the Prior stood up to pace.

"Jean wants to join the order! Well, that's a surprise. He hasn't looked happy lately, he's been glooming all over the place - I suppose if you've been refusing him, that could account for it. What's your instinctual reaction, does he have a vocation? And isn't he still a little young to make profession? Despite the fact that he's growing like a beanpole..."

Lawrence looked into the depths of his ale cup and frowned.

"He is young - but his voice has broken, more or less, he's old enough to profess. He is very eloquent about his reasons for wanting to join the Order. He talks about finding God in the midst of the community. But I am minded that he's had a privileged position here, with Father Wimer as a sponsor; it seems - I don't know - too soft and easy a road to Damascus."

The Prior took another tour around the room. "Does he need to have had a conversion moment? We have, after all, known him as part of the family for these last - what - two? Three? years. I've never questioned his faith. And he's certainly a useful, and valued, member of the community, although of course he's never lived as one of the brothers. My concern is that, if we allow him to sleepwalk into a permanent vow, we will constrain his soul; he will never have known what he could have become."

Lawrence swallowed a gulp of beer and set the cup down. *I was right to come. He reacts to these problems involving people in a way that I simply do not see. And, informal as he is, I owe obedience to him...*

He knelt and asked humbly

"May I ask your guidance, Father? On both men?"

The Prior came to a halt in front of him and silently regarded him for what felt like a very long time.

"Brother Deacon, we have talked before about your own nature pre-disposing you to require a narrow conformance in others, have we not."

Lawrence bowed his head and waited.

The Prior continued. "I think it likely that Brother Jerome will find formal learning to be his trial, but I am not as quick as you to condemn him to a life of servitude. I require you to give him a further six months of tuition; but this time to imagine yourself in his place, and to lead him gently to learning; find some area he has grasped, add on a small incremental piece of learning, and wait until he has assimilated it before adding another."

"Yes, Father." *that's a waste of time, then.*

"Jean's request is of more concern."

The tall figure in front of him paced up and down the room, halting in the same position.

"I will talk to him myself. I will also ask Brother Wimer to keep him busy and away from you for a few weeks. Wimer could use someone to help him get around; his mind is sound but his body grows increasingly frail. He and the boy are fond of each other; I'll ask Wimer to probe a little, see whether he feels that Jean's vocation is genuine. If so, you can admit him as a postulant, and make the postulancy a trial; test his resolve. Does that please you?"

Lawrence looked up and smiled.

"Yes indeed, Father. Thank you."

"Mmmm. Well. Please keep me informed as to how both those souls prosper. But now, up off your knees, man; be seated, and let's talk about you, and your progression towards the priesthood. I know it's a long road, and sometimes a hard one; what are your feelings about it currently?"

***

"Tell me again what I call him?" Jean tugged his tunic down. He'd chosen it, and the brown and yellow hose that matched the hem border, out of pure vanity; the weave was a little light, and his favourite linen shirt was making it ride up. *I should have borrowed a better shirt too...* He smoothed it again, then swiped at his hair. His palm was sweaty, and he winced a little at the tug. *Oh no! Have I left paw prints on the tunic?*

Wimer smiled at him encouragingly, and repeated himself.

"You call him Earl Bigod when I introduce you, and Sir if he speaks to you after that. Which I doubt he will. Otherwise, just follow my lead. Listen carefully to what's going on and be prepared to hand me any charters I ask for. You'll do fine. Ready?"

Jean nodded, tried to sort out his clothing one more time, and followed Wimer into the courtroom. He nearly messed up before he was properly through the door, being too busy being astounded at the noise from all the people to realise that Wimer had halted at the threshold to bow to the man in the tall chair raised on a dais. Jean stopped just in time, and bowed himself. By the time he lifted his head Wimer was half-way across the room, and he had to jog a few steps to catch up, apologising over his shoulder to people he brushed against.

The Earl was leaning on one carved arm of his chair, listening to a black-robed monk - the Prior of Holy Trinity, Prior Gilbert, Jean realised as they got closer. The Earl saw Wimer and stood to greet him. The hum of conversation around the room died as he did so. Gilbert sent a look that could kill in Wimer's direction, then arranged his face into a neutral expression. Jean shivered a bit at how easily he made the shift.

Wimer was introducing him to the Earl –

"Jean, son of Jean, merchant of Rouen, and my ward." He hurriedly bowed.

The Earl nodded at him and turned away, looking round the room.

"Are all parties to this land dispute here now?" His voice was warm and strong. Jean found himself liking the man. "William son of Hervey of Dodnash?"

"Here, Lord." William swaggered forward. He narrowed his eyes at Jean, but said nothing. *He didn't bow to the Earl - how rude! Unless he did earlier?*

The Earl frowned slightly at William, then said "Good, we'll begin. Prior Gilbert, would you like to make your statement first?"

The Prior tucked his hands into opposite sleeves and stepped forward.

"Sir, I obtained the meadow in question as surety on a loan, made to this William son of Hervey, taken out on…" he snapped his fingers and a monk rushed forward and put a scroll in his hands. He read down it a little, then continued "on 27th March last year. The terms were repayment of the loan by Michaelmas last year, or ownership of the meadow was to come to the Holy Trinity. He defaulted, of course." He bowed to the Earl, holding the scroll out behind him. The monk took it and scurried away.

William was looking worried, twisting his cap between his hands.

"Do you dispute these facts, William of Dodnash?" asked the Earl.

"I was getting married, see, Lord.." he fell silent as the Earl held up a finger.

"I am not interested in why you needed a loan. Are the facts as Prior Gilbert has described? Yes or no?"

William looked at his boots and mumbled "Yes."

The Earl looked at Wimer. "Well, Wimer? That sounds very simple; what's your point of dispute?"

Wimer bowed. "I have no doubt that is happened exactly as the Prior described."

Gilbert took his hands out of his sleeves and started to move forward.

"But unfortunately, William had no right to sign away the land. It is mine."

The Prior's scowl matched William's. "Can you prove that, Brother?" he asked silkily.

"Yes! Prove it!" said William.

Wimer turned to Jean. "The charter of '43 and the waybill, please, lad?"

Jean had them ready and handed them over.

Wimer turned to the Earl. "Sir, I have documentation that proves that my brother Hervey was steward of the land, and had the use of it; your father was a witness to the charter confirming the transfer of fealty after our father's death. Your steward provided me with a copy of a waybill for goods moving through your warehouse. Would you like to see them?"

The Earl shook his head, and was about to speak when William butted in.

"That doesn't prove anything - only that my grandfather owned the meadow in those days, not who owns it now!'

The Earl frowned at him, but turned to Wimer with a gesture of apology. "He has a point. Can you counter?"

Wimer shook his head. Jean must have gasped, because William grinned evilly at him.

Wimer said quietly, "Only my word, Sir, that the land reverted to me when my brother died. I can see that my nephews thought they had use of it; I have, after all, been away from this part of the world for many years; and I saw no point in taking it away from them when I retired to the Priory. I am prepared to swear that it is mine."

William snorted, loudly.

The Earl stood up. "Would you challenge that, William of Dodnash? I should point out that, as a man of the cloth, Wimer is unable to defend his honour himself. However, I would be prepared to defend my old tutor's honour personally, if you insist on taking it to trial?"

Jean almost laughed at William's expression, but smothered it in time. William's cap was being tortured again. He said, a little shakily, "No, Lord, I concede the point."

The Earl sat back down again.

"Excellent. So we have established that Wimer owns the land, by his oath. There is the question of the debt. Can you repay the loan, Master William? What is the amount?"

Jean could almost hear the felt stretching as William pulled the cap through his hands.

"Uh, Lord, it's been a poor harvest…"

"Yes, or no, Master William?"

William visibly gulped. "No, Lord."

"Thank you. And the amount?"

"Twelve shillings, Lord."

Prior Gilbert quickly spoke; "A mark, with interest."

Jean pursed his lips in sympathy. *I'd be amazed if his whole farm is worth that…* Even the Earl looked surprised. William was completely still, knuckles showing white over his cap, eyes shut.

Everyone jumped as Wimer marched over to William and slapped his face, the noise echoing around the court.

"You fool! Are you trying to make my Edeva homeless?"

William just stared dumbly at him, one hand to his cheek. Wimer glared at him for a moment, then turned to face the Earl.

"Sir, an it please you, I will pay this idiot's debt. His wife is the daughter of my manservant Piers - you may remember him? - and I would not see her dragged into penury."

The Earl raised an eyebrow at Prior Gilbert, who shrugged. The Earl said, "Well, if you're prepared to take on the debt, I think that closes the case. Thank you, gentlemen." He turned to his seneschal. "Who is up next?"

Wimer reached for Jean's arm. Jean could feel him trembling.

"Wimer! Do you HAVE that much money? And I didn't know you were the Earl's tutor. When…"

"Hush, lad, I'm exhausted. Just get me home before I fall over, please…"

Jean got him settled in the back of the cart then took the reins and let him sleep. He woke only as they rattled down the hill to Dodnash Priory. As he helped Wimer down, Jean asked a question that had been bothering him all the way home.

"Father, what would have happened if you hadn't been there to swear that the land was yours?"

Wimer clapped him on the shoulder and grinned.

"Less of the what-ifs, lad, I'm here, and that's what counts. And besides, you'd pick up the cudgel after I'm gone, if needs be, wouldn't you? Now hurry up and put the horse and cart away, can't you smell supper's nearly ready?"

Jean nodded back at him solemnly, then his tummy rumbled, making them both laugh. He picked up the reins, Wimer slapped the horse on its rump, and he hurried to settle it down for the night.

***

8th April 1204, Galata, Constantinople

My dear boy,

Once again I write to you, with diminishing hope that this letter will reach you. Or perhaps all the others have been safely delivered, and you are too angry with me to write back? But then, surely Father Wimer would acknowledge them? Or perhaps you have dutifully replied, and your letters have been lost in the chaos surrounding me. I will write this as I have all the others, in the hope that you forgive the repetition should they come into your hands.

I must begin with an apology - a most profound one. I behaved terribly when your mother died; I was so caught up in my own pain that I ignored your needs, when they should have come first. You looked so like her, it was not possible to catch a glimpse of your hair, or the intelligence in those bright eyes, or even, sometimes, hear your voice echo some turn of phrase of hers, and not suffer a fresh knife-strike.

And, too, her death was my fault - if I hadn't urged her to come for a ride out with me, if her horse hadn't spooked at nothing and bolted, if it hadn't stumbled in a hole and thrown her - perhaps my beloved would still be alive today, and we would be a happy little family living quietly on the estate. That burden of guilt is a terrible one to wear, despite having been shriven of it; but it burns me daily.

I pray every day that I did the right thing sending you to England. I had little choice - there was sickness in the next valley, and even though I could hardly bear to look at you, the risk of losing you was impossible to contemplate. If my father had still been alive, of course you would have lived with him, but he wasn't, and your maternal grandparents had gone too. My father had always talked of England as such a gentle, safe place, and of his friend Wimer with such affection. I had no-one else to leave you with, and the correspondence I had with Father Wimer after my father died made me sure he was a good man.

But the years have passed, and what I meant to be a stay of only a few months has stretched and stretched - the reports we get now, of this foolish new King John, fill me with unease.

And then, are you even still at the Priory? I torture myself with the thought that you are dead, your bones rotting in some English field... I have to have faith in the Lord, that he has preserved you. It amazes me that you must now be a youth, not a boy - I will make another attempt to send a letter to my steward and instruct him to forward you an allowance. I have heard from him, once.

I wonder if you are at all curious as to what has befallen me, or if you hate me for abandoning you, or if you are simply indifferent. I have found a place with the Knights Templar, as a lay servant, and am largely content in this new life. I expect to die out here at a time of the Lord's choosing.

You would laugh to learn that I have achieved some mastery in the chopping of onions, vast quantities of which are required to keep the armies fed! There is a large force here, as we prepare to storm Constantinople, and they are all permanently hungry. Indeed, I am considering taking the vows of a lay brother - it would make little difference to my life here, except that I would occasionally have to exchange my kitchen knife for a pike and go into battle - but it may give you a better chance of hearing about my death, the Knights look after their own.

Be sure, my son, that I love you, and I beg you to forgive me for abandoning you. I hold you in my thoughts daily. Pray for me, as I do for you!

Jean de Rouen.

Jean carefully refolded the parchment and set it down in his lap. The trunk of the old oak pressed comfortingly against his back, and he shut his eyes against the sun dazzle and the view of the church and cloisters below him.

Instead he was seeing again the bustle in his father's hall as the hurdle with his mother's body was rushed in, the bearers shoving him unceremoniously aside; his father, from his place at the head of the hurdle, begging her to stay with them - they were nearly there - soon she could rest and get well in her own bed - come on my love, you can make it - the chatter abruptly broken by a single deep-throated scream as the priest shook his head and thumbed her eyes closed. His father dropped to his knees as the women began to wail...

Jean frowned and opened his eyes. *I've never really thought of his loss. Imagine if Edeva should die...* He shivered and made the sign of the cross, then the sign against the evil eye just in case. *Well, I'm glad he has made something of a life for himself with the Crusaders.* He picked the letter up and levered himself to his feet. He ran his thumb across the well-remembered seal, then on impulse kissed it.

"Aye, mon Pere, I will pray for you."

At the Priory the bell rang for the substantiation of the host. He crossed himself again, then snorted wryly.

But right now I have some onions of my own to chop - my monks may be even hungrier than your knights, and they'll be wanting to break their fast as soon as the service finishes!

Chapter 6

POSTULANCY

It had all been so quick! Jean leaned on his broom and stared at the mound of disturbed soil in the centre of the cloister courtyard, flecks of white stone freckling the red earth. It was impossible to think that Wimer was under there, even though he had helped lower his body with his own hands, and shovelled the soil afterwards.

It felt like only minutes since fat old Brother Anthony had come huffing up to him at the fishponds, telling him to hurry, Wimer had collapsed and the Prior was giving him the last rites. He'd run into the room just as the Prior was - oh so gently - smoothing down Wimer's eyelids. He'd given one great cry of grief, from so far inside him it felt like the sound had scraped his heart raw, and after that had only allowed himself to worry about the mountain of practical things that had to be done. He had been briskly efficient through all the preparations for the funeral, insisting on writing the invitations himself, and had even remained dry-eyed when Goda had come, wailing and enveloping him in a warm damp hug.

It only seemed a blink of an eye since the courtyard was full to bursting with the great and good, all come to pay their respects to the man who had been more of a father to him than his real father had ever been. His eyes were getting hot again, and he tried to distract himself by remembering all the visitors. Earl Bigod had come from Framlingham, of course, acknowledging Jean gravely when their paths had crossed. The Sheriff of Norfolk and Suffolk too; Wimer's old job, though the man was no friend of Wimer's. The old fellow had more than once grumbled about political appointees and people buying into their posts, not like the old days... There had been three or four older men who probably felt like that, he thought; who had greeted each other warmly, but had been no more than carefully polite to some of the younger attendees.

There had been a difference in clothing between the two groups, too - the old guard in furs and faded, once-colourful silks that looked ever so slightly moth eaten, the younger men crisp and fashionable in black. Perfumed, too... he had almost brushed against the Sheriff as they'd carried the coffin out, and the resulting hit of rose oil had clashed with the slightly sweet smell coming from the coffin, making a stomach-churning mixture that had actually helped to keep his mind off what they were doing. He stood straight as he realised why the Sheriff had been so close to the step - *he wanted the first place behind the coffin, to get the best spot by the grave...*

Jean had had an excellent view of the grave from his place of honour at Wimer's right shoulder, with the

Prior on the other side of the coffin. The hole had seemed to grow and grow as they got nearer, until it looked large enough to swallow all of them. Then amazingly Wimer's coffin had almost filled it. The Prior - *hey! Had he been crying too?* Jean realised with surprise - had had to remind him to throw the first handful of earth. It had sounded so empty; he had grabbed the shovel and worked and worked, desperate for that terrible hole to be filled, even if his Father's body had to be left in it. Some of the brothers had helped, of course, although he couldn't remember who.

And then there had been the incident at the reading of the will over the grave, the one thing that had broken though the wall he had built against his emotions ever since he'd been summoned to Wimer's bedside. Until William had spoken, it had felt like there was a shell between him and the world. He could move, and talk, and even smile; but nothing could touch him. Nothing except that despicable creep!

Jean looked down for the source of a creaking noise. He realised he was gripping the broom handle hard enough to break it. William had been standing beside him, of course, having paired up with the Sacristor to carry the foot of the coffin. After the Bishop had finished reading the will - most going to the Church, some money for Goda and Edeva, and the bottom meadow to Jean - William had leant down to him with a pleasant smile and remarked

"He never did swear on oath that it was his." He'd left before Jean had realised what he'd meant – the land Wimer had inherited from his father, including that little meadow.

The handle creaked again and Jean started sweeping like a demon - wishing that each jerk of the broom was a fist going into William's gut.

***

This robe was a ridiculous pain in the neck - white was such a stupid colour to have as a postulancy robe, even with a leather apron over it; it picked up every scrap of dirt. He scraped off a flick of muck with a fingernail and tugged the cloth higher through the belt. Brother Lawrence would yell at him again. He sighed. *He's going to yell at me anyway...*

Nothing seemed easy or clear any more. He had been so sure he wanted to be a novice before Wimer had died, and taking the postulancy vows only a few weeks after the funeral had been the only bright spot in that dark time, embedding himself in the priory family. Now he just felt miserable and sad all the time - he was permanently in trouble, nothing he did was done well enough for Brother Lawrence. He was also finding it hard to get used to the hours the monks kept, with such a short time between services, and of course as the postulant, it was his job to make sure that the candles were all lit and the place was spotlessly clean before each service, on top of any other task that came his way. And with Wimer gone, there was no-one at all to tell his troubles to. He shook his head hard to try to drive away a wave of self-pity. *What else is there for me? I've committed myself here, now. And there's nothing for me out in the world anyhow. Until my father can be proved dead, my total worldly wealth is that little meadow that William is going to try to steal. And what could I do away from the Priory, anyway?* He sighed again. *I will just have to tell God all my woes and pray for guidance.*

He was supposed to have the stables mucked out before Nones, but he'd been getting slower and slower. Now he stood leaning on the shovel, chin propped on the top of the handle, gazing out across the meadow at the church, not really seeing anything. For a moment he allowed himself to imagine Wimer bustling over to the woods to tend his beloved bees, shutting his eyes against the pain. The Priory seemed so empty without Wimer, so much less a home...

When he opened his eyes again, there was a rider on a grey palfrey where he'd imagined a slim black-robed monk. He blinked to clear the image and realised that it was the Prior on Dobbin, heading for the stables. He hastily bent to his shovelling again.

"Ah, Jean - I've been meaning to have a chat. How are you doing?"

Jean propped the shovel up against the wall and moved across to take the bridle.

"Well enough, thank you, Father."

"No, really, Jean - I'm interested in the answer!" The Prior swung a leg over Dobbin's broad back and dismounted, putting them on a level. "How do you feel your postulancy is going?"

Jean ducked his head. "I'm afraid I'm disappointing Brother Lawrence - I am trying; but since Father Wimer died, it all seems so much harder. He's left such a big hole!"

"Aye. But don't be too downhearted, Brother

Lawrence's bark is often worse than his bite. Offer up your duties to God, and try to do everything joyfully - He sees all, and knows the workings of your heart." The Prior steered both Jean and the pony into a stall. "I'm missing Wimer too. I've known him for what, 30 years now? His passing is a real blow. Give me a hand with the girth, would you?"

They untacked the pony together in silent harmony. When the beast had been rubbed down, had fresh hay and water, and the tack had been put away, they stood together looking over the valley. The Prior went on,

"I'm also missing Wimer's accounting skills, and I'm sure we'll miss his knowledge of the law, and I wish the priory had another priest! I'm having to take all the services at the moment, it's keeping me very busy. Still, I'm hoping that the Bishop will ordain Brother Lawrence in the next few months. But we should be grateful that the Lord lent Wimer to us for such a long time."

Jean plucked up his courage and tried to get the right words to ask about the thing that had been gnawing at him ever since the funeral.

"Father, I think William plans to dispute Wimer's will - how can I stop him, do you know?"

Down the hill the church bell began to ring. The Prior shook his head and spoke over his shoulder as he hastened down the hill.

"Don't you worry about that, lad. We can deal with Master William if and when he becomes a problem. You should concern yourself only about your postulancy - and praying for the souls of the dead, of course. Hurry up, or you'll be late!" and he moved off almost at a run.

Jean checked that Dobbin had water and followed slowly. *I might feel less trapped if I knew that meadow was safe from William's clutches.*

***

It was so cold outside that most of the monks were happy to listen to Father Adam's money woes for as long as he cared to talk - anything to prolong their time in the warm room. Jean was half-listening - something about having to hand in all their coinage, and no-one in the kingdom allowed to own coin between the end of November and the beginning of January whilst the King changed the currency, which was why the food that the kitchen was producing was so boring right now; they couldn't buy anything, and some of the stored food had been spoiled by the cold. Brother Joseph asked a question about barter, and the conversation started to go round again. Jean shifted impatiently, then schooled himself to serenity. However much he wanted to be out of there...

Jean knew what Cook had been doing instead of cooking, and was really happy about it. A couple of days ago, when they'd finished the last scraps of a scrawny red deer that Father Adam had managed to hunt down, Cook had pulled first one shin bone from the stockpot, then the other; squinted down the length of them; and then looked speculatively at Jean.

"You ever do any skating, lad?"

Jean had felt his eyes go wide, and had shaken his head vigorously.

"Well, if this cold snap continues, mayhap you'll get the chance. Ye can go and play on that bit of meadow of yours, it's flooded as usual. Not on the fish ponds, mind, in case there's anything left alive in there. If we're lucky, a carp or two will be swimming around at the bottom of the deepest pond, but we can't get at them until the frost eases. That meadow will be ready to take your weight in a day or two, I reckon."

Jean had spent as much time in the kitchen as possible, watching Cook sawing, drilling, and eventually grinding the bottom of the bones flat - he'd blown the last scrap of dust away and squinted along the edge one last time just as the bell for Chapter had gone earlier. All they needed was a couple of leather thongs to tie through the holes at the front and around his ankles, and he could try them out! If they ever got out of Chapter. He went back to listening. It sounded like they'd finally stopped talking about money and were discussing whether or not they should break Saint Benedict's rule about the length of time everyone could spend in the warm room. Jean wasn't too bothered about that, given the amount of time he had to spend in the kitchen - but he could really see why some of the older brothers would suffer in this weather. Father Adam was talking...

"...least we have good supplies of wood. I will authorise a brazier in the dormitory, and we will maintain the fire in here for an extra two hours a day. Anyone who has duties that can be done indoors may bring their work in here. When the weather is more clement, and we have a steady supply of food again, we will do some extra penance in compensation. And now, Brethren - let us pray, before going about our tasks."

Jean bowed his head and tried hard to listen to the dismissal. But he couldn't wait to get down to his meadow and try his skates out! *It must be the closest you can be to flying...*

***

The embers of the fire flared briefly as William swept the curtain aside, banging the door shut behind him. Edeva looked up dully, brightening as she saw what he was carrying.

"Here you are, Wife - don't waste a scrap! It was right hard work getting it."

He held out his hand, the hare's long legs trapped between his fingers. She stood up, cold bones protesting, and took it from him, her mouth watering at the thought of it already. It was still dripping blood, so she wrapped her shawl around her one-handed and went straight out to the kitchen lean-to.

She eyed it where it lay on the wood block as she ran the knife up and down the leather strop. *Poor little thing - half starved itself...* It was pretty, as well as bony. Its fur was patched with white in response to the harshness of the winter. William had clubbed it to death by the look of it, there was no rip in its pelt. *If I'm careful skinning you, you might make a muff!*

She slid the knife into the soft place under its chin and down its length. With her fingers, she began to ease the skin away from its skull, but there was too much bruising. She turned her attention to the shoulders, easing the skin free of the flesh as far as she could reach. There was still a bit of warmth in the body, enough to make her relish the feeling - the kitchen fire was out, they only had enough wood for one fire and that had to be in the house. The East wind was cutting through the gaps in the walls that William had never got round to fixing, the sound alone making her shiver.

She picked up one long forepaw, dislocated the ankle joint, then carefully slid the sharp knife into the space between skin and flesh until she could force it through the knuckle. The other forepaw came away clean too, and she clicked her tongue in satisfaction. The haunches were quickly dealt with. Flipping the skin inside out, she pulled it up towards the head. *Yank, or peel? It would be sad if it ripped on that shattered skull.* She held her breath and yanked about a finger's breadth; there were bone splinters stuck to the skin, but it had stayed in one piece. She trimmed around the lips and smoothly pulled the rest of the skin free. Smiling in relief she turned her attention to the body; no longer an animal, but meat to be butchered.

She pinched up the membrane at the point where its breastbone ended and slid the knife in at a shallow angle, blade uppermost, and ran it gently down the length of its belly. Two quick cuts at the top and bottom of the gut, and the entrails spilled into her hands. She sliced first the kidneys then the liver free and set the rest aside for the pigs. The liver was clean and perfect, and just about the most appetising thing she'd ever seen. William would want it all - would expect it, as his hunter's right - but she just couldn't help herself; she lipped one thin slice, then another, off the knife.

She almost swooned with the rich, earthy scent and delectable taste of it and forced herself to chew slowly whilst she dealt with the lights and the heart. *Too much of that too fast, and I might be sick...* Then it was simply a matter of jointing the limbs and blocking out the saddle. The bones went into a stew pot with a double-handed scoop of snow. She emptied the grain jar on top, a thin dusting marring the clean white. *It might thicken the broth a little. I'll see if I can dig a leek to go in there tomorrow.* She hastily rubbed a handful of coarse salt into the flesh side of the pelt and rolled it up for processing later. She was beginning to shake with the cold, and daubed more dripping than she'd meant to into a skillet. Without pausing to put some fat back in the crock, she threw the pieces of meat on top, chopped the liver and kidneys into a smaller pan - *please God he doesn't notice I've had some already-* and hurried back to the warmth of the house, a pan in each hand. They were going to eat well for the first time in days.

Chapter 7

FORGERY!

"Wife!"

Edeva heard the bellow all the way from the stream. She jumped to her feet, abandoning the washing, and hurried up the slope to see what William wanted.

He bellowed again as she came in sight of the house. He was standing there, arms on his hips, red in the face.

"Calm yourself, husband, I am here. What do you want?"

"I expect you home when I need you, woman! Hurry up and pour ale for my visitor and me."

She swallowed down a sharp comment about asking how he expected the washing to get done, or the dishes scoured, or even ale mashing to happen if she couldn't go down to the stream - and ducked her head to obey. He had warned her what would happen if she talked back to him again - she didn't want to try his temper. Particularly in front of a visitor... who was this visitor anyway? No-one ever came here - she even missed William's children, now they were all out of the house.

She poured ale into two matching horn cups, balanced them on a plank, and covered them with a cloth to keep the flies off. The curtain was across the door between the ale house - *well, ale-room, she corrected herself tartly* - and the kitchen, and as she paused to be sure the cups were balanced properly before she pulled the curtain aside, she heard male voices from the main building.

"...advantage of being Prior, dear boy, is that I can instruct any monk to do exactly what I say, and then never mention it again to anyone; and be confident that they obey. Leave it to me."

William's familiar voice replied.

"So what would work best, do you think, Father? A single charter that claims ownership of that meadow and all that block of fields above, or a couple of them spread out a bit? It wouldn't do to look too greedy..."

That doesn't sound like Prior Adam - who's he talking to? And what are they up to?

William spoke again, louder, as though he had turned his head towards her...

"Where is the woman?" - quieter - "So you know how to age the parchment properly, then? - WIFE!"

Edeva pulled the curtain aside and crossed the kitchen. She dropped a deep curtsy to the guest, careful not to spill the ale. *Prior Gilbert, of Holy Trinity! What on earth were he and William plotting? It must be something to disadvantage the local Priory, William would do anything to get even with them after Wimer hadn't left them as much money as William thought was his due.* Suddenly she realised what they were talking about! They were going to forge a charter, and use it to steal the meadow that Wimer left to Jean! Plus some of the land that had gone to the Priory, for good measure, by the sounds of it. *Thieves! And her own husband, too!*

She lifted her eyes and found the Prior studying her.

"You were a long time getting ale, Goodwife. Did you happen to hear any of our conversation?"

"N-no, Father" *think fast, you can shade the truth a bit, it's not a confessional* "Not really, you were talking about parchment, weren't you?" She forced a smile. "Will you be buying some lamb skins from us?" She handed them the mugs and began to back out.

The Prior stared at her, then turned to William. "Keep her close until the matter's settled, if you please. We don't need even that much gossip getting out."

William nodded and grabbed her wrist, hard.

"You will stay in sight of the house until I say otherwise - do you understand?" His eyes were cold; hard grey flints. Suddenly afraid, she nodded. He tightened his grip until she gasped, then pushed her away.

"Make us a platter of bread and cheese, Wife."

She turned to go.

"Quickly!" he spat.

***

The kissing-gate was a giant muddy swamp. William took one look at it, and at the broad sweep of mud that was the path the other side, and trudged up the hill to the stock gate instead. As he'd hoped, he was able to climb onto it and leap off to one side without covering himself in mud. He heard the Priory bell rung for the transubstantiation as he walked up beside the path and crossed himself automatically. *Good timing, I shouldn't have to wait long.*

He slowed his pace a little and looked around to see if there had been any changes since he was here last. There seemed to be more sheep than he remembered. He grinned. Maybe Prior Adam was getting into the parchment business himself... *If I can bring this visit off, I'll steal one hell of a march on the Holy Trinity. Nice of Prior Gilbert to tell me about their fake charter racket, I might have to remind him I know all about it if he gets too cross with me. IF Adam plays ball. If he doesn't, then Gilbert's my back-up plan...*

He reached the church as people were leaving, and sent the gatekeeper monk off with a request to see the Prior. As he'd hoped, he was in Adam's study within a few minutes.

Adam was still fussing with the hood of his robe, clearly having just got changed after the service. He was standing, and didn't offer William a seat.

"What can I do for you, neighbour?"

William thought about sitting down unasked, but decided not to risk annoying the Prior. Instead, he leaned forward, arms propped on the Prior's desk, and smiled in what he hoped was a winning manner. Adam pulled a scroll out of reach and raised his eyebrows.

"What, William? I have a lot to do today."

"Well, Father, I've been thinking about my Uncle Wimer."

"Praying for his soul, I hope?" enquired the Prior, dryly.

"And that," William stood straight and waved a hand in the air. "And also about the land he left to the Priory. I've been talking to one or two of the old boys in the village; they're not sure that the land was Wimer's to give, I thought you ought to know. In fact,..."

The Prior interrupted him.

"Oh, enough, William! Leave be! That land belongs to the Priory; you're not going to get your hands on it. Is that all you came for? Then please leave, I am far too busy for this."

William bowed and left without argument. *Stuck-up old fool! You just wait. You asked for all that's coming to you, and you can't say that I didn't try and warn you.* He side-stepped a pile of sheep droppings and began to whistle. *Filthy things, sheep. Don't think I'll keep 'em when I farm this land for the Holy Trinity.* He flapped his arms at a small flock of them and watched happily as they panicked over the hillside. *Noisy as hell, too... This field is just about flat enough to plough - you could get a good crop of barley off it. What couldn't I do with that kind of money!*

***

Adam couldn't settle. Finally he gave up even pretending to read the Bishop's circular and allowed himself to pace. *That William is a real troublemaker! I thought the land issue was all settled...* He stood and looked into the cloister and Wimer's grave, still slightly mounded. *You'd have tied him in knots, old friend. Nasty little man! I hope he hasn't got anything he can use against us. What did he say, exactly?* He leaned against the wall, looking out of the window where the breeze could sharpen his thoughts. He chewed absently at a torn fingernail and tried to remember everything William had said and implied. Something about asking the old men in the village? And they weren't sure who the land belonged to? The gnawing stopped, finger still in his mouth. What if all the old men, who've known William since he was a baby, could be persuaded that Wimer didn't own the land? Then what?

He took his finger out of his mouth and spoke aloud.

"You've left us without a lawyer, my friend, and it sounds like we need one."

His gaze fell on a figure in a white postulant's robe, sweeping the far cloister. His eyes narrowed, and he half-leaped to the door.

"Jean! A word, please."

When the boy knocked and entered Adam was back behind his desk, trying to look like he was in charge, at least.

"Have a seat, my boy. How's your postulancy coming along? The Novice Master tells me that you are obedient but you can be a little absent-minded."

The boy blushed and hung his head.

"Yes, Father. I'm sorry. Sometimes I get to worrying, and then I can't concentrate."

"Are you concerned about your final vows?"

"Well, a little, Father. I'm studying Saint Lawrence in Divine Reading, and I just cannot open myself to God as he does." The boy twiddled with his rope belt and looked up into Adam's face. "But mostly I'm worried because William wants to steal the land that Wimer left me. I've no real use for it - I'll gift it to the Priory if I take my vows - but it would be too awful if he got his hands on it. I'd feel like I'd let Wimer down."

Adam ran his hands over his head, newly shaved tonsure reassuringly bristly.

"Yes, I have similar concerns." *If. He said if he takes his vows. No longer wedded to the idea, then. He'd make a wiser choice if he'd seen something of the world...*

"Jean, I think that right now, you could serve the Priory better by working out a way to stop William in his tracks, than as a postulant. Inadequate as it may feel, the training you got from Wimer in his last few months makes you the best qualified person in the Priory to pursue it! Would you consider a leave of absence from your postulancy and take the job on? I think you'd need to start by talking to anyone in the area who might be able to cast light on Wimer's acquisition of the land."

He held his breath whilst the young man in front of him sat, hands on his knees, thumbs unconsciously making circles on his robe. Finally he spoke.

"Thank you for the opportunity, Father. May I think about it?"

The Prior stood up, and Jean leapt to his feet.

"Bless you, my son. I will pray that you find a decision that is right for you."

"Deo Gratia."

As the lad turned to go, Adam said

"My own credo is that God helps those who help themselves. And Saint Lawrence must have been an unbelievably irritating man."

Jean turned back, eyes wide open - then a grin lit up

his face. He bowed again and left, a bounce in his step.

***

He walked away from the Prior's office with his head whirling. *It'd be worth it just to escape from under Father Lawrence's thumb for a while! But I can't do it. I'm sure I'd make a huge mess of it and let everybody down... why is he asking me, anyway? Is this the same thing as when I was a boy, give the sickie the easy job because he can't do anything else? Is it a test - am I supposed to say Please Sir, can I remain a postulant?*

Jean lifted the robe of his gown to climb the stairs to the dormitory. *No, I don't think so. I don't think Father Adam works like that. If it were Father Lawrence making the offer... Dear Lord, though, if I am really the best hope that the Priory has to keep that land...* He climbed a couple of rungs and stopped again. *What would Wimer do?* The answer to that came immediately. *He'd want me to do it. He fought as hard as he could to sort it all out before he died. I owe it to him!*

He took a firmer grip of his habit and started to climb again. William was going to roll right over him... Well, not without a fight, he wasn't. *Hey! I can go back to tunic and leggings! And stop worrying about getting my clothes dirty!* He ran up the rest of the stairs in a rush of enthusiasm, stopping at the top - skirts still raised - as a sudden thought hit him. *I could go and see Edeva again...*

He brushed his gown down and walked slowly over to the clothes press. It felt like there were about 4 people having an argument inside his head.

I need to find out about how land deals work. Who would have the local charters before the Priory was founded?

I can't do this. It might mean talking to everyone! He put his hands over his face and rubbed them down over his chin.

It might mean talking to Edeva.

He shook his head. *Don't be stupid, she won't know anything!*

But she might. Wimer might have told her stuff, like he used to explain things to me. I'd have a duty to go and see her! But how can I talk to her, with William around?

He peeled the gown over his head, folded it over his arm, and reached into his cubbyhole for the tunic and leggings he'd shoved right to the back weeks ago. He pulled the bundle out, putting the habit in its place. As well as the clothes he was expecting, there was an extra tunic there, a pleasant shade of blue, inside-out. He frowned and unscrumpled it. Soft... Way too small. He turned it the right way out and gasped. The neck was neatly trimmed with a tablet braid he himself had helped his mother to make; blue and gold chevrons, his father's colours and device. It was the tunic he had been wearing the day he left home... *Home... Could I go back to France, throw all this difficult, confusing, painful life away and live as... What?*

He stroked the braid with his finger, then lifted it to his lips and kissed it. *No - if Father has returned, he wouldn't welcome me, I would still remind him of Maman every day; and if not, I have no claim on it until I am both of age, and have proved that Father is dead.* He snorted with sudden laughter. *Hah - perhaps a bit of legal training and practice would be a good idea!* He folded the tunic carefully and put it to the back of the cubbyhole again. *Am I going to do it, then? Dump the postulancy, maybe forever, and spend my days in a wild goose chase, fighting the Holy Trinity's whole flock of monks with a lifetime's more legal training than I have? I'd be a fool.*

He slowly pulled on leggings and tunic and ran his fingers through his hair. *I owe it to Wimer. If it weren't for him, and Goda, I'd be dead. And I've already proved to Edeva that I'm a fool, can't make things any worse there... The Lord alone knows where I'd start, though.*

He turned and clumped down the stairs again. It was all going to need some thought. He ducked into the chapel and sat on the bench by the back wall, turning it over and over in his head until he had something of a plan.

He knelt and thanked God for his help, then marched off purposefully to find the Prior.

Chapter 8

ON THE ROAD

The Prior had been reasonably generous with money, luckily - once one of the row of men lined up on the bench outside the ale house had taken pity on Jean and explained the way things worked around here, and he'd gone back to ask for some. He had known enough to leave most of it behind - but he thought he'd brought plenty of silver pennies to get the men's tongues wagging freely. He'd sprinted up the hill to the ale-wife's house, hoping that the little row of old boys, sat enjoying the weak sunshine, would be still there when he got back. *I could do with some beer myself after that run...* They were, thank heavens. Now all four of them were talking - at his expense - but no-one was saying anything useful. Jean plunked the last of his coins down in front of the ale-wife, waited until she had filled everyone's beakers, and tried again.

"So what you're telling me is that anyone who feels like it can turn up at a lord's manor court and witness a land deal? And all of you go along as often as you can." He narrowed his eyes at the most talkative of them.

"You like the gossip, don't you! You find out everything that's going on."

"Aye - that and the free ale!" The man raised his mug in a toast. "You're being quite generous, lad. Your pockets are nearly as deep as young William's, a week or two back."

Jean very carefully didn't sound as interested as he felt.

"Oh? Was William after anything in particular?"

"Wanted to know all about his grandsire's holdings, the other side of the valley. Did you know anything about that, Russ? Bigod land's more your thing than mine."

The man on the end of the bench took a long pull of ale, burped, and said "Naw. And I thought he were being a bit pushy, so I told him I didn't recall any court when his Da paid death duties to the Earl. That shut him up fast."

Jean shook his head. "I don't understand - what does that mean?"

The last speaker grinned evilly. "If his Da didn't do things right and pay his dues, like, it means that William's land might not be his'n. Nor all that land that Wimer gifted to the Priory. It'd all revert back to Earl Bigod, less'n he waives the due." He drank again and looked sadly at his empty mug. "Don't I recall that you did well out of Wimer's will, lad? Didn't you get the meadow at the bottom of the slough?"

Jean must have looked the way he felt, not far from tears, because Matt's neighbour on the bench took pity on him.

"Ah, leave him alone, Matt - you know full well that Wimer paid dues on that bit, as well as the fields that he left the Priory, right and proper, with a charter an all, I wouldn't be surprised. Not stupid, Wimer, knew the way the world works, he wasn't made Sheriff for nowt! Sets a wassit, a pre-ce-dent, is that the word? - on the ownership, even if 'is brother Hervey didn't do things properly, which wouldn't surprise me, he was a tight-fisted ole beggar." He chuckled. "'Corse, I don't think William knows about all that. Our paths crossed right early this morning; he was off, all indignant, to talk to the Earl and try and make trouble for the Priory." He drained his cup. "Nasty piece of work, young William. I'll give 'ee a bit of free advice, lad, in return for the ale; stay well away from him."

Jean looked at him open-mouthed. Had he finally found the missing charter?

"Did you witness Wimer's payment, Sir?" *please, please say yes...*

"Naw, heard about it though." He thought about it for a bit. "Think it was ole Geoff told me, and I'm fairly sure he mentioned a charter - but he's been dead these last few years. Sorry I can't be of more help."

The man heaved himself to his feet and nodded to Jean in farewell. Jean looked after him - feeling a little better that there might actually be a charter somewhere in the world that gave Wimer ownership of the land. *I've just got to find it! Hey - and he said that William was away from home. I can go and talk to Edeva today!*

***

There was a strange figure inching up the field from Dodnash brook... it looked like an enormous snail, with a dark blue shell. Jean blinked, and it turned into Edeva, bent almost double and struggling to climb the hill to her house - with a large pot on her head, and a mound of something heavy draped over her shoulders. He called out and lengthened his stride towards her.

"Oh, Frenchy - am I glad to see you! Here, give me a hand, would you?" - she swung the pot over towards him. It turned out to be full of fine sand, and seriously heavy. He clutched it to his chest and stumbled after her - she was still climbing the hill as fast as she could go; quicker than before now he had the pot.

"Hi! Slow down!" he panted.

"Can't!" she called back. "Got to be home with these clothes spread to dry and dishes scoured - and you GONE, by the way! - before William gets back. I'm not supposed to be out of sight of the house!"

The thought of William catching them together lent him extra energy, and he caught up with her at the house clearing just as she was shrugging off her shoulders-full of wet clothes. Her damp robe clung to her in very interesting ways, and he hastily looked away.

"Um - where do you want this pot?"

"Over by the door, please. Don't think me ungrateful, Frenchy, but why are you here? I really don't want my dear husband to think I'm seeing strange men whilst he's away."

"Uh, yes." He very carefully looked at her eyes, and not anywhere else. Especially not at the swell of her breasts, where the wool of her dress was drying off a little, and beginning to move freely again…

"Frenchy! Talk to me!"

He jerked his eyes upwards again and got down to business.

"Uh. Sorry… It's about Wimer's legacy, and the land he left to the Priory - and my little bit too. Um - did he ever talk to you about it, or can you remember ever overhearing a conversation between him and your father? Like, saying whether he'd got his ownership ratified by the Earl - or the present Earl's father, I suppose - when his father died? Or paid death duties? Or… anything?"

She frowned in thought, biting at a fingernail. *She looks so sweet like that…* All too soon she shook her head.

"No, I'm sorry, I don't remember him talking about it ever. It might be worth a trip to Orford and asking my mother? - but I'm no use to you at all. And sorry, but I have LOADS of work to do before William gets home, was there anything else?"

He shook his head dumbly. She bounced up to him, kissed his cheek, and spun him round so he was facing back down the hill.

"Bye, Frenchy! See you sometime!"

By the time he turned round, she was inside the house. He floated down the hill, his cheek tingling all the way.

***

Orford was buzzing; the weekly market was in full swing, a double row of stalls filling a wide market square. Jean had dismounted when the crowds had become thick, pretty much as soon as he'd first sighted the church, and now he was beginning to regret doing so - the bony nag he'd borrowed from Woodbridge Priory after his palfrey had gone lame was very interested indeed in the stalls piled high with early fruit. It might have been easier to control him from the saddle; as it was, he was getting fed up with having his arm jerked to one side and the other, and having to apologise to people he got dragged into. To make things worse, he was getting one of his buzzy headaches, and he really didn't want Goda to fuss. Although finding out where she lived would be a relief...

He gave up, bought a pair of apples from a stallholder, fed one to the nag, and asked.

"It be that house over there, young master, with the red shutters, see? - but you can't tie your horse outside the front on market day, the bailiff'll be after you for obstructing the road. Go down that way, towards the church. Take the first lane on your right, down towards the quay, then first right turn again into the back lane; the healer's garden has a low gate, you can't miss it, there's a quince tree just inside."

He nodded his thanks and started to push his way through the crowd. The church was straight in front of him, tall and beautiful. As he passed the Ipswich road, the crowd thinned a little, and he was able to swing up on the horse, giving him an unobstructed view. His gaze followed the lines of the windows up, and there on the roof was a gargoyle - Wimer had been so proud of that! Jean had lost count of the number of times the old man had told him about it. He mentally saluted it, and promised himself that he'd visit the church whilst he was here and light a candle for Wimer's soul.

He turned into the lane and passed a couple of good-sized houses before he found the quince tree, set at the bottom of a large plot. The house itself was large and sturdy, whitewashed in between the laths, and well maintained, with the same pretty red shutters as overlooked the street. He manoeuvred the horse through the gate and left it loosely tied to a branch, happily cropping the grass and well away from the vegetable beds, and went up the garden in search of Goda.

She was sat on the bottom step stripping beans out of their pods and levered herself to her feet as soon as she saw him, a dry brown curl of pod clinging unnoticed to her skirt.

"Jean, lad! How good to see you! My, you've grown - still getting overtired, I see" - as she combined a hug with a palm on his forehead - "come and sit in the shade whilst I fetch you a drink. I won't be a minute..."

He sank down gratefully on the grass beside the step and idly picked up a pod to continue her work. He had barely got it open when Goda reappeared with a big horn mug of buttermilk. He took a long gulp and licked away the resulting milk moustache with a satisfied sigh.

Goda smiled in approval. "I only churned the butter this morning, I thought the milk would be good. Now, tell me your news, and what's brought you half-way across the county - I see you're not in postulant's robes, you haven't given the church up, surely?"

She sat back down on the step, took the pod from him, and sat silently, fingers calmly busy, whilst he described the doings of far-away Dodnash, and the threat that William and the Holy Trinity Prior were becoming to Wimer's bequest. Her movements got faster and more agitated as he talked. She was shredding the pods, sending bits flying, by the time he'd finished. He absent-mindedly flicked a bit out of his eyebrow, and went on,

"So you see, Prior Adam and I thought it worth-while for me to come up here and talk to you, and perhaps any of Wimer's friends still living, to see if he ever mentioned what happened when his father died, or when his elder brother died. Can you remember anything at all? Anything he ever said to you, or a conversation you overheard with your husband?"

Her hands stilled as she thought. Jean found himself holding his breath. She shook her head before speaking, though, and he knew it was bad news.

"I'm so sorry, Jean - I can't remember anything at all about his land. He would have been more likely to have talked to my Piers, God rest his soul, than to me; or if he ever did, I've forgotten it. I do recall him once talking about his eldest brother - Hervey, was it? - and how glad he was to have escaped the farm labourer's life in Dodnash that would have been his lot whilst his brother was alive; and I think he mentioned a nephew or two occasionally; but that's all I can remember. I wish I could be of more help!"

She looked so woebegone that he leaned forward to comfort her, and nearly fell over as the pain in his head worsened suddenly.

"Enough of this! You need to rest from your journey and take one of my potions. Come on, inside with you..." Jean allowed himself to be gently bullied into lying on a pallet in the front room. He closed his eyes for just a moment...

They walked up together to the church in the morning, and Goda introduced him to everyone they met who might have known Wimer. One after another, they all shook their heads apologetically. He was on the road by noon, still feeling a little light-headed.

***

William kicked the wheel of his waggon and cursed. In response, the iron rim creaked a bit and split further. There was no chance of it making it all the way to Ipswich in this state. He glared at it again. *By-our-lady typical! I have to get up to Ipswich today, or I'll miss the wheat market. And John Blacksmith's laid up, worse luck!* He had an idea and hunted around in his tool box for some hemp twine. *I'll have to go at a snail's pace, but if I'm careful and wrap it well enough, I can nurse it as far as Blacksmith's Corner and see if they can do anything there...*

The bell rang off in the distance as the Priory celebrated mass. He anchored the twine with one firm thumb and crossed himself with the other.

"Saint Christopher, grant that this holds for me..."

The drive up the back roads was uneventful. He'd

met a herd of cows being driven down to the Cattlewade at what could have been a tricky spot, just before the little bridge at the steepest part of the woods; but he'd managed to stop in time to give them room, and the animals eyed him a bit suspiciously but trotted either side of the cart peaceably enough. He and the cattlemen had exchanged a nod through the dust, then he'd shaken the reins and driven on, the ba-DUMP... ba-DUMP as the bound patch on the wheel hit the track becoming almost a pleasant companion.

It wasn't long before that rhythm was counterpointed by the great hammer at the Blacksmith's Corner forge. *Sigwulf sounds busy - I hope I don't have to wait too long, I'm late enough as it is!*

As he drew nearer, he began to hear something else. It was like a roar, or possibly the sea... he puzzled at it for a bit, then shrugged. *I'll find out soon enough.*

The cart pulled clear of the last stretch of trees. He looked ahead eagerly across the field to the forge - and stood up in amazement to get a better view. He could barely see the forge buildings; all the clear area around it was a sea of men and carts. Suddenly the roar resolved itself into shouting. He sank back down onto the bench. "What the..." The horse stopped with the weight shift and he sat for a moment, unsure whether to go on or to try to turn the cart in the narrow lane.

The decision was taken away from him as three horsemen cantered over. All wore swords at their sides, and William sat very still, hands clearly visible on the reins. They circled him once, then the leader pulled up and nodded to him.

"Good day to you, fellow. My name is Fulk of

Canterbury, and I have some bad news for you." He nodded at the younger of the other two, who dismounted and handed his reins to his companion.

"I am one of the King's Sergeants at Arms, and I'm confiscating your horse and waggon to help with the war effort. You can come along and drive it. Every cart in the land is needed to get supplies to the ports so we'll be ready to invade; you can tell your grandchildren that you were part of the King's glorious victory in France."

William frowned at him open-mouthed for a heartbeat. He could feel the blood rushing to his head. *Hell no! He can't, that's stealing...* he realised that the youngster was now at the horse's head, firmly holding the bit strap. *Trapped!* He forced himself to lean back against the back rest, thinking frantically. The leader took his hand from his sword pommel and nodded approvingly.

"Sensible fellow. Tie the reins up, please - that's right. Jon here will come with you up to the camp. Fine strapping fellow like you will enjoy the military life, I'm sure."

Dear Lord. How do I get out of this?

The youngster swung up to the seat, shook out the reins, and clicked his tongue to the horse to start off. He almost immediately stopped.

"Er, Sir? - there's something wrong with that rear wheel?

The sergeant turned his horse and inspected the bodge job.

William seized his chance.

"Yes, Sergeant - I was bringing it in to the forge to be

mended." He swallowed, and steeled himself to carry on with a lie.

"Sir? My wife is heavy with child. She needs me home right now - how long before the waggon can be mended and you need a driver, do you think? Could I go home in the meantime?"

The sergeant glanced over at the hectic scene by the forge and back again at William. He shook his head.

"Yes, all right, I take your point. The King needs your waggon and your wheat more than he needs an unwilling conscript - on this day, anyway! Don't be surprised if the war with France soon needs every man, though! Go on, farmer - back to your wife; and I pray that she is delivered safely."

William scrambled off the seat and made for the safety of the woods before he could change his mind. He didn't look back until he was in amongst the trees, and by then his waggon was almost at the camp.

That was far too close! They nearly got me! How the hell am I going to cope without the waggon and horse? Bastards! Who gives a toss about what happens in France? He spat on the ground and wiped his lip. *I'm sorry that I lied about Edeva, though. Might be bad luck, swearing that she was big with child, when she hasn't quickened at all.* He glanced back through the trees to make sure he was alone, and sank to his knees, hands clasped.

"Please, Holy Mother, don't take revenge for my lie on my wife - it was the only thing I could think of that might stop them from taking me away!"

He clenched his jaw for a moment and went on.

"I'll say one hundred Hail Marys if you promise not to make her barren." He waited, but nothing seemed to have changed. Still, he felt better at the thought of action. He hunted around on the forest floor until he had first ten white pebbles, then nine dull ones, to help him count; the white ones for tens, and the dull ones for the ordinary numbers. He squared his shoulders and started off on the long walk home mumbling the prayer.

"Hail Mary, full of grace..."

***

Jean saw from a distance that the Earl's standard was missing from the Framlingham Castle flagpole, but rode in anyway; perhaps the Earl's steward would be able to help. In any case, Goda had been very specific about how far and how fast he should travel for the next few days, and he was due a break; he might as well sit in a nice dry hall and drink ale, as huddle under a dripping oak and have water from the nearest stream.

The steward was very helpful, and hauled a great armful of charters out of the document cupboard onto the trestle table for him.

"Here you are, lad - that's all I have here. They'll keep you busy for a while!"

He picked up the first stiff strip of vellum and squinted at it. The handwriting was a bit spiky and old-fashioned, but not too bad, and as he'd hoped, was written in a standard formula. *Thank goodness they're using the normal abbreviations. It would take me twice as long to read this lot, otherwise.* The charter was about a gift of land by Roger's father Hugh to Bungay priory, no use to him, but about the right age. The next one off the heap was still creamy white and a bit flexible - from last month, an acknowledgement of a marriage. The ink was a little smudged in one corner, and Jean sniffed disparagingly at the quality of the ink. *No-one's going to find our Priory charters looking like that...* He sighed and began to sort the charters into piles, all the land grants in one heap, everything else in another. Then it took him a fair while just to put the land grant pile in date order, and some were undated. He was a little vague as to the year that Wimer's brother had died, so he looked carefully through everything for four or five years either side of his best guess. Nothing. He had a thought, and made a note of the witnesses on all the Bentley, Dodnash, and East Bergholt ones for future reference, and then did the same for the undated charters. Still nothing about the fields he was interested in - probably. Some charters were talking about strips of land in Bentley, next to woodland in Dodnash belonging to a man called Aelfric. He looked back a few years, and there he was signing charters alongside "Hervey, son of Aelfric" - so at least he now knew what Wimer's father was called. He stood up, stretched, and went looking for a mug of ale, surprised how thirsty he was.

He drained the mug. As he lowered it, the housekeeper bustled up to him and made a quick curtsey.

"Beg pardon, Sir, but have you finished with the trestle? I need to set up for the noon-day meal. I'm sorry to bother you, but..."

"Oh! Yes, I'm sorry, I've been longer than I meant to

be - let me tidy up."

They got in each other's way for a bit, but soon the charters were back neatly in the cupboard, the trestles he'd been using were pulled with others into a U-shape with tablecloths over the planks and benches set up either side, and people began to appear looking hungry.

The steward looked in, spotted Jean, and came over.

"Did you find what you were looking for, lad?"

Jean shook his head. "Not entirely, but I've made a tiny bit of progress. I need to look at some of the earlier charters still - may I borrow them again after the meal?"

"Yes, of course! You'll join us for food, won't you - and for the service? It's starting now." The man smiled and gestured him to follow, presumably towards the chapel, chattering away. Jean missed most of what he was saying, trying to remember what on earth the man was called... *Henry! Of course he's a Henry, I've just been reading some of the charters he's signed.* He realised that Henry had been telling him about his morning's problems...

"...and this new tax, for the King's wars in France - it's all very expensive, and worrying; I'm having to scrabble around to get the money, and I've never yet heard of a war that only needs a single tax. I hear the King's men will be here next week, or the week after at the very latest. Are you ready for them at your Priory?"

Jean was saved from having to answer - just as well, it was the first he'd heard of it - as they turned into the chapel and genuflected to the altar.

The service washed over him without any meaning at all - he'd spent most of it feeling glum, lost in his own thoughts. *Where do I go now? I'm getting nowhere fast. What if there wasn't a charter? What if Wimer never owned my land, or even the land he built the Priory on? What if William grabs it all, can he do that?* His head was spinning by the time the priest said the dismissal.

He did his best to be a pleasant companion over the meal, but could hardly wait to get back to the charters. As soon as the servants had cleared a single trestle, he asked them to move it under the window and got the pile out again. Aelfric had been a model citizen, apparently - signing several of the old Earl's Bentley charters - but frustratingly, there was no proper record of his own land holding at all, only that vague mention of woodland - and nothing that he could see relating to either his own little meadow, or the Priory lands. The light was perceptibly tipping into golden afternoon when the steward came by again, to see if he wanted anything, and to enquire whether he was staying for the evening meal.

Jean shook his head.

"Sir, my apologies - I have an urgent need to pray, to clear my head; if you don't mind, I'll pass up on dinner, and take my leave when I've finished with the charters - I just want to be sure these last few hold nothing of interest to me, then I'm done."

"As you like, lad - I'll have them saddle your horse, and pack something into your saddlebags. Good luck with your quest!"

Jean smiled his gratitude and went back to his

reading. When he finally made it into the chapel, a pair of black-clad women were praying. He moved to the wall to wait until he could have the little space to himself. One of the paintings caught his eye; a human-sized saint holding a club. He went to look up at it. St Jude - the exact saint he needed; his cause was about as hopeless as it could be! He glanced around and found he was alone. He knelt in front of the saint and tried to put in words how he felt. All that came out was a strange little squeak -

"Please help!"

He shook his head in disgust, and gave up the effort to find words. He simply allowed himself to let the frustration, the fear of failing Wimer and the Prior, even the pain of losing Edeva to all well up - to show it all to the saint, and let it flow through him.

When he stood up he felt so much calmer.

The stable boy was waiting for him when he reached the stables and handed Jean a cloth bundle and a leather bottle along with the reins. It wasn't long before he was on the road back to Woodbridge, enjoying the last of the evening sunshine, and very happy at the thought of giving up this jolting, bony horse and reclaiming lovely old Dobbin... He munched a bite of bread. *I'll need to work down that list of charter witnesses and eliminate them. And it'd be worth talking to the Earl; if I'm lucky he might have witnessed the missing charters for his father, when he was a young man, or could at least confirm this Aelfric's holding.* He took a big bite and washed it down from the bottle. *And maybe I should plan another day at Framlingham, and see if*

I could map out where everyone's strips of land are. I wonder if the Tollemache records from Bentley would overlap? That might make things clearer. He folded up the empty cloth into his saddlebag and kicked the borrowed horse into a canter. Somehow the quest didn't seem as hopeless as he'd thought. At least he had a plan...

Chapter 9

EDEVA TRIES TO CONFESS

He was going to miss the service if he didn't get a move on... Jean swung round the pillar at the entrance to the Holy Trinity's scriptorium, slipped on a wet flagstone, and fell over the feet of the woman who was crouched outside. He landed full on his kneecap. The shock of it made him gasp, and for a few heartbeats he was much more interested in clutching his leg to his chest than in worrying about who he'd fallen over. Then he forgot about the pain entirely as she spoke - there was something familiar about the voice, slurred though it was...

"You great oaf! Can't you look where you're going?"

He lifted his head incredulously, swinging round to face her. "Edeva?!"

The woman pulled her shawl hastily over her hair, but not before he'd seen the bruises on her cheek.

"Dear Lord in heaven - what happened to you!"

She spoke from underneath the shawl. "Oh, go away, Frenchy - you really have a habit of turning up at exactly the wrong time, don't you! Just go away before he comes back and beats me for talking to you, again!"

He stood up, a bit gingerly, and stared at her. Slowly he pieced together what she meant.

"W-William did this to you? But that's dreadful! Hang on - he beat you for talking to me? Why? We haven't spent five minutes in each other's company since you got married!"

"Don't be so by-our-lady stupid! He can beat me any time he likes, it's his right!"

The shawl was beginning to shake, like the person underneath was having trouble controlling their breathing. He leant forward and gently lifted it clear of her face. The whole right cheek was one livid bruise, starting to yellow at the edges. Her eye was half swollen shut, and there was a cut on the corner of her lip.

She glared up at him, defiantly. "Oh, shut your mouth, Frenchy, stop looking like a fish out of water!" She dabbed at her eye with her shawl. "Please, just go away before he comes back. He did this because I let slip that you'd been to the house the other day. He doesn't like me talking to other men - and for some reason, he thinks you count!"

Jean blinked a little at the insult, but something was puzzling him.

"Why are you here? I mean, here in this Priory, and looking like that? Surely he doesn't want anyone to know he treats you like this?"

"I'm not allowed out of his sight, hardly. I get dragged all over the place... He's in there somewhere seeing the Prior, and told me to find a quiet corner and stay out of sight. How was I to know that you would come charging round that pillar like a bullock with its head down! You've given me another bruise, look at my ankle!"

Unwillingly, Jean watched as her skirts were hitched up just far enough to show a neat little ankle, sure enough with a new purpling starting to show. He swallowed and looked away. There was a shadow moving down the walkway towards them, and footsteps getting louder. Her good eye was as round as an owl's! He placed a finger on his lips, and hopped round her again, back into the concealing shadow of the scriptorium. He pressed his back against the wall as William's voice cracked out -

"Come on, you - on your feet. I need a drink - too damn tight to offer me one, is the dear Prior. And crawling to him makes me very thirsty. Come ON, I said!" There was a little whimper as Edeva was jerked to her feet. Jean clenched his fists and pressed his head back against the cold stone; she was right, her husband could beat her any time he wanted, and smashing his face against the wall could only make things worse for her. *Besides, the old bastard is still heavier than you - even if he's not much taller any more...*

He waited until the footsteps had died away, then shook his head in disgust and walked back to his borrowed desk. He'd well and truly missed the service, he might as well go back to reading charters. Somewhere there must be a record of Wimer's family getting hold of that land...

***

The list was beginning to look like a flock of

chickens had worked it over, there were so many scratchings-out. Jean turned it sideways to find a fresh spot and tried to work out who was left.

Hmm, the Tollemaches - how did I miss them? I can do them tomorrow. Ah. The de Veres. The Norwich Cathedral cartulary. He stroked his chin with the tip of his plume and ran his finger carefully down the list. *That's really all the likely prospects left. Horribly short list! And not counting nipping over to Bentley for the Tollemaches it's at least two long trips, north and south. Ah well. Then it'll be done, and I'll have tried my best; I can go back to being a postulant, and stop all this running around.*

The Tollemaches' records had been well ordered (and only a single box of parchment, quickly searched through), but were clearly missing anything useful with Aelfric's or Hervey's name on. He sighed and shifted his weight in the saddle a little. It would have been wonderful if he'd managed to find the missing Dodnash charter in the place closest to home, to save both time and his riding muscles. Never mind, he could cross them off his list, he was on his way home now, and there was still the Norwich Cathedral archive.

The rain started as he crossed the river at Bures, a burst of heavy, penetrating rain that quickly soaked his cloak and hood, then settled down to the sort of grey drizzle that wasn't going away any time soon. It matched his mood; despite the de Vere archivist-in-residence at Hedingham Castle helping him to sort through a mountain of parchment, stacked neatly in shelving running round all of one of the turret chambers, there had been nothing much at all about the Dodnash land. Wimer's name had come up quite a lot, which had given him a warm feeling every time he saw it - and once Hervey was mentioned, buying a mill in Flatford - but nothing else. *This whole thing is a waste of time.* He'd been in a hurry to get out of Hedingham so he could be home before dark, and he'd forgotten to ask for a way-meal. His tummy rumbled at the thought. *Fasting is much easier when you meant to do it!* He blew morosely at the drip dangling off the rim of his hood. *Not going to go thirsty, I suppose...* A farm cart was coming up the hill, a pair of thickset cobs beginning to have problems in the mud. He nudged Dobbin off the track to make way. He and the farmer nodded at each other, sending matching sprays of water from their hoods, but passed in silence. *So what can I do if Norwich comes up empty too? I'm completely out of people to talk to. One good thing, I don't suppose William is having much joy proving his claim, either!* He shifted his weight at exactly the wrong moment, as Dobbin was stepping back onto the sand of the track, and the horse stumbled. A few steps later, and there was a definite limp.

"Oh, I'm sorry, old fellow! Hold up. I'll walk for a bit."

He swung his leg over the saddle and down. His heel caught on the edge of the track, and the mud gave way; he ended up flat on his back, left toe still caught in the stirrup. Dobbin looked round, mildly surprised, and took a step forward. This freed his toe, but pulled his cloak up round his shoulders, driving the mud up his tunic. He squealed and scrambled to his feet.

"Great. Just great." He retrieved the reins and grabbed the saddle cantle to keep upright. It was going to be a long walk home!

***

The pan of rabbit stew was beginning to burn her hands through the cloth. She hesitated a little to see if William would move his legs for her, but he kept them stretched out almost to the fire. *If he moves when I go past him I'll spill this horribly expensive stew...* The place where the cloth was thinnest, on the base of her right palm, was becoming unbearable. She took the risk and stepped over his legs.

The two men's conversation continued without a break. John de Vallibus, from Wenham Castle, was listening avidly as William was describing some land... she set the bowl down on the stool beside the fire and held her scalded palm against the fabric of her skirt, still cool from the walk from the kitchen.

"...the clay sits on top of both sides of the valley, with sandy soil underneath, there's a line of good springs at the join..."

She picked up a new piece of wood and settled it onto the fire. *Why he wanted to buy a rabbit for this meeting, I don't know - I'd rather have spent the money on some soap, Goody Kes' stuff lasts for ages...*

"Plenty of woodland too, mostly alder, and there are beehives in the wood nearest the buildings, a good spot..."

Hang on, what buildings? She gathered her skirts up

and stepped over William's legs again. He moved his head impatiently to keep his gaze on his guest, but otherwise continued to ignore her. She moved over to where the eating-bowls were stored, as slowly and quietly as possible, and listened carefully. William was working his way along the valley, describing every field and piece of woodland along it. *Curious...*

De Vallibus drained his cup, and looked around, frowning. She hurried over and refilled it from the ale jug. His frown stayed in place and he continued to watch her. William noticed and stopped talking, too. He pulled his legs in as she went back for the bowls, almost tripping her. In the silence she served first de Vallibus, then William, a bowl of stew, spoon, and a wedge of bread. She turned to close the flap of hide across the doorway, and they were still watching her, stew untouched.

If they hadn't been so secretive she might have ignored it - but now, she had to know what they were doing. She went to the kitchen and got a hunk of bread for herself and tiptoed back to crouch beside the door. Their voices were low, and she strained to hear.

"...then just this side of the Great Way, I have an arable field; but below it there's a lush meadow, excellent grazing."

"And who owns that? Still the Priory?"

"No, it's an irritating little no-account postulant. That meadow's the reason the Holy Trinity are taking an interest in all this - and once the ownership of it is in their hands, the rest..."

William's voice faded out. Edeva frowned and crept nearer. *Ownership? Why is the Holy Trinity priory going* to get ownership? It's Wimer's priory! Well, was - but the Dodnash priory owns it all except Jean's little meadow, what IS William going to do?

"...understand why you're offering this to me. Why not, say, Tollemache?"

"Well, tell the truth, we did offer it to him first, as he's nearer. But his scruples are getting in the way - too bad for him. You could manage the land from Wenham well enough. Are you interested?"

"The charter trail would need to be clear, and unchallengeable. But given that, yes, I think I am. If the price is right."

"No fear of that, the Holy Trinity have had plenty of practice in, shall we say, creative charters! Excellent. Let's drink to it then... WOMAN! Bring more ale!"

Edeva leapt away from the wall as though she'd been stung, and ran to the far door in case William was going to pass out the ale jug to her - but the door flap stayed down. She concentrated on slowing her breathing as she walked towards it. *Would they be able to tell from her face that she'd overheard?* William bellowed again, and she jerked the flap aside and forced herself to go in. He half-threw the jug at her without looking.

Her thoughts were in turmoil as she went to fill the jug. *That's what the Holy Trinity Prior was doing here that time - working out what to steal from Dodnash! And from Jean, too - Wimer gave him that meadow, it's his inheritance! And the Prior knows how to forge the age of the charters, I remember him joking about it to William. Of course no-one would question the source, if the Priory swore that the charters had been in their archive! What a nest of rats! What can I do? Who would believe me, instead of the Prior of Holy Trinity?*

William stormed out of the snug and grabbed the full jug from her and backhanded her for good measure. The flap swung shut again, leaving her in the dark. *No-one, that's who. And William could do whatever he liked, people would say I was God-touched and I should have the wickedness beaten out of me...*

She started to sob, quietly.

***

Adam waved him to a seat and leaned forward eagerly for Jean's report. The cat squeezed out of the Prior's lap, walked over the table, and jumped up on Jean's lap instead. He ran his hand down the warm curve, getting a purr as payment, then swallowed hard and began to list all the people he'd talked to, talking more to the cat than to the Prior. Half-way through, Adam went over and poured them both a mug of water, then sat back down. Jean sipped gratefully and carried on, hearing his voice grow lower and rougher as he finished the litany of uselessness. He got to the end and heaved a sigh, glad that the job he'd been dreading was done.

Adam was silent. Jean looked up at him; he was cupping his mug, staring into the mid-distance. Their eyes met, and to Jean's surprise, Adam began to smile.

"You think it's hopeless, don't you? No, don't hang your head, you promised me that you'd do your best; that's all any man - and the Lord - can ask. Look at me - how's your scripture knowledge coming on, my son?

Do you recognise Isaiah 40, verses 29 to 31?"

Jean shook his head.

Adam was still smiling happily. "Wimer quoted it to me once, you know. I was a young and very inexperienced temporary Prior, and I'd inherited what looked like a hopeless case - the priory I was looking after had been run down for years; the previous Prior had been very ill, and had simply ignored the money side of it. We had a huge bill from the Treasury to pay. I had nothing but beans in the coffers, and I was so new and green that I didn't even realise how much trouble we were in. Then a miracle appeared in the form of this man who understood exactly how the courts worked, and how to make money. He saved us; the Priory would have been disbanded if he hadn't come along. He saved me, too, though I'm not sure he ever realised it. I was prepared to resign as Prior, perhaps even to abandon my vows; I never told him that - he was still excommunicate at the time, it would have been far too cruel a burden for him - but he came upon me one day sitting slumped exactly as you are now, and quoted it to me. 'Young men grow tired and weary, and stumble and fall; but those who hope in the Lord will renew their strength.' So. Let us place our hope in the Lord, and see if there's any stone left unturned in this. Let's go over it again in detail, please."

Jean started off again. Adam listened intently.

"Whoa, hold on - you talked to Earl Roger's steward, not the Earl himself?"

Jean nodded.

"Well, I that's one avenue to explore further. I think

you need to talk to the Earl and explain the problem we have, it may jog his memory. The land may have come to Wimer when the present Earl's father was alive, but Roger was involved in their land management, and witnessing charters, from a very early age. And the Bigod holdings are spread all over the country, it may not have been Framlingham where the petition was made. Carry on!"

Jean worked his way down the list.

"There's another one, lad - try the dowager Lady Tollemache. Bit of a long shot, her husband may have handled all of that kind of thing, but you never know. And I like your idea of piecing together the Tollemache and Bigod charter descriptions to see if you can map Wimer's father's holding. Go on."

Jean was feeling much better about the whole thing. He looked up to say to Adam that he'd go and spend a few days at Norwich next week - and the words dried in his mouth. There was something wrong. The left side of the Prior's mouth was dragged down at one corner - he was trying to say something, but nothing was coming out! Jean watched horrified as he tried to stand up and fell heavily over his desk. *Dear God! Dear God! What's wrong with him?* Jean dithered between trying to pick the Prior up, and getting help. He ran to the door - sending the cat flying - and screamed for help, then ran to the Prior and tried to pull him back into his chair. The old man tried to help, which only made things worse - the whole left side of his body was floppy, like an under-stuffed scarecrow. All Jean managed to do was to cushion his fall as they both ended up on the floor. He nearly cried with relief at the sound of sandalled feet in the corridor outside.

***

"Husband, it's been at least three weeks since I went to church, and I didn't take mass then, or the time before - would you mind if I went down early for confession and mass?"

Edeva held her breath, fingers firmly crossed under her apron, until he looked up from his bowl of potage and waved her away.

"Just don't waste time after the service gossiping! I want you straight home, you hear?"

She ducked her head in acceptance, stripping off her apron and edging out of the door before he could change his mind. It was a glorious morning, sunshine just starting to take the edge off the first crispness of autumn, and she drew a deep breath - one that wasn't tainted with the smell of William's food. Her tummy rumbled at the thought. *Worth it, though, to feed him early so he couldn't go to Mass even if he wanted to, so I get all this lovely time to myself!* She lifted her skirts indecently high and almost danced down the hill, allowing herself to skip across the bridge at the bottom to hear the rhythm of her best wooden shoes against the planks.

She sobered as the Priory came into view. *I'm just going to lay it all at Father Adam's feet, all this business about William and the Holy Trinity Prior up to no good, and let him sort it all out. I'm sure I'll be punished for disobeying my husband and telling on him, either in this world or the next, but what he's doing is so WRONG!* She slowed to a walk and put her hands up to check that her wimple was in order.

A second later she was swept up into a bear hug from behind.

"Edeva! Didn't you hear me calling? It's so good to see you again..."

Edeva turned to return the hug.

"Maria! You look well! How's the baby doing?..." The two girls moved off arm in arm, chattering nineteen to the dozen, and joined a growing group of women enjoying the sunshine against the cloister wall.

After a little while Edeva broke away.

"Please excuse me, goodwives, I must make confession. Does anyone know where Father Adam is?"

"Oh, my dear, you haven't heard! The poor man is deathly ill. I'm not sure if you can confess today - hold on, let's ask, there's that nice young postulant - JEAN! Jean, love, is there anyone taking confession today, Edeva here needs it?"

A startled Jean waved at them and vaulted over the waist-high wall.

"Yes, I think so, Goody. Mistress Edeva, if you'll come with me?"

All Edeva's nervousness was flooding back. She wasn't really listening to what Jean was saying to her until something caught her attention...

"Wait! Say that again?"

"I was saying that we've had to get a priest in from the Holy Trinity priory, because Father Adam isn't up to it yet. Father Gregory is taking confession today."

Edeva stood stock still. *Oh no! I can't talk to anyone*

from Holy Trinity about what William's been up to - they'll be in on it, like as not!

Jean was asking what was wrong? Edeva bit her lip and looked at him dumbly. Finally she made up her mind to go through with it. *Well, I'll just have to be careful what I say. I NEED to hear Mass, I feel so tangled up inside myself! If I can't rest the burden on Father Adam, I will beg God to help me bear it.*

She nodded to herself in relief and smiled weakly at Jean.

"Sorry - I was lost in my head, working out what I needed to say to the priest. Lead on!"

Jean tilted his head a little and frowned at her, but opened the church door and waved her in first. The familiar scent of incense started to work its soothing magic at once, overlaid by the sweet smell of honeysuckle from the flowers that a couple of women were arranging by the altar. Jean pointed her to a corner where the priest had just started the prayers over his confession stole, its purple glowing in a shaft of sunlight. To her surprise, as well as giving her a smile, Jean rubbed the top of her arm in farewell. It tingled pleasantly as she waited for the priest.

Finally she could kneel in front of him.

"Forgive me, Father, for I have sinned..."

The priest stared into the middle distance whilst she worked down the list of things (other than William's lying and stealing) that were worrying her. The only time he looked at her was to scowl when she confessed her growing dislike of William. By the time she'd finished, there was a short queue of people waiting to take her place. The priest gave her a little homily on her duty of care and obedience to her husband and sent her away with 50 Hail Marys as penance. She didn't mind, although she blinked a bit at the amount. She was feeling relieved even by that partial confession, and maybe the prayers would help.

She wandered into the body of the church and stood for a while, head bowed, enjoying feeling at least a little less troubled. Around her the church began to fill, and she reached for her beads to start the penance. She was three Hail Marys in before the priest, followed by the monks, processed down the aisle and the service began. She let the sounds wash over her - the priest's Latin gibberish, and the chattering from her neighbours, all joining to form a comforting buzz of people making a fellowship with her in God's house.

She took the Eucharist almost in a trance, still unable to articulate exactly what she wanted even in her head, but hoping hard that God could see into her heart and understand her predicament, and know that she was being bad for good reasons. It helped, somehow.

Afterwards she laughingly shook off the many invitations to stay and gossip awhile, and ran up the hill to home, calmed by the church rituals, and even feeling good about picking up her duties to serve and obey William again.

CHAPTER 10

WILLIAM'S LUCK CHANGES

Jean had been standing outside the Prior's office - *well, Father Lawrence's lair, now...* for ages. His back was beginning to hurt, and there was a west wind trying to blow right through him. He tucked his hands under his armpits for warmth and slumped against the wall. He shut his eyes. *I do wish he'd call me in. I want to go and look through the Cathedral cartulary - is there any point in taking the slightly longer road and trying the Framlingham records again, or should I just stay the night at Eye Priory? Eye, I think - quicker, whilst the weather's uncertain. And ask for a bed in the Cathedral dormitory for two nights, so I can have a whole day in the archive.* His mind wandered back to a visit to Norwich Cathedral with Wimer, several years ago. He'd shut his eyes to close out the world then, as the bell-clear voice of a boy chorister opened the Evensong service. The tenor voices had joined the refrain, a fine countertenor rounding the sound out to perfection. *There are compensations for having to spend a night or two in Norwich...*

"Look at you! Disgraceful!"

He leapt upright as Father Lawrence's words stung

him like a lash. The Acting Prior was glaring at him, hands folded, lips a narrow slash in his face. He shook his head and pointed towards the door.

"Get inside. You and I are going to have words!"

The whole feel of the room had changed with its new occupant. Jean looked around, trying to work out what was different. *Maybe it's just old sourpuss's smell...* He glanced across at the Prior, who was seated bolt upright in the chair behind the desk. There was no sign of the cat.

"You, boy, are a disgrace. Lolling against a wall when summoned to a superior! Dressed like a mummer! What do you think you're doing? Where is your postulant's robe?"

"But Father,"

"SILENCE! You may not speak until I give you leave to talk. And that privilege has to be earned. I am aware that Father Adam has been lax with you; and for the good of your soul, that will stop right now. You will immediately resume the duties of your postulancy."

Jean opened his mouth to protest. Father Lawrence's eyebrows almost hit his tonsure, and he shut it again. *But I've got to track down exactly what happened with Wimer's land grants! Doesn't the narrow-minded old goat know what the stakes are?*

"Better. The next time I see you, you will be correctly dressed, and in the church on your knees, thanking God for his mercy. Is that understood?"

Jean tried to blurt it all out, so Father Lawrence knew what the problem was.

"I have to find out who owns..."

Lawrence stood up and leaned over his desk,

spitting his words out.

"You, boy, will DO nothing, and THINK nothing, unless I sanction it. Do you understand me? You have just disobeyed a direct order of mine. It is clear that it's high time discipline was restored. You will do exactly as I command, or you will suffer for it. Dress yourself properly; then go directly to the church and start a vigil. A fasting night on your knees may help you to refocus your thoughts. And you are to remain silent, except during service, until I give you leave to talk again. GO!"

Jean turned automatically, thoughts whirling. A bark from Lawrence stopped him.

"Boy! You've forgotten something!"

Jean looked back at him blankly.

"BOW to your superiors whenever you meet them or leave them!"

Dear Lord. I'm trapped! He bowed in submission, then half-ran for the dormitory, very close to tears. *Now what can I do? I've failed everyone! I have to get away from here - this isn't home any more!*

***

Jean took the last curl of peel off the last turnip with a huge sigh of relief and scooped up the pile to carry over to the table by Cook. A lone turnip bounced out of his hands, and Cook caught it as it rolled off the edge.

"Steady on, lad! Are you done peeling these? - good. The next job is to go and get some fish. I'll take perch, eel, carp - whatever you can catch. Enough for, oh I don't know, thirty people. And some sorrel, please, and wild ransom leaves, if you can find any left - it's been so hot recently, they may all have gone over, but if we're lucky there might be some at that boggy bit by the far fish pond. And take the peelings out to the pigs."

Jean nodded and started out the door.

"Hey! Put a leather apron over those pretty robes of yours, or Father Lawrence will give you a piece of his mind again! You don't want another week of silence, either, do you - wondrously peaceful though it was!"

Jean grinned and rolled his eyes, and lifted the heavy apron off its hook by the door. *As if the robe isn't hot enough...* It wasn't until he was half-way over to the fish pond that he started to wonder at the amount. *Guests, obviously - I wonder who? Glad we're having fish pie, anyway...*

Of course Cook had him gutting and scaling the fish, so he had to go down to the stream and wash before running back up to serve. He'd forgotten about the guests until Brother Cellarer thrust a flagon of wine at him.

"Where have you been, boy?! You're late! Get in there and top up their glasses. I had to pour the first round myself!"

He apologised over his shoulder, and nearly fell over one of the hounds at the doorway to the refectory. He managed not to spill any wine, and thought he'd recovered the situation well - until he looked over at the high table, and saw Father Lawrence glaring at him. *Great! Of course he would have to see me stumble!* His cheeks were hot. He hurried over and offered Father

Lawrence some wine.

"Stupid boy! The Earl has precedence!" he hissed.

The Earl? It was Roger Bigod! Looking like he'd aged a couple of decades, rather than the scant months since Wimer's death. Jean carefully filled his cup, and got a nod of thanks in response. One of the Bigod retainers further down the table waved his cup, and Jean moved to obey. *I need to talk to the Earl!* He moved along the table and made sure everyone's cup was full of wine. Then he took up a station behind the Earl, and a little to one side, ready to talk to him in a break in the conversation - and be handy with the wine. It would have been a good plan, if Lawrence hadn't seen him. Actually, he smelt him first... Jean watched with horror as Lawrence started to frown, then sniff, then begin to try to work out the source of the smell... Jean looked down at his gown and saw a little trail of silver scales all along the hem, and decided that the kitchen was the safest place to be right now. *I'm going to have to pick them all off by hand, yuk...*

He'd just finished when Brother Cellarer found him again and drafted him into carrying one of the pies to a lower table. He carefully avoided looking in Father Lawrence's direction. He did steal one glance at the Earl - but his place was empty. *Where's he gone? Is he talking to someone? His men are all still here, thank goodness.* That puzzle was solved as he took a bowl of slops out to the pigs. The Earl had clearly been emptying his bladder and brushed past Jean on his way back to the hall. Jean plucked up his courage and spoke;

"Lord? May I ask a question of you?"

Bigod turned, looked him up and down a little quizzically, but gestured for him to continue.

"I am Jean, Wimer the Chaplain's adopted son. You recall Wimer's will gifted several parcels of land to the Priory, and also one to me?" Roger nodded. "Well, I cannot find either charter or witness to the original land grants to Wimer. Do you know anything about charters confirming the land to Wimer when his elder brother died, or when his father Aelric passed?"

Roger had crossed his arms and was frowning thoughtfully.

"Nay, lad - Jean? - I'm sorry; I don't think I remember witnessing such a grant myself, nor coming across one in my reading. I'll have my chaplain look it out for you, if it exists." He turned to leave.

"Lord, I've looked through your charters at Framlingham myself, there's nothing there." Jean could feel the skin across his forehead tightening. *He must know something, please…*

"Hmmm. There are other charters in Derbyshire - I'll try to remember to ask my chaplain to look for you next time he's up there. Now I must get back into the hall." Roger nodded at him, and left.

Jean looked up to heaven. *Please Lord, let him remember…*

***

The road to Brantham was a little busy for comfort - there was someone riding over the hill from Ipswich and he could hear the sounds of a driver shouting to encourage a team coming up from Manningtree. *A real pain in the neck having to come all the way over here to pray, but I'm not going to start mouthing off about a good crop in the monks' hearing, they'll raise my tithing, tight bastards.* He wasn't going to make it to the church, and the privacy of the graveyard. *God will have to wait a bit until I can give thanks for the harvest without my legs crossed...* He was not far from the sunken path leading to the Hall. *That'll do.* He walked a few steps down the path, then as soon as he was out of sight of passers-by, climbed the bank into the little stand of woodland that screened him from anyone's view.

One of the scrubby trees against the bank had fallen recently, the earth still crumbly at its roots. He aimed his stream of urine at the root ball, enjoying the way he was able to clear the muck so fast - and something shiny fell down. He followed its motion, and then hurriedly aimed away. *What on earth was that? Looked like silver. Can't be!* He finished and tied his clothing back up as quickly as he could, then picked up a stick and searched in the damp leaf mould for whatever it was. *There!* It was a coin! He picked it up and wiped it off with his thumb. It wasn't like any money he'd ever seen before - the face was sideways instead of full on, with one great staring eye and a crest of spiky hair. There was writing round the outside, but he didn't know any of the letters. He turned it over, and there was more writing around a long cross. *French money, maybe?* It was about as heavy as a normal penny in his hand. *I bet it'll spend like real money!*

He picked up his stick again and began poking the soil of the root ball. There was another of the strange coins - and another! He poked until all the roots were clear, but didn't spot any more. He turned his attention to where the tree had ripped from the bank. Almost immediately his stick made a dull thunk as it hit something just underneath the soil. He scraped with the stick until he could see something green, then used his hands to brush away the dirt. There was definitely something metal in there... He pushed his fingers underneath, then lifted. *Huh! That's heavy!* He was holding a large bronze cup, with more of the strange coins visible through the sand packed inside.

He sat down with his back against the bank, clamped his legs together, and dumped the contents onto his hose. He brushed away as much loose soil as possible, then started counting. His hands were trembling so much he had to count the coins twice. He picked the cup up and looked to see he hadn't missed any, shoved all the money back in, then carefully stood it upright whilst he checked the bank where it had been. Sure enough, some frantic digging brought up three more shiny coins. He stood holding them. One of these had a picture of a sword on one side... he stared at it for a long time. *Well. That was a better reward than I expected, for walking over here to pray. Uh... Thank you, Lord, for your bounty, and...*

Someone shouted something on the road, and he ducked and closed his hand protectively over the coins. *94 pieces of silver! By God's teeth, I'm worth robbing!* He picked up the cup and added the loose coins. The whole was a solid weight in his hand. *I've never seen so much money in all my life! How am I going to get it home? I don't even have a purse with me.* In the end, he used one part of his hose to wrap the cup and its coins tight, and the other to sling it round his waist. An armful of dead wood later, and he had an excuse to clutch the cup tightly to him, under the firewood. He stomped off in the direction of home wearing his best glare, daring anyone to ask him why he was half naked, gathering wood all the way over here. Luckily he met no-one... He stopped just out of sight of the home clearing, tucked the cup up in a high hollow in a tree on his own land, and sorted his clothing out. *Now what?*

He took a couple of the coins to the tavern on the Manningtree docks that Saturday, carefully cut along the lines of the cross into farthings. They looked much less foreign that way - the pot-girl was happy enough to take them. He bought a jug of ale for the bar and was careful to look like he'd drunk a lot more than he had. When he suggested they play a game of peg-knife quite a few of the sailors and hangers-on followed him outside. It took him a surprisingly short time to turn his farthings into whole pennies before no-one would gamble against him any more, and he decided it was safer to head off home.

Edeva was down by the stream, with a pile of dirty clothes beside her. He watched her scrubbing for a while without her noticing. None of the washing looked like it was hers - it was all his shirts and jerkins, by the looks of it. *She's a good lass - works hard, no complaints. And easy on the eye... Don't look like we'll have children, and that might be because of that stupid lie I told that sergeant that time. I should put some of this money aside for her, give her a bit of a cushion in case I go first.* He nodded and marched purposefully up the hill to home. He filched one of Edeva's pots and dropped in all the English pennies he'd won. He wrapped it in a bit of leather, and tucked it in the tree hollow with the bronze cup.

The next week he took his winnings to one of the richer taverns on the Ipswich dock, where they gambled with whole pennies - and still weren't sharp enough to spot a farmer's son who'd been throwing knives at hares and partridges since he was a boy.

*****

The felt was a little thin in one spot. Edeva pulled a hank of her best green wool free from the batt, dipped it into the pail of hot soapy water by her side, and put the hat back over the upturned bowl she was using as a form. She squeezed the hank almost dry and patted it onto the thin spot, then started gently massaging it. As the fibres began to knit she was able to put more and more effort into it - so much so that she only noticed William watching her when she stopped to wipe her forehead with the back of one soapy wrist.

"Oh! Husband! I'm sorry, I didn't see you there - do you need anything?" *Damn - what kind of mood is he in?*

"Nay, Wife - I was enjoying watching you working away there. What are you making? It's a pretty colour."

Edeva smiled at him. *Thank the Lord - a good mood!* "It's a birth day gift for Maurice - a cap, like the one I made you last year, he's grown out of his old one. I'm pleased with the colour, it was an experiment; it started off yellow, from dyer's rocket, then I…"

William had come close and put a forefinger on her mouth.

"Shush, woman, I don't want a lecture on the mysteries of dyeing! Can you leave that cap alone for five minutes without it spoiling?"

At her silent nod, he scooped her up into his arms and made for their mattress.

Oh my - a very good mood! Edeva flung her arms round his neck and nibbled his earlobe. *Five minutes, huh - I'll have to see about that. I'll need to heat up that water again, but it'll be worth it!*

***

The leather ties had swollen tight with the damp, and there was no way he was going to be able to lever his clogs off without undoing the laces. Jean balanced the trug of spinach he was carrying on a barrel of butter, tugging at the laces until they came loose. *If I go in with hands this muddy, Cook will kill me…* He sighed, then shuffle-kicked his way outside again, balancing on the loose clogs, and trying not to trip himself up. The water trough outside the door was growing a skin of ice across it, and he hissed through his teeth as he pushed his hands under the water and hastily scrubbed.

He rubbed his hands dry-ish on the tails of his cloak and tried to get in quickly out of the cold. Of course he stood on a lace and went flying, knocking the trug off the barrel and spilling spinach all over the floor. By the time he'd got everything sorted out, Cook was bellowing for him. He ducked under the curtain and held the trug in front of himself, defensively.

"There you are! What the Hades have you been doing, talking to the veg patch?! Get out there again and pick another tray of leeks and two of spinach, right now! Roger Bigod and his men will be here for the feast tonight, I need to crack on! What are you waiting for, boy? Leave that spinach on the table and get out of here!"

Jean did as he was told and retraced his steps. The brief time in the kitchen had been just long enough for his hands to start tingling painfully, and it took him forever to tie the clogs on again. *This rain is awful! I can't ever remember it so wet. I suppose the Earl's feeling half-drowned too, if he's been travelling. The roads must be appalling, for him to spend Easter here instead of with his family.* He stopped, so suddenly that he splashed more mud up his tunic. *Oh dear Lord, he'll watch the Resurrection play!* He snorted and started slogging through the mud again. *Well, one good thing about this latest sentence of silence - I don't have any lines to mess up!*

He began pulling spinach leaves as fast as his frozen fingers would go.

He could have picked twice as much spinach again and still not have had too much - both the Earl, and Prior Gilbert of Holy Trinity who turned out to be travelling with him, loved Cook's tansy cakes, and even Father Lawrence was indulging himself. Jean stopped a little short of the hall, balanced the platter laden with them against his hip, and filched one. They were too good to risk not getting any himself! After he'd offered the platter to everyone at the top table, he went to stand behind the Earl, to be handy when they wanted more. He hadn't meant to eavesdrop, but their conversation was fascinating…

"…Trinity's position is clear; Hervey of Dodnash gifted to us several of the areas that Wimer wrongly re-dedicated to you, Father Lawrence. The land is ours." *Wimer wrongly re-dedicated? What's he on about?*

The Ipswich Prior bit into a capon leg, and the Earl spoke into the gap.

"Are you sure of that, Father? I happen to have taken an interest in Wimer's legacy recently, and I've been unable to discover any charters. I suspect he made a verbal arrangement with either my father, God rest his soul, or with the de Veres directly, as my father's overlord." *Oh! That would be impossible to trace!*

Prior Gilbert waved his chicken leg. "Not so, Lord; we've been lucky enough to come across some references to land grants in our own cartulary." *Oh, no! Where were they hiding - how did I miss them?* The Prior shook his head and took a bite, then continued. "But we do recognise that a more natural recipient of the land would be Dodnash Priory itself." He took a swallow of ale.

Father Lawrence asked eagerly, "Do you rescind your claim, then?" Jean edged a little closer.

Gilbert tossed the bone to the nearest hound and delicately wiped his mouth before answering. "Well, Brother - I cannot throw away such a grant, you understand, I have to look after the affairs of the Holy

Trinity. However, there is a solution; we are prepared to give Dodnash Priory free use of the land, on two conditions..." he picked up the last tansy cake on the trencher he was sharing with Father Lawrence, and chewed appreciatively. Jean held his breath.

"What conditions?" Father Lawrence's voice wasn't entirely steady.

Prior Gilbert swallowed the last of his cake. "Dodnash Priory will become a daughter house of the Holy Trinity, and our candidate will be nominated, and voted in, as Prior here. I'm sure you can manage that without too much difficulty, Brother? Perhaps a way could be seen for you to continue as Prior here, if so?" He swivelled in his chair and reached for Jean's platter. Jean was shaking so hard the cakes were bouncing a little. *The nasty, evil little man! He wants to steal all Wimer's land, AND control his Priory!* Jean looked at Father Lawrence, who had also turned. *What's he going to do to stop this happening?* To his surprise, Lawrence was glaring at him as if it was his fault...

"Thank you, Jean, you may leave the cakes and return to the kitchen. In silence." Somehow the fake smile was scarier than when he was being yelled at. Jean bowed reflexively, put the platter on the table, and backed away. Father Lawrence watched him go, all the way across the hall and out.

The slap of fresh air as he ducked through the doorway made him gasp and seemed to shock his brain into action. He finally understood why Father Lawrence was so upset with him. *He's going to give in! He's going to throw away everything Wimer created, and*

Father Adam nurtured - dear Lord, you can't let him! He became aware that his palms were hurting where he had driven his nails into them. *Please, Lord, help me find a way to stop them!*

CHAPTER 11

BACK IN THE CLOISTER

It was so good to be outside, even in the frost! He seemed to be spending all his days either peeling things in the stuffy kitchen, or on his knees, scrubbing or praying… He aimed one more blow at the branch that had fallen half across the hive, and it came away cleanly in his hand. He tossed it onto the little pile of brushwood, ready to be hauled away. *There you go, bees - a free path to and fro for you, for when you wake up again. It's not going to be too long now, the year's on the turn.* He put his hand on the hive and thought he felt a faint thrumming. *Does anyone come and talk to you now, I wonder, since Wimer died?* He looked around. There was no-one in sight to see him idle, or to hear him…

"I've been having an awful time recently. Father Lawrence has put me under yet another vow of silence, the only time I'm allowed to speak is in Chapter, that's one of the Rules, he can't shut me up in there, but I never have much to say, anyway. Does talking to bees count? I don't care, my voice will go rusty from lack of use, and it's not like a proper conversation… He says it's for the sake of my soul, but I think he's making sure I can't carry on looking through the archives - I promised Father Adam that I'd try and stop Wimer's land being stolen, and Father Lawrence is getting in the way! You know he's acting Prior, don't you? Father Adam is so ill, I don't think he's going to get better, but he doesn't seem to be getting much worse, either..."

He poured his heart out to the bees, and it wasn't until the bell rang for Chapter that he became aware of the time again.

"Thank you so much! I feel much clearer now in what I need to do - wish me luck; I'll ask the brothers for help!"

There was some shuffling in the cloisters as the monks got lined up in the new order that Father Lawrence had decreed; he wanted everyone to sit along the wall in order of ordination, to improve discipline, apparently. Jean leaned against the wall and waited for the monks to get themselves sorted out. There was quite a lot of grumbling going on, as people argued about dates. He was last, that was easy. Finally they were ready and trooped in. Father Lawrence had, of course, been inside waiting for them, and the delay clearly hadn't improved his mood.

Jean waited politely for all the monks to be seated before sitting down himself. *I want them to listen to me; and I do not want to give Father Lawrence any excuse at all to shut me up...* He sat rigid through the reading and through Father Lawrence's little homily to them all on the virtues of good timekeeping, going over and over in his mind what he wanted to say. Finally it was the open part of the meeting. He leaned forward a little, so he could look down the line of monks to see what their body language looked like. *Is anyone going to speak? I'll let them go first.*

Brother Michael stood up and told the meeting about a robbery that had happened in Bentley - the barber had had all his money stolen and no-one knew who'd done it. Everyone agreed that the village just wasn't as safe as it used to be, and how the thief must have been a stranger passing through, there had been a lot of robberies in Manningtree, they'd probably come over the border from Essex.

Finally that topic had been exhausted. Jean looked down the line again; everyone was still. Out of the corner of his eye he could see Father Lawrence drawing in a breath to close the meeting, so he stumbled to his feet hurriedly.

"Brothers, may I ask your advice on something?"

There was a general rumbling of assent. He very carefully didn't look at Father Lawrence.

"Thank you, Brothers." He took a big breath in to calm himself. "It's about a task that Father Adam set me, and of course I don't want to worry him with it. You recall that Father Wimer left land to the Priory, and a meadow to me?"

Nods all round.

"Well, Father Adam asked me to check that the land had been properly registered at a land court, just to be sure the title was all clear; and I haven't been able to find a charter that confirms that. I've checked at the Holy Trinity priory, and at the Framlingham archive, and at Hedingham, with no result; Norwich Cathedral is the only main place left, and I don't know what to do if that fails too. My vows keep me here, would one of you be able to go there and look for me?"

There was a little flurry of raised eyebrows, as the monks took in the implications of what he was saying. No-one was volunteering to take on the job, either…

"There's another thing, as well; William of Dodnash has twice tried to steal my piece of land…"

Father Lawrence leapt to his feet and roared -

"That's quite enough of that, young man! You will not defame our neighbour like that. Sit down and be silent. And your incompetence is not a matter for the general chapter." He stood waiting, arms crossed, for Jean to obey.

There were a few nods of agreement. *Oh no! What an idiot I am! I've lost them!* He bit his lip and tried to think of something to say to rescue the situation.

"SIT!"

He sank down, mentally kicking himself. *Now what?*

***

Jean was becoming intimately acquainted with the patterns in the floorboards in front of Father Adam's desk. Studying them was much safer than meeting Father Lawrence's eye; he'd be sure to take it as insolence. Lawrence had been yelling at him for a while now, and Jean had mostly stopped listening. There was a knock on the door, and the rant stopped. *Thank heavens…*

"What is it?" snapped Lawrence. "I'm busy!"

"I'm very sorry to disturb you, Father…" shy little Brother John poked his nose around the door "But I have sad news; he's gone."

It took Jean a heartbeat or two to realise what he meant. *Father Adam! Sweet Jesu, rest his soul!* Father Lawrence too was taken by surprise, then bent his head in prayer for a few moments. He crossed himself and stood up.

"Thank you, Brother, I'll be there shortly. You, boy!"

Jean was still dazed by the shock and turned too slowly to face him.

"You are the sorriest excuse for a probationer I've ever seen! You will stay within the priory grounds unless I give explicit permission to leave them. You will take part in services and Chapter, but you may not speak to a living soul otherwise until I think that you have learned proper humility and respect. You will spend the work hours of your day in the kitchen, doing whatever Cook directs; at least you have a use, there. Do you understand?"

Somehow, Jean managed to bow. Father Lawrence made a Pfft! noise and swept from the room.

Jean sank onto the stool behind him and rested his head on his hands. *Trapped! I'm trapped here until he releases me, which will be the day Hell freezes over. What can I do - run away? Where? To what?* The enormity of the world outside the priory threatened to overwhelm him.

He shook his head to push it away and stood up. There was one thing he could do; pray. For himself, and for the souls of Wimer and Father Adam. He headed for the church.

The evening light was gilding the cream-coloured

stone of the window enclosure. From where Jean stood in his place at the back of the church, a slanting beam of dancing motes fell just short of the altar.

Falling short - sums me up. I've made such a mess of everything... and I've let Wimer, and Father Adam, down. His mood blended exactly with the opening words of the service, and he found himself singing with all his heart.

"Deus, in adiutorium meum intende. Domine, ad adiuvandum me festina." Oh God, help me. Lord, make haste to help me! *I could really do with some help right now, Lord!*

Usually he enjoyed Vespers, in a peaceful kind of way; it was pleasant to think back about the day just gone, and what had happened. Today had been so awful that it felt like the whole service was a cry for help, and he became lost in the words and the music. He had sung the Magnificat with his eyes closed, understanding for the first time how Mary had felt when God had come to her aid, and raised her whole people up. It wasn't until the Amen that he realised that his was almost the only voice left singing; everyone else had tailed off.

He opened his eyes. Father Lawrence was stood in front of the altar facing them, the hood of his habit pulled far forward over his head. The last notes of music died away, and he spoke.

"Brethren, it is with deep sorrow that I have to tell you that Father Adam has just passed away in his sleep. We will go on to sing a mass for his soul..."

Jean stopped listening. Lovely, warm, human Father Adam - he was going to miss him so much. The Prior had been almost as much a father to him as Wimer had been - and now they were both dead. *Oh Lord. Father Lawrence will be Prior, and he hates me. And he won't listen to me, and there's no way he'll release me from my vows. It's hopeless!* He didn't care if it was sacrilegious or not. He bent his head and whispered the English words from that evening's psalm.

"Lord, out of the depths of despair I cry to you. PLEASE, Lord, hear me. And Lord, please welcome in the soul of Father Adam, who was a good man and a loving one, and I am lost without his help. Domine, ad adiuvandum me festina! I can't fight this fight on my own!"

***

The first hint Jean had of trouble was the raised voices in the cloister. Admittedly, Jean was on his hands and knees scrubbing the floor tiles in the church porch, so the speakers couldn't have known he was there - but still, it was the morning study hour; no-one should have been talking at all, let alone yelling. The puzzle was too great to resist - he peeked over the wall.

To his surprise it was the sacristan breaking the rules. He couldn't quite see who he was talking to, so he settled down with his head below the wall, ears wide open.

"…won't do at all." The stranger was speaking - the voice was strangely familiar somehow. "…closed coffin, and as short a service…"

They must be talking about Father Adam's funeral! Who

is that man? And why on earth would they have a closed coffin, everyone will want to say goodbye to him?

The sacristan was clearly trying to fight back. "…community will want to say farewell… assumed…"

"…orders from the Prior, a closed coffin to prevent any unseemly displays of emotion and to hurry the process up; it's how it's always done at the Holy Trinity. And in any case, the Prior has to be back in Ipswich for a meeting this evening - there can be no delay. He will be taking the service himself."

Jean suddenly realised that the voice had been growing much clearer and louder, and grabbed his scrubbing-brush just in time.

The man, a monk in a black robe, was talking over his shoulder as he and the sacristan walked towards the church.

The stranger spoke again. "It will be done as I command, according to the Holy Trinity customs. I'll leave it to you to arrange; and I will come and inspect your arrangement after Nones. Out of my way, boy!"

Jean hastily moved his bucket as one of the senior monks from the Holy Trinity brushed haughtily past. Their own sacristan followed, head bowed, looking so sad that Jean wanted to hug him.

There was more unauthorised noise later, as the congregation filed into the church for the funeral. The monks had been almost silent, although many hands had reached out to stroke the coffin on the way past, and Jean - last in the precedence order as ever - had spotted more than one wet cheek. But the lay people, crowding in behind him, were less circumspect.

"Closed coffin? What the…" "Shhh! Don't blaspheme! It is unusual, though…" "Here, what did he die of? Why have they shut the coffin?"

The speculation continued until the Ipswich Prior, Gilbert, made his appearance, coming through the side entrance by the altar and glaring everyone into silence.

It felt to Jean that the service was as cold and short as Prior Gilbert could make it - none of the warm, comforting grace notes that Father Adam had loved so much. Jean picked up more snatches of conversation from the congregation as he followed the monks carrying the coffin out to the cloisters, where Father Adam's last resting place had been dug next to Wimer's.

"… too modern!" "What a short sermon! Like he wanted to be out of here as soon as possible" "…like he didn't want to be here at all, shame they didn't get someone who knew the old Prior…why was that miserable git from Ipswich taking the service, anyway?... Father Lawrence elbowed out…"

The oration at the graveside was the bare minimum too, and it felt like no time at all until Jean was helping to shovel the soil onto the coffin.

Chapter was a very subdued affair. Neither the Ipswich Prior nor Father Lawrence were present, which should have lightened the atmosphere a bit - but Gilbert had travelled with a servant, and no-one wanted to discuss the day's happenings with a stranger in the room. He was clearly ill at ease too. As he left in response to a call from his master, he'd thanked them for their hospitality a little too cheerfully, and said that they'd no doubt see much more of each other once the Prior had completed the arrangements to make Dodnash a daughter house of the Ipswich Priory.

It wasn't until the door had shut behind him that the uproar started.

***

Lawrence smoothed the front of his hassock for the tenth time and told himself not to be ridiculous. *The sin of usury isn't contagious... it's not my soul at stake! This Jewish moneylender is the one whose palms should be sweating.* Still - if this man wouldn't lend him the money he needed to pay off the Sheriff's rogues, he just didn't know what else to try.

He took another turn around the room, noting the depth of the Turkish carpets - three or four piled on the floor, and a beautifully patterned one on the good oak table against the far wall. *Plenty of money here...* The walls themselves were remarkable - covered in a dark green silk. He reached out to touch it, and flushed as he left a greasy fingerprint. He tucked his hands inside his sleeves and backed away from the wall.

He was standing, head on one side, wondering what the paler patches on the walls were - several, in rectangular and oval shapes - when the door opened, and what could only be the moneylender himself walked in. His clothing - white robe, tasselled shawl, both in fine linen - made a startling contrast against the dark solidity of his reception room. Only the rich embroidery of his hat - black thread on black silk -

seemed to fit.

Lawrence started to take his hands out of his sleeves, then remembered the grease. *Besides, do you shake hands with them, anyway?* The Jew watched his decision process and smiled, eyes showing no amusement whatsoever. He bowed and started speaking.

"My apologies, Father. I don't make a habit of keeping my customers waiting; but I was forced to deal with the Sheriff's men, and they weren't interested in making an appointment."

Lawrence winced in sympathy. *I wonder if they're the same men who were so unpleasant when they visited me last week? I'm glad they didn't see me. They might've put the amount they claim we owe up, if they knew I would come here for help!*

"Well, now they've gone. Can I get you some refreshments?" He looked across at the oak table and frowned, as though something he expected to see there was missing.

"Nuh- No." Lawrence blushed, irritated at his incoherence. "No, thank you. Uh - what do I call you?"

The man bowed again, this time the smile reaching his dark eyes.

"That's more interest in me as a person than the Sheriff's men showed! My name is Levi ben Tobiah. Very well, Father - let's get straight to business. I assume you need to borrow some money? How much?"

Lawrence blinked a bit at this lack of finesse. *But then, simply being in this man's company for this purpose may be a sin. I will be glad when it's all over and I'm back home...* He swallowed, and said with equal brevity,

"50 marks."

The Jew looked like he was making some internal calculation, then nodded.

"You do understand the rules I operate by, Father? I can lend you the money today, and you must pay me back the original amount plus interest."

Lawrence shook his head slightly at this blunt admission of usury.

"Yes. I understand your practice."

"Very well. Quarterly, and ten percent?"

"I- I beg your pardon?"

"You will owe me interest, payable quarterly, at a rate of ten percent - plus, of course, the principal of the loan, which you can pay at any time. So in three months you will owe me 5 marks' interest, and 5 marks more every quarter after that until you redeem the loan. Is that acceptable?"

Lawrence swallowed hard and nodded. *I hate putting the Priory in debt - but the Sheriff won't take anything less than 6 marks per knight's fee for this latest French war of the King's. Plus, of course, the fine because I can't go to fight myself. The amount they're asking for ought to be a sin, and they're leaving me no other option. It's either this or sell half our land to pay them - and then how could we live? Or pay them next time they called!*

"Thank you, Father. I was presumptuous enough to draw up the terms. Let me fetch the contract and fill in the details. Are you sure you don't want any refreshment?"

Lawrence, feeling nauseous enough, waved him away. The Jew - smiling his all too knowing smile again - bowed and left, returning quickly with parchment, pen, and ink.

"Let me just fill in the amount... there. Place your mark here, and here, please."

Lawrence signed, feeling numb. *How on earth are we going to raise an extra 5 marks every quarter? What have I done?*

The man took a knife from his belt and carefully sliced the parchment in half, forming a wriggly line. He handed one half to Lawrence.

"Here you are, Father. Your half of the contract. Is there anything else I can help you with?"

He found himself expertly eased onto the street, clutching the parchment and a small, heavy bag of money. The seagulls wheeling over the Ipswich docks sounded like they were screaming contempt at him. It took almost all the long walk back to the Priory before he remembered to pray for the soul of the Jew, prevented by law from any occupation other than money lending, and so condemned to heresy. *And Lord - I was so sure I knew how to run the Priory, and now I've stumbled at the first hurdle.* He flushed a little at the memory of the Bishop's homily at his ordination service. *I promised to be buoyed up by the prayers of the whole community, and to be humble in asking them for support. Lord, I need help on that...*

CHAPTER 12

PLEA TO THE EARL

Edeva took the letter out of her pouch one more time. The handwriting was a scribe's, of course, but he'd caught her mother's ways of saying things exactly; and that was unmistakeably her own mark at the end. Somewhat to her surprise, Edeva lifted it to her lips and kissed it, then hugged it to her chest. *I can't wait to see Mama again! It's been far too long...* She tucked it back into her pouch and let her hand rest there for a moment.

She looked around her front room with a frown. *But everything is so small and mean here! How can I make it look better?* She spotted a cobweb and flailed wildly at it with a broom until it was all gathered up. *What else?* She picked up the sheep's fleece in front of the hearth, took it outside, and shook it until it had stopped releasing clouds of dust. She put it back in place and turned her attention to the kitchen.

Oh dear, I wish William had found the time to make this a proper part of the house! It looks... so shabby and make-do! She stuck her hands on her hips and glared around the little lean-to. *It isn't a tenth as nice as Mama's kitchen in Orford! I shall have to pick some herbs to dry, that will make it look a bit better - and I wonder if William could be persuaded to redo the thatch, that would help. There's not much else that can be done before she comes. I wish she'd given us a little more notice about wanting to visit!*

Edeva ran the edge of her nail between her teeth and found a rough patch to worry at. *She knew I'd regret marrying William.* She put her little finger in her mouth and tried to find a bit of nail not already bitten down to the quick. *I won't give her the satisfaction of knowing she was right!*

She looked around again, barely taking anything in. She fished the letter out of her purse again and hugged it. *I've missed you so much...*

"I'm not having the interfering old witch here, and that's that!"

Edeva stared at him open-mouthed, shocked into silence.

"And don't quiver your lip at me like that, Wife! Where's my supper? I've been working my guts out all day to keep you clothed and fed, I expect supper ready as soon as I'm in from the fields! Come on, hurry it up, or you'll get the back of my hand!"

She ladled a big portion of pottage into his bowl and silently took her place opposite him at the fire. She pushed her mush around with her spoon until he had finished. To her horror, a big fat tear splashed into his scraped-clean bowl as she bent to take it away from him.

He grabbed her wrist, fingers grinding her bones.

"Cry all you like. She is not coming here." She stood mute, holding her breath to keep back the tears, until he let her go with a push.

***

He tossed and turned all night. Eventually he gave up, and crept downstairs and over the cloister wall to his favourite thinking spot, an old oak at the top of the slope overlooking the priory. He sat there for what seemed like forever, back pressed against the trunk and hugging his knees, his body slowly relaxing as the feeling of being trapped drained away into the night. As the first light of false dawn lightened the skyline he began to be able to work through his problems again. By Matins he had made up his mind. He stayed behind after everyone had left the church, knelt in front of the altar, forehead resting on his joined fingertips, and spoke aloud.

"Dear Lord, please forgive me - I see no other way! I must break my postulant's vow of obedience; ignore the sentence of silence I am under; and speak to the Earl of Norfolk before he leaves today."

He opened his eyes and fixed his gaze on the crucifix.

"I know it may be the end of my chances of becoming a monk. I'm so sorry that I've failed you in this and messed up on my first real test; but I have to do it, the Earl is the only realistic hope of stopping the Holy Trinity from stealing Wimer's Priory, and I gave him, and Father Adam, my word that I'd defend it as best as I could. It's not their fault that I rushed into a postulancy that maybe I should never have taken up." He bent his head, then raised it again on a sudden thought.

"I was afraid! I made a bad decision because the thought of leaving the Priory terrified me, and now I might lose it anyway, because I can't be a monk if I can't be obedient, and I don't know how to stop William and the Holy Trinity, and now I'm letting down everyone I ever loved. Dear Lord, please help me to accept whatever is your will; but I don't believe You want the Priory to be destroyed. I must act to stop that, *Deo Gratia*, with your help! And Lord, if I am then to leave the Priory, I cast myself on Your mercy. I have no idea how I might support myself."

He bent his head in silent prayer. *Ave Maria, gratia plena, Dominus tecum. Benedicta tu in mulieribus, et benedictus fructus ventris tui, Iesus. Sancta Maria, Mater Dei, ora pro nobis peccatoribus, nunc, et in hora mortis nostrae.*

"Amen." *Despite what a terrible mess I'm making of everything.*

He swallowed, then prostrated himself, arms wide. He lay there calmly for a short while, then got up, brushed off his robe, and went to look for the Earl.

He found him just in time, rather impatiently waiting in the stables for his horse to be saddled. The Earl saw him coming and nodded a greeting.

"God give you a good day - you're Wimer's adopted son, aren't you? Do you have a message for me?"

"Good day to you too, Sir. No, I want to talk to you about Wimer's legacy to the Priory, if you have a few minutes?"

"Ah! You mentioned that once before, and it slipped

my mind!"

Roger looked over at the stall, saddle still balanced on the half-door, and led the way over to a straw bale. "Might as well be comfortable whilst we talk - have a seat, lad, and tell me what's on your mind."

Jean held back nothing - not his fears about the Holy Trinity, nor William's threats, nor his own failure in finding a charter that could help. By the time he'd finished, the Earl was listening very carefully, and frowning.

"Hmm, well, I suspect your assessment of those gentlemen's ambitions is correct. I'm having a few issues with the Holy Trinity myself... You said that you'd searched the Framlingham archive?"

Jean nodded.

"Well, I'll have it searched again. There are also some records held on my estates in Derbyshire, my father may have taken a batch of charters up there for some reason; I'll have them thoroughly looked over."

His groom was standing waiting with his horse. Roger took a carrot from the basket behind them, snapped it in half, and held it out on a flat palm for his horse.

"It would suit me ill for the Holy Trinity's influence to grow too great. Rest assured, lad, if that land grant exists, I'll have it found."

He rose, took the reins from the groom, and led the horse outside, Jean following. He swung easily up into the saddle and leaned down to Jean.

"But be warned - unless we can produce that proof of ownership, the Prior may be able to argue his case in the de Vere court - he wouldn't be stupid enough to try to argue it in front of me. And I'm not in the de Vere good books at the moment, an intervention from me would be counterproductive."

He tuned his horse to leave, then turned back.

"I'll also ask my lady wife if she knows anything. She and Wimer were friends; a long shot, I doubt he discussed land ownership with her, but worth a try. Keep praying, monk - we need the Lord's aid in this!"

He raised his hand in farewell and rode off, retinue jangling behind him, down the short slope to the Priory buildings, where there was a group of people waiting to bid him Godspeed. Jean shrank back into the warmth of the stable in case he was seen. He puttered around for a bit, picking up a discarded curry comb, folding a horse blanket, generally straightening the place out. He felt strangely light, despite the breaking of his vow.

Dear Lord, please let the Earl succeed in his search. He tried to think of something else to pray, but that seemed to cover it, so he checked the coast was clear then made his way down to the kitchen to start the day's work.

***

He had taken the pots and pans far upstream of the fish ponds, to a shallow bend lined with blackthorn bushes - well hidden from the path and anyone who might spot him and pile on another job or two.

His scouring action had been getting slower and slower, and had now stopped altogether. *The problem is, the only way to fight them properly is to get a case together in court; and Father Lawrence would never do that. He's just not the type to make waves...* He scooped up a fresh handful of sand and rubbed once or twice at the neck of a butter crock. *And anyway, I don't think he could even if he wanted to - Father Adam was very clear that I had the best chance of anyone at the Priory to win a case. I wish I didn't feel like I was fighting this so much on my own!* He giggled at the thought of the whole Priory showing up at court, surrounding William, and praying him into submission. Even in his head, Father Lawrence wasn't helping. He bent to work, and the crock got some proper attention for a while.

He sat back on his heels and rolled a kink out of his shoulders. *Actually, getting the whole Priory to help might be the answer. If I asked Father Lawrence, he'd just say no without even thinking about it. But if the Chapter meeting asked me to prepare a case, he'd have to let me - at least until he's elected Prior, and can overrule the chapter's decisions.* He finished off scrubbing the crock, rinsed it in the stream, and set it aside to dry.

But how can I get them to see how important it is? It was a disaster last time I tried to tell them about William! He picked up a cast iron pan and scrubbed vigorously at some burnt-on pease pudding. *They were at least listening, though - until I bad-mouthed him.* The pan was clean enough. He set it beside the crock and hugged his knees to his chest to think.

Of course, I'll have to wait for a day when Father Lawrence is away, or he won't even let me speak. But then I should remind them about the risk to the land, and how the Holy Trinity wants to take us over, and put their own Prior in Father Adam's place... By now he was standing, pacing up and down. *And I should say how Father Lawrence is getting in the way and keeping me cooped up...* he stopped abruptly. *No! Don't be an idiot! That's where I went wrong last time!*

He gathered the pots together and began to walk slowly back to the Priory. *Mmmm. Just stick to the threat from the Holy Trinity, I think. Nice and short and simple. Don't ask them to support anything complicated.* Someone was coming down the kitchen corridor, so he stepped back outside to let them through. Father Lawrence pushed past and bustled up the path to the stables. Jean stared after him, then bowed respectfully to his disappearing figure. *Well! Looks like today is the day.*

"And so, Brothers, the Holy Trinity's claim to the Priory - and to nominate a Prior - would be much weaker if it could be proved that Father Wimer's ownership of the Priory lands was indisputable. It is this task that Father Adam set me, shortly before his death. Will you allow me to carry on with it, on your behalf? I'd need to beg Father Lawrence to temporarily suspend my postulancy, of course, as Father Adam did."

Jean stood, hands clasped in front of him and eyes modestly downcast, as the monks discussed it.

"...very young ...but Wimer's boy, and acted as his apprentice ...something has to be done or Holy Trinity ...let him try."

The murmuring died out. Jean looked up at Brother Michael, the senior monk. He was looking round the room, gathering consensus. At last he turned to Jean;

"The Chapter accepts your offer. Please act on our

behalf on this matter. I'll speak to Father Lawrence for you."

Jean bowed and sat down quickly, before his knees gave way. *Oh thank you, Lord! Now please give me the strength and courage to see it through to the end!* He closed his eyes and swallowed, hard. *And deal with Father Lawrence, when he finds out what I've done behind his back…*

***

Lawrence sat leaning slightly forward, elbows on his desk, fingers steepled. He pressed his fingertips hard against his lips, trying to use the pressure to stop a yawn… *was Brother Michael ever going to get to the end of his account of the Chapter meeting?* Lawrence was trying to look interested, so as not to insult his friend, but his thoughts were miles away. Seven miles, to be exact; at the Priory of the Holy Trinity in Ipswich. Solving the problems caused by that power-hungry institution was a better use of his time than listening to the litany of petty issues brought up at Chapter.

Of course, when - IF! - I'm Prior, I shall have to be on top of all this. But it merely underlines the importance of having a local man step up, someone who understands the people. Who else would know to allow Brother Jerome's request for an extra hour in the warming room to ease the pain in his bad knee, but refuse the same to Brother Antony, who just hates the cold? It would be chaos if some upstart from Ipswich were installed over my head. And as for this business of becoming a daughter house to them - well! Father Wimer would spin in his grave! I think the Bishop saw the sense of my argument when we met last week... I'm glad I went over the pros and cons so thoroughly with him. Shame he had to leave for another appointment before I could tell him why I would be the most suitable candidate for Prior; but maybe it'll all be for the best. As God wills...

He turned his attention back to Michael, and noticed his cup was empty.

"Do help yourself to more ale, Brother?"

Michael smiled, shook his head, and carried on his interminable report.

And as for this question of land ownership – it's threatening to become a ridiculous waste of time! I'm certain that Father Wimer had title to the land he gifted us. I vaguely remember seeing a charter about it once - I must have a look in Father Adam's chest. I suppose the position on young Jean's meadow may be less clear...

As if in tune with his thoughts, Michael mentioned the boy.

"Oh, and Jean gave the Chapter a run-down on the difficulties of proving ownership of our land, and asked permission to prepare a case on our behalf to present to the manor court. We agreed that he should."

Lawrence frowned and held up a hand to stop him.

"Really, Michael? What's your view on that? Is he capable of such a trust?" He stood up and absent-mindedly went to fill both their cups whilst Michael spoke.

"Well yes, I think so. He's very young, of course; but very bright. And he's really the only one of us who spent any time at all with Wimer. If anyone else had any training in the law... but they don't; so Jean looks like our best bet. Do you not see it that way, Brother?"

Lawrence sat back down and sipped, thoughtfully.

"I see him as far too young and scatterbrained. I do take your point about a scarcity of other options, though... I take it that the Chapter agreed nothing about releasing him from his postulancy?"

Michael looked horrified.

"Oh no, Father - of course not! That's your prerogative, we wouldn't presume!"

Lawrence nodded. "Thank you, Brother - please continue."

Well, so long as the boy appreciates that he's still under my authority... I may have to remind him of it - what was it that Father Adam counselled? "make the postulancy a trial, test his resolve" - perhaps this was another opportunity to do just that. And maybe the boy did learn enough from Father Wimer to make a difference. Certainly I don't want to take it on myself, I'm far too busy and not at all sure I'd win, and that wouldn't be good for the Priory at all... I wonder if this is the Lord's way of testing me, a trial of humility, at the hands of the least of us?

He sipped again, slowly, and nodded to himself; then began to actually listen to Brother Michael.

CHAPTER 13

INTERDICT!

"...and I do NOT appreciate you talking to the chapter about this matter without discussing it with me first! I am your superior, you should have come to me! What's more..."

Jean, head meekly bent in submission, allowed himself a small eye-roll. *I wish he'd stop frothing at the mouth and get to the point. Is he going to let me, or not?*

"...not for Brother Michael, I wouldn't be considering it at all..."

Oh! That's decent of Brother Michael to put in a good word for me! And I bet the old windbag is going to let me take the case on! He wouldn't bother to say he's thinking about it if he wasn't, just send me away with a flea in his ear!

"...so don't think you can slack one iota in your postulancy duties! I expect you to put in exactly the same hours in the kitchen; to attend all services; and to carry on your Latin studies, and your lectio Divina. You can use your spare time to research the land matter - and don't think that I will fail to check on you! The punishment..."

Oh, fabulous! That's amazing - I really did expect him to

shut me down altogether! Although when he thinks I'm going to sleep...

Father Lawrence had finally ground to a halt. Jean raised his head and spoke:

"Thank you so much, Father! I'm very grateful for the chance to redeem my oath to Wimer. I promise I'll keep up with my studies, and thank you for letting me continue with the postulancy. There is one thing, though - some of the records I need to consult are in the Norwich Cathedral archives and elsewhere - may I have your permission to travel occasionally? If I make up for the lost time?" *Pleasepleaseplease...*

There was a knock on the door, and Brother Michael stuck his head into the study.

"Beg pardon, Father Lawrence, but a courier has arrived from the Holy Trinity with a message he insists on delivering to you personally - shall I keep him busy?"

"No, no, send him in, please. We're finished here." Lawrence scowled at Jean and flicked a hand in dismissal.

"Get out of my sight - and remember what I said!"

Jean bowed and turned to go, almost bumping into the courier; they had to do an awkward little dance around each other. Finally, though, he was on the right side of the office door. He leaned back against the wall for a moment, huffing out a breath he hadn't realised he'd been holding, feeling the tension fall from his shoulders.

Well! He didn't say no - and that's as good as a yes!

He pushed himself off the wall and went to talk to Cook about maybe building an extra shelf in the kitchen where he could keep his book for lectio Divina out of the way of his vegetable peeling duties. *What's that thing about making the best use of time? Um... is it in Ephesians?* - "Look carefully then how you walk, not as unwise but as wise, making the best use of the time, because the days are evil." *Yea. Do as many things at once as possible, and walk carefully to avoid Father Lawrence like he was a mad dog, or he will make my days even worse! Hah!*

***

The Priory was in a gentle sort of uproar. Father Lawrence had received notice that Henry de Guisnes, the Holy Trinity's preferred candidate to replace Father Adam as Prior, was coming to visit. Everyone wanted to give him a good impression - even those who hated the thought of the Holy Trinity muscling their way in were aware that this man might be their superior for many years. Father Lawrence had scrapped the usual job allocation, and everyone was cleaning, trying to make the place shine.

Jean had been issued a bucket of lime-wash and told to smarten up the church porch; he'd spent the morning brushing off all the dust and loose flakes from last year's coat, and was just starting to dampen down the top of the first wall so that the lime-wash would soak in properly when Father Lawrence came bustling by.

"Good heavens, boy - what have you been playing at? This needs to be finished and dry by tomorrow morning, get that whitewash on right now!"

Jean opened his mouth to explain what he was doing and shut it again. *He's in no mood to listen - I don't want another silence sentence...*

"Yes, Father." He replied humbly. *And if it turns to powder and gets everywhere, don't blame me!*

He climbed down from his ladder, got the bucket, and started to slap on the wash, being quite generous with it in the hope that it was wet enough to sink in properly even without the walls being dampened first. It was a pleasant job for a warm day, and he'd finished two walls by the time the Chapter bell rang.

Pretty much the only topic of discussion in the Chapter was de Guisnes. No-one had met him, and no-one had any idea what kind of man he was; one or two thought he must be something to do with the old Earl of Oxford, for the Holy Trinity to take an interest in his career. Perhaps a by-blow? Finally Jean leaned forward and asked:

"Forgive me brothers - but I don't understand; if he isn't one of Holy Trinity's monks, why are they putting him forward as Prior? Has he been a sub-prior somewhere? How do they know he can do the job?"

There was plenty of head-shaking and muttering along the lines of "we don't!". Brother Michael clapped his hands.

"Enough of this idle chatter, Brothers. Let us return to our labours; we will meet the man himself tomorrow, and can form our own opinion of him."

Jean had been posted up on the dormitory roof, looking over to Haugh Bridge, so he could give the community a bit of warning when their august visitor arrived. De Guisnes surprised him, though, by cantering his horse off the path, down the hill and across the meadow, scattering the sheep - Jean only just managed to get himself back down to earth in time, and was still trying to control his breathing when de Guisnes tossed him the reins. As he turned the horse to walk it up to the stables, he caught the man's first remark;

"Pretty enough, I suppose, if rather provincial. I prefer my lamb on a trencher, rather than getting under my horse's feet..." the man's laugh was almost a hiccough. It took a couple of heartbeats before Father Lawrence joined in with a polite titter.

Jean walked the horse around until it had settled, and was cool enough to be given a drink.

"There, that's better, fellow, isn't it! He worked you hard, didn't he... hang on a bit, there should be a bag of carrots somewhere... yes, there we go. No, you can only have one! Into this stall with you and have a rest. I'll come and get you when your master needs you again."

The horse whickered softly and moved over to the hay-net. The bell rang for Sext, and for the second time that day, Jean had to sprint.

After the service there was to be a special treat in honour of their visitor; the normal rule of silence at the mid-day meal was to be suspended, and instead of a reading, de Guisnes was to give a speech, and possibly even answer questions. Jean waited eagerly for his turn to leave the church and process to the refectory, but there was some delay - all the lay people attending service had left some while before the monks were given the nod to start the procession. Jean slotted in at the end, as usual.

Father Lawrence was waiting to close the door behind them, looking like a thundercloud. He grabbed Jean by the arm and growled

"You stupid boy! Did you do it on purpose? You can go without food, and serve it instead. And woe betide you if you spill a crumb!"

Jean must have looked as puzzled as he felt.

"His habit! Just look at his habit!" Lawrence shook him a little, then let him go. Jean watched, fascinated, as he forced a smile on his face and turned back to their guest, who was brushing ineffectually at the great smear of lime-wash dust across his gown. *Um - I told you so! Shame it's costing me my meal!* Jean sighed and headed for the kitchen.

De Guisnes' address to them was more a series of statements of his accomplishments than a campaign speech. They did learn where he was before, though; at a priory in his native town of Calais, where he had been both Sacristan and Cellarer.

"And let me tell you, Brothers, both are taxing positions indeed in a priory in such a great city, with travellers coming and going all the time." He paused, and took a swig from his wine cup, which Jean had just refilled for the third or fourth time. His voice grew low and confidential: "You fellows may be happy here with your sheep, but I have bigger plans. I've been promised a decent-sized Priory shortly - after all," he sipped again, "There won't be much left of this one soon."

Father Lawrence asked him sharply, "What do you mean?"

De Guisnes blinked at him, surprised. "When the election is done, this will revert to a daughter house, of course. There's some local landowner or other," - he waved his hands - "who has a claim on part of the land, but the Holy Trinity will make proper provision for you fellows, of course, after it's confirmed ownership of the rest. No need to worry." He peered into his cup, and when Jean didn't move, took the jug out of his hands and refilled it himself. "I'm sure there'll be enough land left for you to keep a sheep or two if you want!"

Jean had to get out of the room before he hit the man. The peculiar laugh followed him - this time no-one was joining in.

***

All Jean could see of the two candidates for prior, kneeling at the altar, was part of Father Lawrence's tonsure. It was going redder and redder as he listened to the Bishop's homily:

"...goodness of life and soundness of teaching; and the worst thing a community can do is to choose a leader who will do what they want him to do..."

He's sure he won't get elected! I wonder which bit is worrying him. Maybe he's regretting being so mean to me, and from now on he'll be trying to make his teaching kinder... Well, I can hope, anyway...

At long last the Bishop stopped lecturing them.

"Brethren - let us stand and pray in silent contemplation, asking God to strengthen our hearts and send us the inspiration of the Holy Spirit to aid our choice of the right candidate."

The silence seemed to go on forever. Now he was standing, Jean had a better view of the two kneeling candidates. Father Lawrence had begun to sweat, droplets turning the back of his tonsure to a dark iron grey. De Guisnes was completely still and poised, head upright, looking straight at the altar.

Finally the Bishop led them in the Lord's Prayer and the dismissal, then he held out a hand to help each candidate to their feet. They genuflected and left the church, so that the monks could begin their discussions. Jean waited until they had gone past him and turned to follow them out. Brother Michael put a hand out to stop him.

"Stay, lad - weren't you listening to the Bishop? The whole community must choose its leader. And besides, as the youngest of us, you might have to live with the decision the longest, if you complete your vows!"

Jean smiled at him and leaned back against the wall to listen. The flow was going against Father Lawrence, surprisingly - almost everyone had some tale of him being petty or too rigid.

He's going to lose!

Brother Michael was clearly concerned by the direction things were taking too.

"Brothers - is Father Lawrence lessened in our regard because we know him too well? Is it possible that we're blinded to his better qualities because we see him day in and day out? I'm certain that Henry de

Guisnes has habits that would grate. The question is, which of them has - as the Bishop said - more goodness of life?"

The debate rumbled on. So far as Jean could see, no-one was looking beyond Father Lawrence's personality issues.

For heaven's sake, can't they see that De Guisnes doesn't care a jot about us? He's only standing because he's been told to, and sees us as a stepping stone.

He pushed himself off from the wall and moved until he could see most of the monks' faces.

"Brothers, may I speak?" He waited until they were mostly silent.

I can't believe I'm defending him, but here goes…

"Thank you, Brothers. I've been listening to all that you've been saying, and I'm sure you've seen that I myself have suffered at Father Lawrence's hands." He paused whilst they muttered agreement.

"But Brothers, I'm convinced that he has acted out of a desire to bring me closer to God. I know he is a more Godly man than I am - is it possible that the petty slights he has given many of you have been because he is driven by a desire to get as close to heaven on earth as can be? That he's seen some small imperfection, and has felt bound by his love of God, and us, to correct it?"

He paused again and waited for that to sink in. When most of the monks had again fallen silent, frowning in thought, he continued;

"I would rather put my faith in Father Lawrence, impatient though he can sometimes be, because I am sure he loves the Priory. Can any of us say as much for de Guisnes? Has anyone heard him say anything positive about the Priory, or about us, since we've met him?"

Everyone was shaking their heads No.

"Then, Brothers, on one hand we have someone who we know is God-fearing, who understands us and our tribulations, and who we understand and have compassion for in our turn. On the other hand we have a stranger who has shown us nothing but indifference and arrogance."

Sides! I wonder if I can make them physically take his side!

"Brothers, stand here with me if you will support Father Lawrence, and please move over there if you prefer de Guisnes."

He held his breath, but no-one moved. Brother Michael broke the silence;

"Thank you for clarifying things for us, Jean. I can see how you've benefited from Father Wimer's training in clear thinking! Brothers, raise your hands if you choose de Guisnes as Prior?" – not a single hand went up.

"And for Father Lawrence?" Some hands shot up, some were slower than others; but before long everyone was agreed.

"Well, Brothers - let's go and tell the Bishop of our unanimous choice of Father Lawrence as Prior. Deo Gratia!"

Jean was still feeling victorious when he visited the privy and found de Guisnes there ahead of him.

In for a penny, in for a pound...

"I've been admiring the gracious way you've accepted defeat, Father. I hope Prior Gilbert will be equally gracious. Perhaps he will be less eager to pursue his land claims, now that Dodnash Priory is unlikely to become a daughter house?"

De Guisnes looked him up and down as though he'd crawled out from under a rock.

"Ah yes, the youth with the golden tongue. I hear you used it to good effect earlier. Not, of course, that the wishes of this witless clutch of field-monks will make much difference to the outcome." De Guines adjusted his robe.

"Be sure, boy, that I will urge the Holy Trinity to rip land away from this God-forsaken muddy hole, until they have so little left that they beg to become a daughter house."

The man leaned forward until his face was inches from Jean's.

"And I will start with your strip of meadow. I will take personal pleasure in leading the case against you at the next Hundred court. Did you know I studied law at Oxford?"

He stepped backwards into a bow, then slammed his shoulder into Jean as he left. Jean stared after him, open-mouthed.

***

Edeva was so furious that she could hardly walk; every few steps she had to stop and lean against a house wall and wait until the film over her eyes had cleared.

Deciding how long to wait was a bit fraught too; she had to keep moving, or the tears would overwhelm her. She could feel them building in her chest, like a wall that must sooner or later fall and crush her.

I've got to keep going until I get my hands on that little rat of a priest!

She used her hands to push off the wall and staggered on in the direction of the church. It was such a little way...

It must take three or four times as long to get from the Priory to East Bergholt, or even Bentley, and they've never let anyone down like this!

She got to the last house in the short stretch of Orford High Street and stopped to gather herself.

He'd better be dying himself, that's all I have to say! With Mama maybe in Hell right now...

She gulped back a fresh wave of tears, then took a couple of deep breaths and launched herself across the road towards the church. As ever, the sight of it calmed her; it held so many happy memories for her as a child, riding on her father's shoulders to a service, or holding Wimer's hand whilst he patiently explained the meaning of every wall painting to her, and why he had chosen it.

She was feeling merely determined, rather than furious, as she reached the door and lifted the latch. Nothing happened. She lifted it again and pushed, hard. Solid! It felt like the door was barred! She put her ear to it but couldn't hear anything.

Well! How odd! Why on earth is the Church shut up? Maybe the priest is dead! That would be a good excuse!

She took a step or two backwards, pulling her shawl

tighter, and set off down the hill to the rectory.

That door was barred too - but she'd seen a glimpse of a white face at a hastily shuttered window, and she wasn't going to be denied an explanation.

"Get out here, you rotten excuse for a priest, and tell me what's going on!"

She set up a rhythmic banging with her fists, only stopping to shout.

"You left my mother to die unshrived!"

-thump, thump...

"You just come out here and answer to me, you craven piece of dog turd!"

- thump, thump... she was beginning to draw a bit of a crowd now.

"My mother was a good woman!"

-thump, thump...

"And where were you when she needed a priest on her death bed?"

-thump -

The door was thrown open. The priest stood there, swaying a little and blinking in the sudden light.

Edeva took an involuntary step backwards as his stench hit her - he'd clearly been drinking, and there was a trail of vomit down his gown.

"Please, Goodwife, be silent! It's not what you think..."

"Look at you! You drink-sodden piece of rubbish! You let my mother go straight to Hell because you were drunk! You..." she ran out of words and lifted her fists, ready to pummel him instead of the door. A hand fell on her shoulder, stopping her, and a well-dressed man behind her said,

"Wait a moment, sister - Father John is a sober, god-fearing man, who has served us well these many years - there's something wrong here. Father, what is it?"

Edeva crossed her arms tightly and glared at the priest, her foot going tap-tap...tap-tap...

"Father?" the man from the crowd prompted again.

The priest gulped, a shuddering breath that sounded suspiciously like a sob. He waved his hands at them.

"Wait here, I'll get it..." and he disappeared into the rectory. Edeva uncrossed her arms and thought about following him before he could run away through a side door, but in a moment he was back, clutching a scroll of parchment. There were clearly tears on his cheeks now. He waved the scroll at them.

"Brethren, this arrived last night. It's an order from the Bishop."

He stopped and wiped his cheeks with the back of his hand.

"It's terrible - I can't tell you how terrible - I'm just going to read it to you, let you hear it for yourselves."

He unfurled the first bit, sniffed, and began to read slowly, clearly translating from the Latin as he went.

"My son - he means me - it is my grave duty to inform you that His Holiness the Pope did, on the 23rd March of this year of our Lord 1208, place all our King John's holdings under an interdict, and in that parlous state the entire country must remain, until our King ceases his opposition to His Holiness' appointment to the See of Canterbury."

The priest rolled up the scroll and stared at them, woebegone.

Someone in the crowd shouted out.

"But Father - what does it all mean?"

He shook his head and sighed.

"It is a cruelly hard punishment that is visited on us. It means no church appointments. No church services. No confession. No Mass. No marriages."

He stepped forward and put a hand on Edeva's shoulder.

"And I'm afraid no burials in consecrated ground."

Edeva heard his voice from a long way away. It felt like the world was narrowing to a single point of light at the end of a tunnel, which then slipped sideways. Someone behind her was beginning to wail.

CHAPTER 14

WILLIAM GONE

Jean was standing on a bench dusting cobwebs out of corners in the church, trying equally not to breathe in the acrid dust coming off the thatch, and to dedicate the service to God.

He was also attempting not to think about how frustrating the whole business of the charters was - even though he was getting much quicker at reading old, cramped handwriting and could spot the various standard formulae of charters at a glance, he was clutching at straws. He'd spent so much time reading through any old charter at all, just in case the proof he needed had been mis-filed, or stuck to the back of another charter by accident, or re-used, or.... Anything!

He banged out his broom against his foot and wiped his face on the inside of his sleeve. *I wonder if the Wenham castle archives would be worth a visit? They're far enough away that they really shouldn't be, but I can't think where else to look...*

Father Lawrence made him jump.

"So, boy -I haven't seen much of you lately - have you solved our little land dispute puzzle yet?"

Father Lawrence's smile was obviously forced. *What's he after?*

Jean hopped down and bowed, tucking the birch broom under his arm. "Not yet, Father, I'm still working on it - although I must admit, I'm running out of things to try."

"Well, Nil desperandum, eh - perhaps you haven't gone to a high enough authority? Keep trying, lad - unless you'd like me to help? I seem to have a lot more time on my hands since the Interdict..."

For a moment Jean was tempted. *Dump the whole messy problem on him and just walk away... but no. I promised Father Adam that I'd make sure everything was sorted out properly. I can't give up now...*

"Thank you, Father, but I'll carry on with it. And thank you for the advice, I'll take it on board."

Lawrence tucked his hands into his sleeves and wandered off again, looking aimless. Jean moved the bench out of the way and swept the debris across the church and out of the door, trying not to think about charters. Again. Finally he gave up, put the broom away, and headed for the kitchen - one place where Father Lawrence was unlikely to follow, and he could think in peace. *Maybe he's right, though. I'm not getting anywhere looking in the archives. Maybe I should go up the tree. Although I suspect the Holy Trinity Prior is hand in glove with the Bishop. Next stop; the Archbishop of Canterbury! Except there isn't one right now, that's what all the issue is between the King and the Pope, they both want their own man in the job.* He stopped and leaned against the kitchen lintel, enjoying the way the last of the evening sun was gilding the priory meadows.

I can't write to the Pope! Can I? What would I say?

He plucked a stray blade of grass and chewed the end. *Dear Your Holiness, please get the Holy Trinity off my back?* He spat out the grass stem. *Well, why not? Father Lawrence should be pleased that I'm going straight to the top!*

He bypassed the kitchen and headed for the scriptorium to beg a waxed tablet and stylus. *If I'm going to do it, I might as well do it properly. It might need more than a few drafts to get it right!*

***

She knew the church was going to be shut up, of course - no-one except the monks had been allowed inside for weeks - but being as near to the saint as possible felt really important. She'd come round by the East Bergholt road, not wanting to meet any of the monks, and hadn't seen a soul.

There had been someone talking in the cloister, so she'd crept round to the back of the church. She got as near to the altar as she could from the outside, and put her hands on the wall, feeling a bit of a fool - but it did help, somehow. She shut her eyes and started to pray; *Saint Walstan, please help my husband William, who is a farmer like you - he's been looking so ill and tired recently, although he says he's fine, and I don't know what else to do...*

There was a touch on her shoulder and she squealed in surprise. She spun around - and there was Wimer's adopted son, Frenchy -no, Jean - looking almost as shocked as she felt.

"I'm ever so sorry, I didn't mean to startle you, I was coming back from tending the bees and saw you - you looked so sad, are you all right?"

She started to answer him and the enormity of just how NOT all right she was hit her all at once. Before she knew what she was doing, she burst into tears. A pair of arms hugged her and for a moment she allowed herself to cry into his shoulder and be comforted.

"I'm sorry - I didn't mean to cry on you like that!" She pushed back a bit and tried, not very successfully, to dry his tunic with her shawl.

"It's just that I'm so worried about William - oh, I am sorry, your tunic's soaked through..."

"No, it's fine, don't bother - what's the matter, is he ill?"

She looked up, and the concern in those dark eyes, so close to hers, nearly made her cry all over again. As if reading her mind he reached over and patted her arm. Suddenly she had to tell someone - and she trusted this man. She sniffed, scrubbed at her face with the damp shawl, and pulled him down with her to sit with their backs against the church wall.

She poured out all the worry about how William's health had just kept getting worse and worse over the past few months, and how nothing she did seemed to make any difference at all. Then she took a steadying breath and told him the big worry before she could change her mind.

"And with the interdict, and us living so far away and everything, I'm horribly afraid that he'll die suddenly and unshriven - and he has a terrible sin on his conscience."

She stopped and brushed the hair out of her eyes. Jean took the hand as it tried to return to her lap again and squeezed encouragement. She looked up at him solemnly.

"Actually, it's partly you he's sinning against."

She shook her head, and said the rest in a rush, to get it over with.

"William and Prior Gilbert of the Holy Trinity have been forging some charters, to put the ownership of Wimer's land granted to you and to the Priory here in doubt."

There! She'd said it! She looked up at Jean. His eyes were as round as they could go. *Oh my, I've shocked him! He knew nothing about it, then.* She sniffed and used her free hand to wipe her eyes again. *Well, good. I'm glad I told him. It's just not right, what they're trying to do!*

Someone was shouting for him, over by the stables. He lifted her hand, still clasped in his, and kissed it.

"I'm so sorry, but I have to go. Many thanks for telling me that, it really helps to be forewarned!" and he leapt to his feet and bounded off.

She touched the back of her hand to her own lips. She felt so much better for talking to him...

***

It was probably a sin to waste the prayer potential of the one service a week the Priory was allowed to hold - behind barred doors. Jean muttered the responses entirely by rote, as he argued with himself about what to do with the information Edeva had given him.

If I was able to take a sworn statement that they've been

forging charters to a court, I think the case would be watertight - but how on earth would I get William to do that? I couldn't tell him that I knew, or Edeva would get into trouble. And I can't just go and bang on his door, he's never liked me, he'll tell me to go and jump in the lake, or worse...

With a start he realised that he'd almost missed the elevation of the host. He quickly crossed himself and tried to pay more attention.

He went back to thinking about the problem during Chapter. His silence was noted - Brother Michael held him back afterwards.

"Hold tight, lad, let's have a look at you - hmm, you're looking a bit peaky, not got one of those headaches of yours coming on, have you? No? Well good, in that case I have a job for you that should put a bit of colour in those cheeks. William of Dodnash's wife has asked for some of my goose fat and coltsfoot ointment for his chest. And don't tell Father Lawrence, but I added a drop or two of holy water for good measure - he wasn't looking too healthy when I saw him a week or so ago, he could do with a bit of divine help, I suspect. A walk over there should do you the world of good, too - here you are; off you go!"

Jean had bowed to the inevitable and set off. *Well, I suppose the worst he can do is throw the pot at my head...and I will see Edeva again!* The memory of that stolen kiss on the back of her hand made his cheeks as rosy as any mentor could wish.

There was no-one visible at the cottage, although the door was propped open, a curtain drawn across the entrance. He banged on the lintel. A voice he barely recognised as William's - shrunk to a fraction of his usual bellow - bade him come in. Immediately there was a long series of hacking coughs.

Jean ducked under the curtain and waited for his eyes to adjust to the dark. The room was hot and close, and there was a sharp undertone of urine. Jean crossed himself against the presence of illness. The coughing was coming from one dark corner. William sat in a high-backed armchair, feet on a low footstool. He was covered in too many blankets - clearly he was sleeping there, and feeling the cold.

The coughing finally stopped and William was left with a ratcheting wheeze, filling every pause in his speech.

"Why... look who it isn't... the little scared... French boy... Wimer's brat... what do you want?"

He started coughing again and waved Jean frantically towards the ale jug on the table by the door. The bad smell got stronger as he got close enough to hand William a mug of ale. *Dear Lord, he looks dreadful! He's lost such a lot of weight. I suppose the poor old sod is pissing himself every time he coughs...*

"I'm here with some chest lotion for you, Sir. Brother Michael's best; and he put a drop of holy water in it too." he said cheerily. *He hasn't stopped wheezing once, and his skin looks waxy. I suspect this lotion is too little, too late...*

"Mmm...well...I appreciate...the gesture...but I think...I might...be well past...helping..."

The effort of talking seemed to tire him out, and he fell asleep with his head thrown back, tunic open at the neck. Before he could think about it too much, Jean scooped out a double finger-full of ointment and rubbed it on what he could see of the old man's chest. It smelt good - maybe simply leaving the stuff on the table beside him might help. It was certainly sweetening the air a bit.

William startled awake, and for a horrific few moments was unable to get his breath. When he did, the coughing had left him visibly weaker.

"Where are you… boy… sent Edeva… for Maurice… not long… to go now."

The only sound in the room was his rasping breath, but the eyes looking into Jean's were steady.

"Did you… a wrong…"

The curtain was swept aside and Maurice bulled in, closely followed by Edeva. Both Jean and William blinked in the sudden light.

"Father!" Maurice fell to his knees, neatly blocking Jean out.

"Wait!" William commanded him, his voice stronger for just a moment. He beckoned Jean closer.

"The Trinity Prior and I… forged charters… to Wimer's…land. Used a…travelling scribe… sorry…. wronged you. Paying for it… now… sin! Run… and fetch… a priest… I need… to confess." He burst into a cough again. Maurice started to wail. Jean exchanged a helpless look with Edeva, then turned and ran for the Priory. Behind him the coughing stopped abruptly.

***

Edeva's whole soul felt like the raw place in your

gum when a tooth is lost - a deep dark blackness that made it difficult to concentrate on what nice old Brother Michael was saying. The contents of William's will would shape all of their lives from now on, hers perhaps most of all, at least until she was forced to remarry. *I suppose Maurice will want me out of the house as soon as possible, to make way for a bride of his own. Unless he wants me to stay and look after the household! Oh, that would be awful - some little slip of a girl, changing everything about, and I'd be no better than a servant!* She shivered a bit at the thought, and Becky, sitting next to her, put a hand over hers. Edeva managed a watery smile. At least Becky was safely clear of her brother's temper tantrums, the carter she'd married over by Woodbridge providing for her well, from the quality of her cloth. And a child on the way... *Did I make a mistake, not having any children of my own?* She shook her head, refusing to add regret to her burden. She made an effort and tried to listen to Brother Michael again.

"...and to my heir, Maurice..."

All she could think of was little Billy who should have been the heir. She could remember how silky his hair was when she stroked it down, its clear fine blonde such a contrast to William and Maurice's wiry sandy curls. *He was the only one who was fond of me...* That same fine hair had clung to his face, dark and limp with sweat, as he lost his battle with fever. She had plucked a damp strand away and kissed his forehead before closing his eyes and going to tell William his son was dead. *At least we were able to bury him in consecrated ground, and have masses said for his soul*

- poor old William is burning in hell right now!

It was too much. She burst into racking wails, the grief from the older loss mixed with the new shock. She was barely aware of her stepdaughter leading her out of the room.

She was all out of tears by the time Brother Michael came looking for her. They sat on the bench that William had built against the house wall, gazing out over the little valley. The gentle sounds of birds preparing for the night were coming from the woodland, and the old barn owl ghosted across the clearing on silent wings. This time she was able to listen to what he said.

"You are reasonably well off, my dear. Maurice gets the farm land, of course, but no money. You have the right to live in the house for a year and a day, then that reverts to Maurice too. It turns out that William has - had - done surprisingly well for himself. He's been lodging sums with Prior Gilbert of the Holy Trinity for safekeeping; I took the liberty of asking him to send it over when I saw the terms of the will. Young Rebecca has received ten marks, I've taken that out and given it to her. The residue is yours."

Oh that is good! She is well provided for.

The monk turned and looked at her, his expression difficult to read in the twilight.

"I understand Brother Wimer left you a marriagiatum of 15 marks?"

She nodded. He reached into his sleeve and held out a small bag.

"Here is one mark of it, so you have some money in

hand. I have the rest, and the money William left you, at the Priory - I didn't want to carry so much silver around. You should think long and carefully about what you want to do with it. Maurice of course would expect to manage it for you until you remarry, but the sum is considerable, and wasn't explicit in his father's will. The stipulation was simply that you had the residue in your own right, and I haven't felt the need to tell Maurice how much is involved."

Good heavens - how much has he left me? And then a new thought - *how did he get a lot of money, anyway?* She frowned and gestured for him to go on.

"You have 45 marks in total, my dear - Wimer's 15 plus a further 30 from William. Enough, if you wished, to buy a corrody and have the Priory provide your shelter, food, and clothing for the rest of your days. William has done very well by you."

She stood up, wrapping her shawl close, and walked to the edge of the little clearing. A last raven flew overhead, going to its roost. She could feel tears welling again. She blinked them away and turned to face her guest.

"I am most grateful, Brother, for your thoughtful treatment of me, and for your sensitive handling of the situation. Would you be kind enough to hold the money at the Priory for me? - as you say, I need to contemplate how to use it best."

She knelt for his blessing, then stood to watch him walk away. When he was gone, she checked to see no-one else was watching, and allowed herself a twirl.

Free - he's left me freedom! I could buy the right to remain unwed! She closed her eyes at the delicious thought.

Thank you, husband…

***

Jean was a little late to Chapter. He slipped into his place at the back. Father Lawrence was speaking:

"…and so, Brothers, I had to give the Jew some surety, or he would not have lent us the wherewithal to pay off the amount the Sheriff is demanding for the King's latest fine. It's not the first time I've had to borrow from him, either; we owe him a large sum of money."

It was so quiet in the chapter house that the drip-drip-drip of the rain falling from the thatch was almost painfully loud. Father Lawrence had his eyes shut. His face was white as he continued;

"I agreed that if we default on the loan, all the farm land from the old pathways to the south of us all the way to the river would revert to the Jew."

He knelt and looked at each one of them in turn.

"I'm sorry, Brothers, but I could see no other way to satisfy the King's demands. We will now owe the Jew twenty-five marks each quarter, plus the capital. I ask you to judge me; if you find my actions wanting, I will step down from acting Prior."

He bowed his head. The silence lasted for just a couple of raindrops before everyone started talking at once.

Jean sat where he was, frowning in amazement. *Dear Lord, how could he DO that? He's thrown away almost half of Wimer's endowment - it makes my worries about losing a field here, a field there look silly! What was he thinking?!*

But he must have had a reason, he's not stupid, and he cares about the Priory…

He found himself on his feet. "Can I ask a question?" Nobody was listening. He drew in a lungful of air, and tried again, bouncing his voice off the walls. Gradually, the hubbub died down. When he could hear the rain again he spoke.

"Father Lawrence, I don't understand why you were forced into this bizarre act. Can I ask what the Sheriff demanded?"

Father Lawrence looked almost grateful for the question. He stayed on his knees to answer, though.

"The Sheriff showed me the King's letter, which has gone out across the land. The King states that every religious house which has obeyed the Interdict has defaulted ownership of its land to the Crown, for failing to serve the people."

The hubbub rose again. Father Lawrence levered himself to his feet and patted the air until they were prepared to listen to him.

"The King gives a way out; we can get back our land from him on payment of a fine. Shhh, brothers, please - let me speak!" He waited again, then continued. "The Sheriff, using the King's tariff, has judged our fine to be two hundred marks. Yes, yes! Please listen! He has also assessed our four-and-a-half's knight's fee to be worth a further 30 marks; and our failure to send both this number of knights and a Prior to battle to personally fight in the French wars is fined at a further twenty marks."

The noise level was astonishing. Jean was shouting himself, shaking his fist in the vague direction of

Ipswich and the Sheriff. Father Lawrence was trying to make himself heard again, but to no avail. He knelt and bowed his head, back upright. One by one the monks fell silent. Jean noticed that it had stopped raining... Father Lawrence raised his head started to speak again, quietly, the monks straining to hear him.

"The King offered us an alternative to paying the fine ourselves." He swallowed and went on. "We could ask the Sheriff to supply four men, who would rule the Priory on behalf of the King; we would be subject to their every whim, and in return they would be responsible for raising the sums required from us by any means they saw fit." He shook his head. "The Sheriff thought that was an excellent idea, Brothers. He even suggested one or two of his soldiers might like the job - maybe run a whore-house in the cloister, as we wouldn't be using it much? - I couldn't stand their smirks! May God forgive me, I told him to go to Hell. After that there didn't seem much point in negotiating the terms. So I went to see the Jew." He bowed his head again and opened out his arms. "Please judge me, brothers - do you want me to step down? I would understand if you did, my outburst and my actions have endangered us all."

It took only a heartbeat before people started shouting.

"No!" "No - stay!" Jean shouted out "No" once himself, then sat back down. Twenty-five marks per quarter, just to pay the interest! How on earth were they going to manage that? He'd probably have done the same as Father Lawrence had, caught between a rock and a hard place - but it had made his task all the harder. *If I lose any of our land at all to a legal challenge, it will just make things worse - make us even less able to pay the Jew.* A sudden thought hit him. *If the King is doing this to every religious house, the Prior of the Holy Trinity will be hungrier than ever...*

CHAPTER 15

INK STILL WET

The destrier was blowing hard as it trotted up to the stables, as though its rider had not spared him for many miles. Roger Bigod reined him in and swung off his back, landing a little stiffly. Jean reached for his reins, but Bigod shook his head.

"Nay, I thank you - I'll walk round and cool him down myself for a while, I've been pushing his pace - and I could do with working out a few kinks in my back, I seem less able to ride hard every year... Would you hurry to your acting Prior instead, and beg a favour from him? I have half a dozen companions and their men arriving shortly. I need a place where we can talk undisturbed - would you beg Father Lawrence for the use of his office for an hour or two? And a meal and a drink for the men?"

"Yes, Lord - and congratulations on the birth of your grandson!"

"Thank you! - Jean, isn't it? - that's a ray of light in an otherwise very troubled time."

Jean bowed and set off down the slope to the Priory at a sprint. *What on earth is the Earl up to? And why is it so hush-hush that our little Priory is his venue of choice?*

With no notice! Father Lawrence is not going to be pleased!
He found Father Lawrence in his office, desk covered
in parchment. The news made his eyebrows rise
almost into his tonsure, and he could be heard
bellowing for extra chairs as Jean headed off back to
the stables.

Bigod's retinue had caught up with him, but he was
still walking his horse, accompanied by a tall thin man
who Jean didn't recognise. There was no clues as to
who he was in the man's clothing, which was a formal
dark-red robe. As Jean walked up the slope a young
fair-hared man trotted down the path from the west to
join the two lords. *Do I go and take their horses off them,
or do they want their privacy already?* Bigod saw him
hovering and raised his chin in a summoning gesture.
Jean walked up and took the reins from the Earl.
Bigod's destrier was restless, tossing his head and
glaring at the path from Ipswich.

"Someone coming, is there, old fellow? Excellent,
that'll be de Vere," murmured the Earl. Sure enough, a
small party of horses cantered past the Priory and up
the hill. The lead horse, richly caparisoned in red with
a single huge blue boar, split away from the group and
came towards them. Jean grabbed the destrier's
chinstrap and leaned back just in time, as it tried to
challenge the incomer. Bigod reached across and
rubbed its nose soothingly.

"Ah, Robert, well met." He said to the lord, who was
wisely staying in the saddle until the destrier settled.
"You know Roger de Cressey, of course, he's
governing Norfolk and Suffolk for us at the moment"

waving at the man in red, "and this is the Marshall's son, William Junior. Gentlemen, may I introduce Robert de Vere, Earl of Oxford."

The Earl dismounted smoothly, tossing his reins to one of his men, and came forward with his hand extended. Jean extricated the Bigod horses and headed for the stable. Before he got there, a couple of the Earl's retainers came across and took the reins from him.

"Do me a favour, lad, and get down there and serve them yourself?" asked the older one. "My Lord is sailing closer to the wind than I'd like, I'd prefer someone he trusts listening to the conversation."

Jean could feel his eyebrows lifting. The four lords were almost at the Priory. *I'd better hurry!* "As you wish." He said, hurriedly, and sprinted off again.

De Cressey was speaking as he entered the study, having detoured to the cellar for wine and mugs.

"...sticks in my craw. I don't mind the Sheriff's officers lining their pockets a little, the King is demanding more and more from us too; but the fines and 'gifts' they're extracting is putting justice beyond the reach of the common man. It's not right!"

Jean took advantage of the break in the conversation to lean into the middle of the crowded room and pass out the mugs. De Cressey accepted the wine with a nod and shrank back in his chair.

"Money is the only grease in the Kingdom at the moment, it seems." De Vere drank half his cup off in one gulp, and didn't object when Jean leaned to refill it. "I am being nibbled away by fines - it appears that every pipsqueak sheriff in every county I own land," -

Jean noticed the dark glare that de Cressey sent his way, even if the Earl did not - "is imposing ridiculously large fines for nothing at all." He sipped more moderately. "And as for the forest courts..." he shook his head.

"Yes, well, there's a subject we can all agree on." Said the blond man, glancing at de Cressey, who was still looking sour.

Roger Bigod held out his cup for a refill. *I didn't bring a big enough jug...* "It's happening at every level, too; we barons are not the only ones being gouged. One of my tenants - a boy called de Bruin up in Lincolnshire - sent a message begging me for help; the greedy rogue the King has installed as his guardian has decided to marry him to the daughter of one of his freemen - an entirely unsuitable match. And there's nothing he can do about it; he'll come to his majority with his estate stripped and wedded to some chit of a girl with no lineage at all. That is, if weddings are possible ever again, thanks to John's dispute with the Pope and this damned Interdict!"

De Vere interrupted him. "Have a care, Roger! You skirt perilously close to treason." He glared at Jean.

Hey! Don't look at me like that, I agree with him!

Bigod followed his gaze and smiled at Jean. "Jean here is my old tutor Wimer the Chaplain's adopted son. He is trustworthy." The Earl sipped thoughtfully. "I have sworn an oath to uphold King John as my liege lord, and I keep my oaths. But the country is groaning under his yoke. I see naught wrong in accepting Langdon as the Archbishop of Canterbury, if that is Pope Innocent's price for lifting the Interdict. My grandson has croup; it would tear my heart if he were to die unshriven, and be condemned to eternal flames." He drained his cup. "For that matter, it may not be too long before I meet my Maker myself, and my soul needs all the masses it can get. It frankly terrifies me how little the King cares for the suffering of the people."

De Vere nodded. "Yes; we must heal the rift with the Pope, and give up this foolish vendetta against Philip of France which is such a drain on the country's coffers."

Into the silence de Cressey asked, "And if the King cannot be persuaded to take these actions?"

There was no answer.

***

It was astonishing how much William had done for her that she'd taken for granted. She pulled her shawl tighter round her head, smiled regretfully at the stall holder, and moved on.

How do you know when alum is good, anyway? All she'd ever had to do when he was alive was to ask him to get some, and after the inevitable grumbling about how spendthrift she was, he'd come back with a bag of the stuff that worked just fine. Now she was finding that even the journey into Ipswich on her own was scary, as well as time consuming.

She took another aimless turn around the market. She really only had a choice of two stalls - or of course she could go without, and simply not fix her dye colours... The thought of wearing only washed-out shades of grey spurred her over to the far stall. She stood fingering the hanks of wool, very tempted by the blues and golds, whilst the stall holder dealt with another customer. The cost of the wool they were discussing made her wince. *Good heavens! If I paid that, my little nest egg would soon be gone. I hope the alum's cheaper!*

Finally the man turned to her and smiled.

"Well now, pretty lady - what can I do for you?"

Edeva could feel the flush rising in her cheeks. *When's the last time anyone called me pretty? Before I married, I should think!*

"God give you a good day, Sir - I need some alum. How much is yours, an you please?"

"Well, you've come to the right place, little lady. Just look at the quality of that! You'll not find better quality alum anywhere."

The man's smile was very warm, and he had kind brown eyes. She found herself smiling back.

"To be honest with you, Sir, I don't know how to judge the quality at all." Her throat was tightening with tears again. "My husband always used to take care of these things…"

"Used to? - ah, that's sad, I'm sorry to hear of your loss. And of course you've no chance of marrying again whilst this terrible Interdict continues. You need a protector, though, or you'll be taken advantage of all over the place!"

To her surprise, the man leaned over the stall and patted her on the cheek. His smile was looking more like a leer…

"Pretty young thing like you, you don't need to

struggle on alone - I'd look after you any day!"

She backed away in alarm as he winked, nearly getting run over by a cart. She ducked around it as he bellowed after her,

"I mean it, mind! Just ask for Aelfbert of Chantry when you get fed up with being lonely!"

"Edeva of Dodnash! Are you all right, child?"

Edeva looked down to where the voice was coming from. It was Goody Parnell from Brantham, sitting behind a cloth spread with the wooden bowls her husband made.

Edeva crouched down beside her and told her all about the leering stall holder.

"Well really, child - what do you expect? You need to remarry, they'll all be after you if you don't. Unless you want to take on widow's weeds and live in a convent? Yes, well, I didn't think so."

Edeva must have looked as woebegone as she felt, because the goody leant over and patted her on the hand.

"Never mind all that now. You sit here and look after my bowls, and I'll go and get you some alum - and then you can walk most of the way home with Will and me."

The woman struggled to her feet and stood looking down at Edeva, arms crossed.

"And dearie - you really should tell that Maurice of yours to find you a husband."

***

There was a tentative knock on Lawrence's doorpost. He frowned and carried on adding up the columns of figures. *Whatever I do, they're not going to add up right... We're about a mark and a half short of the amount we need to pay the Jew off, next week...*

The knock came again, along with a cough. He gave up, and scowled at the figure in the doorway.

"Yes, yes - what is it - come in, man!"

The figure shuffled into view apologetically. He was wearing farmer's brown leggings and tunic, and was clutching an incongruously smart cap - black velvet, with a single long feather. *Not a monk... Good heavens, it's young Maurice! Getting to be as big as his oxen.*

"I beg your pardon, Father - I didn't mean to disturb you, it's only that..."

"Yes, what is it, Maurice - spit it out!"

"Yes, Sir. I, um, wanted to ask you about my father." The hat was going round and round. Lawrence dragged his eyes away from the feather before his nose could follow the same circle.

"About William, God rest his soul? - Come and sit down, lad. Stop looming."

"Sorry, Father." The stool creaked a little as he sat down. Mercifully, the hat dropped in his lap. "It's his soul. I don't see how he's got a chance, with not being buried in consecrated land, like." He picked at something on his knee. "I want to see as best I can that he stays out of hell." The boy - no, young man - raised his head and looked expectantly at Lawrence.

He frowned. "Yes, it's all terribly unfortunate. But really, it was the best we could do, whilst this dreadful Interdict continues."

"Oh, yes, Father, I know you did your best, I didn't mean…" He shook his head, blushing. "But is there anything I can do to help him along? In the old days, I'd pay for masses for him, but with no church…"

"Well, that's not entirely true. The Priory has a dispensation to hold one mass a week. We already pray for the dead, but we could add your father's name explicitly, I suppose."

The ox leapt to his feet, the hat sent flying. "Oh, thank you, Father! That would mean so much to me - you won't regret it! Here!" He shoved a piece of parchment onto the desk.

Lawrence tilted his head in confusion, then picked the parchment up. "*Sciant presentes et futuri…* It's a charter!"

Maurice nodded. Lawrence carried on reading.

"From Maurice of Dodnash… to the Priory!… your two fields on the far side of the Great Way… for perpetual masses for the soul of William of Dodnash. Well, Maurice, that is very generous of you. Under normal circumstances, this would pay for daily masses. You do understand that we are unable to do that whilst the Interdict is in force?"

Maurice nodded again. "Yes, Father - you just do everything you can for my Da, all right? He needs all the help he can get."

Good heavens, is he going to cry? Lawrence stood up himself and stuck his hand out. Maurice took it - Lawrence's hand disappearing entirely inside his fist - and shook it solemnly. Then he made an awkward half-bow and left. Lawrence caught sight of the hat on the floor and opened his mouth to call; but Maurice trotted back in, scooped it off the floor, and made his escape. Lawrence looked down at the charter still clutched in his left hand and pursed his lips. *I know exactly what use to make of this gift! A Godsend indeed!*

***

The elderly Abbot from the Cistercian abbey at Coggeshall was enjoying the attention. The countryside was becoming too dangerous to travel, thanks to the numbers of people unable to pay the King's tax demands - it seemed like every day the village gossips were talking about some new unfortunate made an outlaw, his family turned out of their house and their property confiscated. It meant that fewer and fewer people were travelling, except in large retinues like the Abbot's, so the whole Priory was starved of news of the wider world. Everyone was hanging on the Abbot's words. The old man drained his mug and Jean leaped to fill it.

"But I've saved the best until last."

He took another swig of the Priory's dark, strong ale and sighed happily.

"Well, 'best' might not be the right word. Probably 'portentous' would be better."

He sipped again, and every monk in the room leaned forward, wondering what might come next.

"Brothers, I am reliably informed, by a man who heard it directly from the Papal Nuncio that the King…"

He sipped again. Jean thought briefly about hitting him with the ale jug…

"The King has been excommunicated."

He sat back into a silence, draining his mug. All around him the monks all started to speak at once.

"About time!" "What?!" "The King? What about us?"

Yes, that's the big question! What about us, does it mean we can go back to proper services? Or will it make things even worse?

Father Lawrence had obviously been thinking along the same lines. He leaned forward and asked the Abbot,

"Tell me, Father - does this mean any change to the Interdict?"

The old man shook his head.

"Nay. That was the first question I asked, too - the Interdict stands."

He looked sadly into his empty mug, and Jean moved automatically to fill it.

"No, this is a personal punishment for the King, on top of the one we carry for him."

He sipped thoughtfully.

"Let us hope that the King cares enough about his soul for it to make a difference, and to bring him - and us - back into the Pope's favour."

Jean glanced across at Father Lawrence. His face was dark and grim. *He doesn't think so! No early end to this terrible time, then.* Unbidden he sat on a bench, his duty to the Abbot's cup abandoned. He was remembering where they'd put William's grave - not dug in the church graveyard, where he could join the hosts at the trumpet sound, but in the triangle of waste ground opposite. Even that forlorn little patch was beginning to fill up... *How many more families are going to have to send their loved ones to Purgatory for lack of masses, knowing there can never be redemption for them? Or see their daughters living out of wedlock because they are denied a wedding sacrament? What sort of man is this King who cares so little about the state of his soul - and ours?*

He shook his head and poured his own mug of ale. *God preserve us from such a King!*

***

Jean had finally found the lord of Wenham Castle at home - it had seemed like every time he visited the castle, the family were at their estates in France - and gained permission to look through their charters.

There were a mixed bag - mostly land transfers around Wenham itself, a few around Capel, and a couple relating to East Bergholt - one of which Wimer had signed!

Jean put his palm on the familiar name for comfort, then frowned and lifted it off again. Why would Wimer sign with a mark, when he was perfectly capable of writing his own name? Maybe the charter dated to when he was very young, before he'd gone away to the Norwich Cathedral school? But that couldn't be right. Jean was sure his grandfather had met Wimer when they were boys, long before they would be expected to witness charters.

He picked up the parchment again and had a closer look. No date... He wasn't familiar with the land it referred to, a piece of meadow between Wenham and East Bergholt, by the old Roman road. He noticed that the edge of the parchment was grubby where he had been touching it. He hastily licked a finger and rubbed it clean - or at least cleaner - then examined his hand. There was a big black splodge at the base of his thumb! He scrubbed it against the dark wool of his travelling cloak until it was clean.

Carefully holding the charter by the edges, away from any ink, he took it to the window of the room being used as a scriptorium for a better look. There were definitely places where the ink was darker than others...

He scratched the start of the charter gently with a fingernail. The first word - "Sciant" - stayed put. He did the same with the cross next to Wimer's name; that was good too. When he rubbed a thumb over it, though, the whole name smeared! He looked around for a cloth, then gave up and used a corner of his cloak instead.

Underneath, it seemed to say something different! It was becoming a bit difficult to read, but it looked like Viner? No, Vinar! Someone had definitely added extra pen strokes to make it look like Wimer! He rolled his finger in a fold of cloak and spat on it, then rubbed until the extra ink was completely gone. *There! No-one's going to use Wimer's name on a dodgy charter! That's a disgraceful thing to do! - it's undermining the whole system of land transfer - who could be sure who owns what! I need to tell someone about this - but who? Earl Bigod, maybe? Would he believe me?*

There were a few other suspiciously dark areas where the ink hadn't sunk into the skin properly. Apart from the Prior of the Holy Trinity in Ipswich, none of the other witnesses were names he recognised. There were steps coming down the corridor, so he chucked the charter back into the bag and grabbed another one, which he was pretending to study closely when the steward popped his head around the door.

Sir John had just ridden in, he should go and pay his respects to him.

The first thing he did when he got back was to look for the suspicious charter. It had vanished... *No-one's going to believe me now! All I have to show for it is some ink smears on my cloak - I bet that charter's been hidden somewhere very safe. Hell fire! I wonder if I should go back round all the charters I've already looked at, just to see if any others have been amended - maybe a bit more skillfully? I need a lot more evidence before I can go to the Earl!*

CHAPTER 16

THE KING'S WAR

The gate was hanging by a single strip of leather, and the courtyard was eerily quiet. All that could be heard was the scream of a seagull from the nearby docks. Lawrence pushed the gate wider and winced at the squeal from the twisted wood. *What has happened here? Is it safe to go in?* He stood undecided for a while, until the continuing silence soothed his fears. *Come on! All I have to do is walk in, give the Jew his gold for this quarter - and this gift of Maurice's, which should go some way to clearing the debt - and get out.*

All looked normal at the house; the door standing open as though a servant had popped out to the well a minute or two ago. Lawrence rapped on the door jamb. The house remained silent.

"H-haloo the house?" Nothing.

He lifted the skirts of his robe and stepped over the threshold, for some reason unwilling to let his clothing touch the floor. There was a sweetish smell that was unsettling... *Where is the Jew? Why is no-one answering?* He followed the corridor to the waiting room and jerked to a halt at the entrance. The room looked as though all the demons from Hell had been dancing in it - the panelling half-ripped from the walls, the table overturned. Even the curtains had been torn down. The carpets he remembered from his last visit had gone.

The smell was stronger. He followed his nose, through the door which the Jew always came through. *To his private apartments, presumably...* The stench hit him like a cosh and he staggered back, his hand, still holding his robe, covering his nose and mouth. *Urgh! What IS that!* Carefully breathing through the cloth he cautiously peered round the corner again. The cause of the smell was plain; the Jew lay stretched out, one hand towards the door, his head stove in. A pool of dark blood stained the floorboards beneath him, and dark droplets splattered his prayer-shawl. Lawrence spun back into the waiting room and leaned against the wall, fighting a gag reflex.

Nothing I can do for the poor fellow. Thieves, I suppose. Peace be on his soul... Can I say that for a Jew? Yes, of course I can, he has a soul like any other. Although I do not know what happens to it after death, by his way of thinking.

He stayed where he was for a few heartbeats, head resting against the wall, remembering the smartly dressed man in life. *I wonder what happened to his prayer cap?* He frowned. *Does he need it, when he meets his maker?*

Without conscious thought, he pushed off the wall and stepped into the other room. This room had suffered much less, as though the thieves had run as soon as the Jew was dead. The cap was lying upside down next to a dark wood cabinet that had been overturned. Lawrence bent to pick it up, then noticed something pale sticking out behind a sprung joint of the cabinet. Out of curiosity, he pulled at it. *It's a charter!* He scanned it quickly. *Not mine... Hey! There's more!* He wrenched the wood up a little further and fished out a score or more pieces of parchment, all of them with the same kind of wavy edge as his own acknowledgment of debt. The fifth one he scanned was his own... On an impulse, he swept them all up into his pouch.

He carefully set the cap on the Jew's head and made the sign of the cross over him, before snorting at his own foolishness. *I'm sorry you've come to this, old fellow. And I'm sorry to take your loan documents, but you have no more use for them...*

A seagull screamed again, and the noise startled him into movement. In a moment he was outside on the street, breathing deep of the clean air, on his way home.

***

Lawrence slid the heavy satchel off his shoulder and onto his desk and sighed with relief. Placing a hand on either side of his back, he arched his neck backwards and twisted gently from side to side, trying to ease out the kinks. Finally he was rewarded with a satisfying string of pops. He bent over and rescued one of the Jew's scrolls that had bounced onto the floor.

Idly, he unrolled it, and glanced at the contents. Half-way down the length and he could feel his eyes widening. He patted the air with one hand until he found the back of his chair and sank into it, keeping the scroll open enough to read with spread fingers. When he reached the end and let the scroll curl up again he shook his head in amazement. Carefully putting it to one side he reached for the next scroll.

After the third he stood up and pulled the curtain across his doorway that meant on no account was he to be disturbed, poured himself a cup of water, and settled down again with a note tablet and stylus.

The rest of the afternoon was going to be very interesting indeed...

He was still undecided what to do with the scrolls - and with the information they contained - by Compline. He robed early and went to pray for guidance. *Do I keep them? Use them for bargaining levers?* He allowed himself a delicious image of a particularly obnoxious wine merchant going purple in the face if he discovered that Lawrence owned his loan bond... *He'd be practically giving us the Communion wine! It really isn't a very Christian thing to do. But it could make such a difference to the Priory's finances...*

He was becoming aware of the soft sounds of the monks gathering behind him for service, but tried to ignore them. Only when he was sure of the best course of action did he rise and take the monks through the service at a brisk pace.

Afterwards he led the procession out towards the dormitory as usual, but stopped a couple of stairs up and turned to face them. The handful of monks - and the two postulants bringing up the rear - stared up at him; a few looking curious at the break of routine, but all obeying the rule of silence. He felt a sudden rush of affection for these, his brothers. Protecting their interests was the right thing to do. He looked them over one more time then broke his own silence.

"Brethren, I will make time to discuss this with you at a later date, but I wanted to let you know immediately that the threat from our debt to the Jew is no longer hanging over us; he has been murdered."

He forced down a giggle at the way all of their mouths opened in unison, and continued

"Before you ask - I have no idea who did it; I discovered the body by accident, before the Sheriff's men were told, I think. I have recovered and burnt our own debt charter, and have come into possession of the Jew's halves of many more - for those who haven't come across this practice before, that means that we are owed the debts."

Some of the faces below him - Brother Michael's in particular - were becoming troubled, as they absorbed the implications of that. Lawrence smiled at him and said

"As the Lord's Prayer says, *ne nos inducas in tentationem, sed libera nos a malo* - lead us not into temptation, but deliver us from evil - I intend to return the charters to their rightful owners as soon as may be. Brother Michael, Brother Geoffrey, you will provide an escort."

His back twinged a little as a draft blew across the stairwell. *The boy can come along and carry that ridiculously heavy satchel*

"Jean, you will act as servant and accompany us as well."

He frowned a little at the boy's obvious enthusiasm then mentally shrugged.

"We will leave for Ipswich as soon after Matins as possible - Jean, see that the horses are ready. We will be away for much of the day; there are several charters to return in the town. There are others further afield to be dealt with later. Now, brothers - let us to bed."

***

The pike was delicious, served on a bed of buttery wilted spring greens. Jean was paying far less attention to the reading than he should… He eyed the slice he'd taken out of the side of the fillet to avoid the Y-bones. Was there still a morsel of safe flesh there, or would he regret it? He knifed off a small chunk and carefully put it in his mouth. *Gah! I knew it!* He shook his head at his own stupidity, and set to the task of picking out the vicious little bones without losing the last of the meat or swallowing. His gaze drifted round the refectory, most of the monks still wrestling with their own fish.

Poor old Brother Stephen, stuck up at the lectern, had a face like a wet week. He was never a fluent reader, but he was jerkier than ever - he seemed to be looking more at the scene below him than at the book. *Heh - he's hungry and wants his own fish!* Jean grinned, and the motion sent a wayward bone into the inside of his lip. *Ow!* He stuck his little finger in his mouth and dragged it out. *Never mind, Brother - not long before you get to eat too!*

Father Lawrence was talking quietly to one of the servants. The man bowed and left the room, frowning.

Finally Jean decided it was safe to chew. *Oh that's good!* He washed it down with a gulp of small ale and sighed contentedly. There was something going on at the top table - there was a little knot of servants gathered at the end, looking tense. As he watched, three or four more joined them. *Huh? That's pretty much all the servants, isn't it? Except Cook, I don't see him - oh, no, there he is now. What's going on?...*

Father Lawrence had been watching the gathering too. As Cook arrived Lawrence held up a hand to Brother Stephen, who looked delighted to be let off early. He almost ran down the stairs to his cold fish. Father Lawrence banged on the table twice and stood up.

"Brothers in Christ, and servants of the Priory. I have some grave news that I wanted to tell you all together, monks and servants, as it concerns all of us."

He paused. The only sound was Brother Stephen, making happy little chewing noises. Father Lawrence continued.

"The Sheriff's men brought me this earlier today. I'll read it to you." He was holding a short piece of parchment that shook slightly as he read. "It is the King's wish and command that every man in the Kingdom capable of bearing arms gather together at a mustering point to be made known to them, and from there join me in the fight to punish the usurper Philip and banish him from my domains in France, which he has unjustly seized. Signed, John, King of England, Duke of Aquitaine and Normandy, Lord of Ireland, et cetera, et cetera."

Lawrence put the parchment down and held out his hands to the servants.

"I cannot stand between you and this summons, I'm

afraid. The Sheriff had a list of all your names and read them out to me; he knows about you all. You must all be at the Hythe docks in Colchester by the Nones prayers next Monday, with enough provisions for ten days."

One of the men pushed forward to the front. *James! His new babe is only a month old, and I hear his wife's not doing too well.*

"But Brother - what about our wives?"

"Your wives and children will be under the protection of the Priory. I am sorry, my sons - there is nothing to be done about this edict; it is the King's direct command, and to disobey it would risk outlawry. I release you now from all duties, so you can answer the summons prepared. Go in God's grace, and may He watch over you."

The men started to file out, raising their voices as they did so. Jean watched them go, feeling a weird mixture of pity and envy. *Hang on - who's going to do their work whilst they're away? There's only one postulant right now - me! I can't do it all!*

Lawrence waited until the servants had left the room and banged the table again.

"Brothers, with our servants gone we must make shift to look after ourselves. I will draw up a schedule of tasks and present it to you at Chapter this evening. Let us pray." He waited for everyone to bow their heads. "Lord, thank you for this fine meal, and give us the strength to meet this challenge that the King has put in our path. Amen."

The monks and Jean murmured the response.

"Now, I would suggest that we start by clearing the

trenchers and trestles away and cleaning the kitchen. Jean - as you've spent most time in the kitchen, you can go and show people what to do. See if you can work something out for the evening meal."

Jean stared at him open-mouthed. *B-but I can't cook! I don't know the first thing about it!*

A pair of monks trying to work out how to stack the table boards nearly side-swiped him with a wayward plank. Father Lawrence moved to get out of their way too, and called what was probably meant to be a reassurance.

"Just keep it simple! Stew will be fine."

Oh my. He grabbed a stack of trenchers and headed for the kitchen. *Stew. All you need to do is to throw things in a pot, right? How hard can it be?* He avoided another pair of monks and their lethal weapon. *Please God that the King releases the servants soon!*

***

Brother Jerome was proving to be remarkably good with a fish net. Jean was kneeling on the bank of the deepest fish pond with a basket, ready to grab the fish that Jerome caught, when he thought he heard voices. He glanced at Jerome; he had his head cocked to one side, listening too. They stood up and started along the path that eventually lead to the Roman road. The voices were definitely cheerful - as they grew closer, the words they were singing became clearer;

"Um fa la la it's a lovely day, um fa la la lady, um fa la la..."

The singers came up over the rise and Jean raised a

hand to greet them.

"Good heavens above!" said Brother Jerome. "Isn't that Cook? And Aedwin, and Godfrith, and the rest of the men?"

"Praise the Lord, it is!" said Jean. "But that can't be Cook, he's far too skinny."

The men's song had stopped, and they were waving and calling to them. Jean and Brother Jerome ran to slap them on the back and be the first to hear the news - and it WAS Cook!

They walked in a happy crowd along the path to the Priory, the men refusing to do more than drop hints as to what had happened to them, saying that they'd only have to tell it all again to the monks, and demanding news of the Priory and the village people.

Cook was very impressed that Jean had held the kitchen together all these weeks, and was demanding a day-by-day account of what all the meals had been, and how were the fish stocks, and had he used all the cabbages? - then they reached the church door and Father Lawrence was waiting for them.

All through the service, a thanksgiving for bringing the men safe home, Jean felt sadder and quieter. He had enjoyed his brief reign over the kitchen, choosing what they would all eat, managing a budget, and having a little team of people to work with. Now Cook was back, of course he'd just take over again...

He perked up a bit listening to the men telling the whole Priory what had happened. They'd had to march almost the whole way to Portsmouth - and even before they'd got all the way there one of the King's sergeants had ridden up the line telling everyone that the invasion had been cancelled; the King thanked them for their willing service, and they could go home.

"And on short rations too!" grumbled Cook. "All the monasteries and such along the way were short of food, with people marching in and being turned straight round. Look at this!"

He paused dramatically, fumbled at his waist, and whipped off his belt. The effect was slightly spoiled by the need to grab for his braies...

"This went comfortably round me when I left. Now look at it!"

and he restored his decency by wrapping it twice around his bulk, almost losing his braies again in the process.

Father Lawrence leaped to his feet.

"Yes, well, thank you, Cook! And thank you all, men; you've done the right thing in to obeying the King's summons and going all that way, even if his plans changed in the middle. You can all have a day's extra holiday to spend with your families, I'm sure we can cope without you for one more day!"

Jean rounded up Brother Jerome to continue their fishing trip, a spring in his step at the extra day in charge. Although he was beginning to worry about the state of the kitchen - was everything back in its proper place? Cook would spot the smallest problem... Then Jerome caught the edge of the net on the bank and Jean was far too busy wrestling a double handful of wriggling fish into the basket to worry about it.

Tomorrow was another day...

CHAPTER 17

LIFTED AT LAST!

Jean was getting really rather fond of Matt the Roofer, who had been one of the Priory's patients for some months now, ever since he'd stepped backwards off a ladder into a pile of stakes that his apprentice had set ready. Of course, he'd laughed off the injury until it started to go bad and his wife had forced him to ask for help. Over the summer months Brother Richard, the Infirmarian, had tried several different kinds of salves and poultices; some of them had seemed to work for a few days, but eventually the red, angry look of the wound had returned.

Through it all, though, Matt had remained cheerful; cracking jokes that sometimes made Brother Richard cough and which went straight over Jean's head, or telling them long, involved tales of when he was a youngster. He'd stopped being able to visit the Priory some time ago, and Jean had been sent over nearly every day to help change the dressings and wash the wound. He was beginning to get more of Matt's jokes, too.

By late July the flesh of his calf was almost black and red streaks reached all the way up his leg. There was a smell there now too that caught at the back of the throat. Brother Riccard had walked over with Jean one day, looking very unhappy. He had pressed two fingers against the swollen flesh beside the wound and asked if it hurt there, then walked his fingers up Matt's leg. He didn't get very far before Matt had grabbed his hand to stop him going further up.

Brother Riccard had shaken his head. "I don't like that at all, Matt - you couldn't bear the lightest pressure at the top of your leg, yet I was pressing quite hard at the wound site. Those red streaks shouldn't be there either. I'm wondering whether there's been a sliver of wood in there all this time, rotting away inside you, and making your flesh mortify. I'm afraid we need to cut away that dead flesh, or you'll lose that leg."

It had taken four of them to hold him down whilst Brother Riccard had cut away as much of the black flesh as he dared, and Matt had mercifully fainted when he used a hot poker to cauterise it. For a while, as before, the wound looked like it was responding - there was even a thin layer of bright-pink skin growing over the bottom part of the new wound; but before long the smell and the red streaks were back.

The operation had taken something out of Matt, too - his store of jokes had almost dried up, and he was spending more and more time reliving the days of his youth. Brother Riccard had tried a couple of times to persuade Matt to let him get in the butcher to take off his leg, but Matt was having none of it - "Nay, thank-ee, I'll meet my Maker in one piece." It was clear to all of them that Matt was going downhill, and the oppressive August heat was speeding up the process.

One day, when a thunderstorm had blown through and it was slightly cooler, Jean found Matt a little brighter.

"Ah! Just the fellow I want - come here, lad, I've got something for you."

Jean had gone over, taking shallow breaths, and had been handed a parcel wrapped in a scrap of cloth.

"You've always listened to my stories, I reckon you've got a feel for old stuff. I found that when I were a boy, and the priest said it were made by the Elven folk - well, I don't want any of that kind of thing around me when I die, and I had a mind that you might like it."

Jean had unwrapped the parcel gingerly. Finally it was free of the cloth - an amber flint elf-shot arrow, so fine as to be translucent, side-wings still in place and looking like it could be fitted to an elf-bow that very day. He'd picked it up between thumb and forefinger and looked through it, marvelling at its beauty and the skill involved in making it, before remembering his manners and thanking Matt profusely. Matt had waved his thanks away -

"Nay, lad, take it with my blessing. I don't think the Lord will wait much longer for me, and I want no stain on my conscience when he calls. Especially as I'll be buried outside the churchyard, thanks to this by-our-Lady interdict; the Lord will have a hard enough time finding me as it is."

Matt's death was the first thing that Jean thought of after Father Lawrence had finished reading the

Bishop's proclamation saying that the Pope had finally lifted the Interdict in response to the King's submission to him. The other monks were all on their feet cheering - one or two were even dancing. Jean leaned back against the wall and looked past them, sorrow rising and threatening to drown him. *Ah, Matt, my friend - just one more week and we could have buried you properly - you could have been shriven!* He felt around in his belt pouch until he found the arrowhead and clenched his fingers around it so hard they hurt. *I will pray for you - and if I ever get any money, I will pay for masses for your soul.*

***

Jean poked his head out of the church door and whistled silently. The queue of people wanting services from the Priory stretched half-way up the hill. He glanced back inside - the couple at Father Lawrence's table had only just sat down, and the queue beside the confessional wasn't moving either. He could take a few minutes to give the people outside an idea of the waiting time.

The spring sunshine felt wonderful, and the hawthorn blossom was making the hedges bright. He'd been afraid that some of the crowd, at least, would be grumpy, but the atmosphere was almost festive; everyone was relaxed and enjoying catching up with all the gossip. He had a sudden thought and popped back into the church. The candle clock was getting very low - it wouldn't be long until the Sext service. He walked back out and asked people to pass the word up the queue.

"Oh, we won't be coming in, lad." said motherly Goody Aedith.

Why ever not? They've waited years to come to church - and they clearly still need the Priory?

"Oh? Why's that then, Goody? You couldn't take communion until you've confessed, of course, but wouldn't you want to hear the service?"

"No thanks, lad. I might when I'm properly shrived, but I'm in no tearing hurry. It's been, what, five years? Six? - I guess the Lord can wait a bit longer for me to go to church. I might come on Sunday, if it's raining."

Jean watched, amazed, as people all up the queue made the same decision. In the event, only a handful came to service; the rest just sat on the grass, more or less in queue order, and carried on chatting. Someone had brought a jug of ale, and that was making the rounds.

It worried at him whilst he went through the motions of following the service himself. *Have they simply fallen out of the habit of coming to church?* He crossed himself as a darker thought occurred to him. *Surely they haven't fallen out of the faith?*

Father Lawrence raised the same concern at Chapter.

"I've had plenty of people needing the banns said for marriage, and we'll have a big First Communion class - but attendance at service was much lower than I was expecting, and we haven't had nearly as many people wanting masses said for the dead as I thought we would. It's as though they've decided that they don't need us very much any more. If that doesn't change, we're going to have a problem with the Sheriff

- he'll expect us to pay our taxes just the same, whether people are paying for services or not!"

He ran a hand over his tonsure, newly shaved - as they all were - in honour of the Interdict being lifted.

"It scares me, brothers. Their souls have been starved of God's love for years. We cannot let them continue to wither now the means to bring them back into the fold has been restored to us!"

He slapped a fist into his palm.

"We need to have a care to our pastoral duties. This is the most important task we have, brothers, and we are uniquely suited for it, because of the life we have chosen. Each one of us can speak with authority about a relationship with God. I want each of you to get out there and talk to everyone you come into contact with. We must get them back into church! Go out into the village and preach - remind them of God's love, and if necessary, throw a bit of hell fire in there too! Go with God, brothers!"

Then in a quieter tone, "Not you, Jean, I'd like a word with you, please."

Oh no, what have I done wrong now! He couldn't think of any particular sin as he manoeuvred around the monks, some still sitting gazing at Lawrence in surprise, most chatting to each other as they left the room.

"Ah, Jean. I have some news for you. The Sheriff has advised that the hearing regarding our dispute with the Holy Trinity over Father Wimer's land will be held in the Samford Hundred court in a fortnight's time. I'm afraid it's very bad timing, given the blessed lifting of the interdict and all the extra work it's thrown on us -

but I'm sure you're prepared for it. I have faith in you!" He slapped Jean on the shoulder.

Jean stood rooted to the spot, his mind blank, a dark unease growing in his stomach.

Father Lawrence picked something up from the bench beside him and continued. "And that's not all - read this." He shoved a roll of parchment into Jean's hands.

Jean looked at it in surprise. The seal caught his eye; thick and heavy, with the crossed keys of the Holy See stamped deep into the lead. He frowned and glanced up at Father Lawrence, who waved impatiently at the scroll.

"Come on, boy, open it! I need your thoughts on it!"

He needs MY opinion on something? What on earth?… Why is he getting letters from the Vatican?

Jean unrolled and began reading quietly to himself. The opening sentences were standard greetings… He stared at Father Lawrence in surprise.

"A Papal Nuncio? Visiting us?!"

"Yes, yes. He's also been appointed the Bishop of Norwich, which is why he has an interest in us. Carry on."

Jean got to the meat of it and read aloud.

"…enjoin you to give all possible aid in the matter of the charge that our brethren in Christ, the Prior and Canons of the house of the Holy Trinity in the city of Ipswich, have raised against the house of St Mary de Alneto in Dodnash…"

He could hear that his voice had got higher and louder in surprise. Father Lawrence waved him to continue.

"To wit, that St Mary has, for these past several years, misappropriated tithes belonging to Holy Trinity, and has failed to send its servants to the mother church in Ipswich, as is right and proper. Know that our Nuncio has full powers to resolve this case in any way that he sees fit."

Jean shook his head in amazement.

"But that's not right at all! We don't owe tithes to them; we're part of Battle Abbey's gift, originally, it says so in our founding charters. And we certainly don't need to send the servants to Ipswich to go to church, when we have our own right here!"

Father Lawrence was beaming at him.

"Good lad! I knew you'd have an answer. Well, it looks like we'll get all our legal worries out of the way at once - the Nuncio wants us to go to Ipswich to make a response the week after the Samford court."

Lawrence gave him another slap on the shoulder and went off in the direction of the church, and the queue of people waiting patiently for him.

Jean stood rooted to the spot. It wasn't until he was jostled by a pair of toddlers running riot that his thoughts started to race again, and the fear began to rise.

***

Jean started to straighten up as the latest parishioner left Father Lawrence's study, full of thanks. The topmost tablet in Jean's pile began to slip, and he noticed it just in time to snap his arm straight and rescue it. As soon as he had everything balanced again,

Father Lawrence stuck his head out of the door and apologised...

"I'm so sorry, Jean, I have to run - I have a meeting with the Port Master in Ipswich. Can we rearrange our chat to tomorrow? And please would you bring my horse around?"

His head disappeared back inside and Jean slumped against the wall. This time the errant tablet got away, clattering to the floor. *Not again, for heaven's sake! That's the fourth time he's put me off!*

He remade his pile and successfully balanced it over to the bookshelf in the corner of the cloister. *Might as well leave these here. Then I can just run and get them if he ever deigns to talk to me...*

Relieved of his burden he stomped off towards the stables. *Honestly, am I a lawyer or a servant? One minute he wants me to fetch his horse, the next he wants me to pull his bacon out of the Holy Trinity's fire...*

The sunshine was pleasantly warm on his back, and the tension in his shoulders was easing as he walked. A skylark rose from the grass in front of him, and he smiled as he followed its flight. *Dear Lord, I'm grumpy today! He can tell me to do anything he likes, he has my vow of obedience... I really would like his advice on my arguments for the case, though!*

He pulled a saddle and tack from the wall hooks and balanced them over the palfrey's stall door. The horse snorted at him, and he laughed.

"Well, all right, Apple, if you insist- I'll rehearse the case with you instead; don't tell Father Lawrence, but you probably know as much law as he does, anyway!"

***

It was so HOT! And every step he took rubbed a bit more skin from underneath the strap on his right sandal. He was going to have to start limping in a minute, and once he did, he wasn't going to be able to stop… *I am not going to walk into that courtroom feeling like I'm beaten already!* He pinched up a bit of gown from his chest and flapped it to and fro, trying to get a bit of air down there. *Of course, I might melt first…*

Father Lawrence had been most firm about the proper clothing to wear to court, once it was clear that he wasn't going to be able to get out of a meeting with the Bishop and Jean would have to go alone. Jean was dressed better than the acting Prior himself - in fact, in the best, darkest-dyed, thickest woollen robe that the Priory could come up with. To add to his woes, it was just a little too long for him.

He stumped along a bit further, feeling hotter and crosser the further he went. He got to where the path began to dip down to the stream separating Bentley from Tattingstone and eyed the wooded hill on the other side with relief. *Nearly there…*

The planks across the stream were dry, the little brook happily burbling underneath them. He looked at the water with longing. Suddenly making his mind up, he trotted across to the other side and turned left, upstream, instead of up the dusty path towards the village. As soon as he was out of sight he pulled off his gown and sandals. Dressed only in his loincloth, he sat on the bank, feet in the blissfully cold water, and splashed handfuls of the glorious stuff over his head and body.

He leaned back and tilted his head back to enjoy a bit of breeze. His hand fell on some moss. *So soft! Hmmm...* He picked a clump of it and gathered up his bag, gown, and sandals. Careful of his bare feet, he ghosted half naked up the hill through the wood until he could see the path to Alton Hall. He got decent again - the moss stuffed under his sandal strap made it possible to walk without pain. Even the itching of the heavy wool felt less irritating on cool skin.

He started rehashing his arguments as he walked.

We have usage on our side, and custom; the whole village knows that Wimer owned the land, and his father before him. I wish we could have found the charters from when Wimer registered the land - but it can't be helped. I should be able to call plenty of witnesses to say it was his. He walked on a bit further. *But why is the Holy Trinity going to all the trouble of bringing the case? I wish I knew what they were up to, they must know I can get half the hundred to swear the land was Wimer's!*

He came over the last rise. The Hall was visible a little way down the slope, a curl of smoke rising from the kitchen building. A few people were standing around, but none of the bustle you'd expect if the Sheriff's retinue were present. *Thank heavens, I'm in good time.* He glanced down to check his gown. *And looking as respectable as I get, I suppose.*

There was movement away to his left. A line of horses were cantering along the Ipswich track. *That's too many to be either the Sheriff or the Prior - I bet they've travelled down together, and the Sheriff's had poison against us dripped in his ear all the way...*

His mouth was dry, and the robe felt unbearably claustrophobic again. *Please, Lord, may I at least get a fair hearing - and whatever the Prior is planning - make him speak the truth!*

He arrived into the middle of chaos, servants running everywhere, people spilling out of the Hall. He stopped someone -

"Brother, what's happening here? The place looks like an ant's nest, there's no delay to the court, is there?"

"No, it's just moving outside, is all. Sheriff De Cressey arrived, took one look in the hall - or maybe one nose-full, it was a bit ripe in there - and decreed that the court will be held out here. Waste of time me getting here early!"

Jean nodded thanks and wandered off to find a shady wall to lean against. *Well, I'd rather be outside too… de Cressey. De Cressey… I know that name, I'm sure.* He glanced across to where the servants were finishing putting together a makeshift dais. Waiting for them were the court officials, including one man who did indeed look familiar. Jean stared at him then snapped his fingers. *I know! He's the Earl Bigod's friend, they came to the Priory together a while ago. He was concerned about court officials taking too much in bribe money, I think - well, I might get a fair hearing, then!*

Feeling much better, he walked over to stand in the crowd forming in front of the dais.

"Jean! What are you doing here?"

Edeva! He whirled round. *Her hair's all covered up… Silly, of course it is, if she's attending court.*

"Edeva! Great to see you! You're looking well. Oh! I

suppose Maurice is here too then? Why are you here, have you got a grievance with someone?" *shut up, fool, you're babbling.*

She was smiling and frowning at him at the same time.

"No, I'm here on my own, I want to ask for the right not to be wed. Er - that's an unusual bit of headgear you're wearing? Hang on…"

She reached up and plucked something from behind his ear. It was a piece of weed. He blushed at the thought of what she'd saved him from. *Oh! That would have been awful, standing there covered in green slime!*

"That's better! You're here for the Priory, I take it, given the way old sourpuss from Holy Trinity is glaring at you? - Hey, you're on, look - the steward's just waved at him."

Sure enough, the steward called "Case of Trinity Priory against Saint Mary de Alneto Priory, Dodnash. Representative from Saint Mary, come forward, please."

She smiled at him. "Good luck!"

He smiled back, then started to work through the crowd. *Did she say, she wanted the right not to be wed?* He shook his head and tried to concentrate on his own case. *What trick will he try to pull, I wonder? Does that mean someone's been asking for her hand?*

The steward made them state their names and who they were representing. De Cressey waved at the Prior to go first. He bowed and half-turned so that he was speaking to the crowd as well as the dais.

"Thank you, Lord. My case is in two parts; the first

concerns the fields to the west of the Priory, between the great elm and East Bergholt's outfield, which the Priory have set to corn this year. I can prove that this land does not belong to them, as it was gifted to the Holy Trinity several years ago by Wimer the Chaplain in cognisance of a debt he owed us."

What? That's ridiculous! There's never been any question of the ownership of those fields! What's he playing at?

There were grumbles from the crowd. De Cressey glared around and the noise stopped. He turned back to the Prior.

"And the second part?"

"That concerns the land claimed by this young man here." The Prior smiled sweetly at him. Jean concentrated on not balling his fists up. "I'm afraid that it never belonged to him in the first place, as it was passed to his eldest nephew on the death of his brother. This nephew, William, farmed it as his own, and it has never been under the control of either Wimer nor this Jean. William asked me to clear up ownership of it before he died; carrying out that promise is a sacred trust." He looked smug again. Jean gritted his teeth.

"Very well; let's examine those claims one at a time." De Cressey turned to the crowd. "Is there any person present who witnessed the transfer of the land west of St Mary's to the Holy Trinity, as the Prior has described?"

No-one came forward. Jean heard someone behind him mutter "what rubbish!"

"Silence speaks! Well, Prior - you said you had proof; can you produce it?"

"Indeed I can, Lord! The charter is dated from some time ago, perhaps it's not surprising that there are no current witnesses." The Prior turned to one of his monks who put some parchment in his hand. "Here it is. It even has Wimer's personal seal on it." He started to read it out loud.

"Yes, yes. I'm sure it's precisely as you described. Hand it to the steward for lodging in the records, please."

The Prior crossed in front of the dais to had the charter over.

"Hold! Let me see that!" de Cressey took the parchment and turned the seal to the light. He looked up, frowning.

"How did you come by this, Prior?"

"It was found following an extensive search of our cartulary, Lord. Why do you ask?"

"This is not Wimer the Chaplain's seal. It's close - it was created by someone who knew that he used a cormorant as his emblem - but this one has its wings shut; Wimer's has them spread for drying. He told me the story of how he chose it once."

De Cressey had taken a small knife from his belt and was carefully scraping at the parchment.

"And this ink is purely on the surface, hasn't soaked in at all. I'm surprised it's dry. No, you'll have to do better than that, Prior. This charter is obviously a forgery."

That must be one of the ones that Edeva told me about! I didn't realise they had cooked up charters so far away from William's land - I thought they were just after the fields next to his!

The Prior's voice was smooth as silk.

"Good heavens, Lord! How terrible! I'm so glad you spotted that before an error was made. I withdraw my claim at once, of course, and I'll check for any more incorrect seals in the cartulary. Dreadful business, I wonder how it came to be there!"

The same voice behind Jean muttered "because you put it there, you old fart!"

He tried hard not to grin. *Did the corners of de Cressey's eyes start to crinkle there too? What luck that he knew Wimer's seal and was able to shut the Prior up! I don't much care about losing my bit of land, so long as the Priory is safe.*

"Yes, well. I think I'll send one of my men with you to check. It would be safer, I think, now that I've told the world what Wimer's seal looked like."

Oh! I never thought of that! The Prior's face had turned purple. *And he's not happy at all! Is there a whole sheep's worth of fake charters in his cartulary? Wouldn't that be funny!*

The Prior bowed stiffly. "As you will."

De Cressey turned to Jean.

"To the other charge, then. What is your claim to the land? Exactly what is involved, anyway?"

Jean swallowed the lump in his throat and bowed. "My adopted father Wimer left it to me in his will, Lord. It's a piece of meadow from the Great Way along the banks of the stream separating Dodnash from Bentley, until it turns into a marsh; and the field above it, known as Big Fish from its shape."

The Prior spoke up. "Of course, it was not Wimer's to give, Lord."

De Cressey nodded and turned to the crowd. "Are there any witnesses to the reading of Wimer's will? The steward tells me that we have the text of it lodged with the court, it all appears in order."

Silence again.

"Well, it was some time ago, was it not, perhaps it's too much to ask. What about the usage of the land - has it been in the hands of Wimer's nephew, as the Prior here describes?"

There was a general mutter of agreement. The steward leaned over and pointed out someone in the crowd to de Cressey.

"I'm told that William de Dodnash's widow is here, is that so?"

"Yes, Lord." Edeva's voice was subdued.

"Come forward, woman... do you confirm that your late husband farmed the land in question?"

"Yes, Lord." *Oh, poor Edeva - what a terrible position they've put her in, she doesn't want to lose me the land!* The voice behind him muttered "Don't matter nohow." Jean turned, puzzled, but couldn't identify the source. De Cressey went on, and he turned back.

"For as long as you knew him?"

The steward was scrolling frantically through the court records. Jean watched him curiously, consciously not looking at Edeva.

She finally spoke, voice almost a whisper. "Yes, Lord."

De Cressey nodded dismissal at her and she turned to go.

The steward had found what he was looking for and leaned over again. De Cressey said something to him, and the steward nodded vigorously. De Cressey said something that Jean half-heard - it might have been "Really! How interesting!" *What's going on?*

"Wait, Goodwife, if you please."

Edeva turned back to him, puzzled.

"Did you know Wimer the Chaplain?"

"Yes, very well, Lord; my parents were his servants. We lived in his house in Orford whilst he was Sheriff, and often visited him here after he founded the Priory."

"Your husband's family - can you describe it?"

"Yes, Lord - William had an elder brother who died as a child, and a sister who is married over Elmstead Market way. His first wife, God rest her soul, gave him two sons and a daughter. The youngest boy died only a few years ago."

The Sheriff nodded, thoughtfully.

"And the generation before that?"

"His father, Maurice, had an older brother, I believe; I think he was a monk too. I'm not sure of his name. William had a couple of aunts, both dead now, of course."

"What about Wimer's generation, your husband's grandfather's?"

"Wimer was the youngest child, by a long way. I think he had two older brothers - Hervey was William's granddad... I can't remember the other one."

The Sheriff sat up straight.

"You're certain Wimer was the youngest son?"

Edeva looked puzzled. "Yes, Lord."

De Cressey turned to the Prior. "I doubt you're aware of this, as you're clearly not a local man. I wasn't until a few moments ago when my steward pointed it out. This manor has a rather curious inheritance pattern. Jean, are you aware of it?"

Jean frowned and shook his head.

De Cressey continued. "Yes, I've come across it once or twice before, but I didn't realise that it applied here. The term is ultimogeniture; by ancient custom, not the eldest, but the youngest son inherits!" He sat back in his chair, arms crossed, and watched them all.

The youngest… That's Wimer! Wimer should have got the land, not his brother Hervey! So it wasn't really William's - or Maurice's! He shook his head in amazement. *Hang on - if it was Wimer's, and William was his next in line blood relative, wouldn't it have gone to them anyway when he died?*

De Cressey stood up and stretched.

"I'm afraid that's another one you lose, Prior. It sounds to me like Wimer's brother Hervey had use of the land. With Wimer in Holy Orders, that would be entirely proper. But the ownership remained vested with Wimer; so the clause in the will giving that piece to Jean here is valid. With Wimer's death the remainder of the estate passed to his nephew William, and so land ownership and land usage came under one man. Case closed."

He sat down again. "Next case?"

Jean stared at him, open-mouthed. *I've won! Dear Lord, I've won! Thank you for answering my prayers!* He glanced across at the Prior. Curiously, he didn't look upset at all. Jean frowned, then shrugged. *I won!*

***

The band of her wimple was unbearably tight. Edeva raised her hand to ease a finger under it and stopped herself. *Wouldn't do to have even the tiniest wisp of hair showing, they'd take that as disrespect to the court...* She picked up the skirt of her apron and fanned herself instead. *Dear Lord, it's hot! I bet my face is as red as Jean's was when I pulled that bit of weed off his head!* She smiled. *He must have bathed in the river; but then how did he miss it when he combed his hair? Caught in all those lovely tight curls, I suppose... Shame he has to tonsure them...* She wiped her face with the apron, leaving damp smears on the cloth. *I'm so glad he won his case! Despite them hauling me in...*

The memory of the case - the formal group in front of the stern judge, the whole disgraceful thing of that rotten Prior from Ipswich lying through his teeth and nearly getting away with it, and her own terror at being called up herself - made her flush again.

I do wish they'd hurry up. I want to get this over with! Her tummy griped. *And I'd better get to the latrine pit before I have a nasty accident!* She looked over at the dais. It looked like they were having some kind of break - the Sheriff was out of his chair, having a chat with the Tollemache father and son, and the steward was nowhere in sight. *I've probably got time to go and get back before they start again, if I hurry...* She picked up her skirts and half-ran to the latrine.

She was feeling so much better when she came out - almost skipping in relief. She curtsied to the man going to the pit and stepped out of his way - then realised it was the steward. Without thinking, she spoke.

"God give you a good day, Sir - an it please you, do you know how long it might be before my case is heard? I'm Edeva, widow of William of Dodnash."

The fellow halted, smiled, and very slowly ran his eyes up and down her full length. His gaze came to a stop about a foot below her face. Edeva shivered a little. *I wish I hadn't talked to him! Dirty old man...*

"Beg pardon, Sir, I shouldn't have interrupted you." She moved to leave, but he put out a hand to stop her.

"Stay, Edeva of Dodnash. I recall you - didn't you speak in that Church matter? Yes. I remember admiring your figure at the time. You're younger than I thought - and prettier! What brings a lovely little thing like you to court?"

She edged away a bit before replying and kept her response as business-like as possible.

"I am going to plead to pay a fine to choose my own husband, or none at all." *So I don't end up with a slime-ball like you!*

"Ah, now, that would be a pity. A lass like you needs a man!" He leaned over and fingered her sleeve, clearly assessing the quality of her weaving. "I might consider taking you on myself - if the wife would let me!

He chuckled as she took half a step back.

"Besides, you need a deep purse for that - the King has made it clear that we're to fine people every possible penny to help the war effort. The last widow we allowed to buy her own disposal - and she was nowhere near as pretty as you - paid us 400 marks for the privilege."

Her hand crept unnoticed to her purse, tied for security under her skirt. *400 marks! I have nothing like that much!*

He was watching her face now, and smiled again, showing his teeth.

"Don't have it, lass? There's a shame! You'll have to hope your lord doesn't give you to some smelly old peasant... But with a face like that, you could earn your price on your back; I'd help!"

He grabbed for her. She twisted away just in time and ran as hard as she could - the direction didn't matter - so long as she got away! His laughter followed her.

She didn't stop until her foot caught in a rough patch of grass, sending her flying. She sat up and looked around, rubbing her ankle. There was no-one in sight. *Good heavens, I'm almost at the mill in Holbrook!* The millpond was just visible, further along the path. There was no noise from the wheel - come to think of it, Aelfburt the miller had been at the court. Her wimple - still stupidly tight - had become wedged, painfully, across one eyebrow. She glanced around again and pulled it off, shaking her hair out, light-headed with the rush of cool air. She hobbled over to the bank and washed her face, then sat on the bank with her feet in the pond, mind churning.

Eventually the peace of the place soothed her. *I'm thirsty - and I can't spend the rest of my life sitting here!* She dressed her hair decently again and got to her feet, wincing at the pain in her ankle. She hobbled upstream from the pond a little way and drank from the stream, then hunted around until she found a stout branch to lean on.

Oof! I wish I'd run the other way! It's a long walk back. What am I going to do now? I suppose the first thing to do is to go home, stay in my little cottage in the woods, live as quietly as possible, and pray that no-one remembers I exist. And work out some way of dealing with Maurice...

She limped on a few more steps.

That creep of a steward might remember me - I gave him my name! But he's married, thank heavens. Ugh it was horrible, feeling his eyes crawl all over me! She stopped and shook out her arm. *Lucky I didn't kick him in the balls, I suppose - that would've given him something to remember, all right!* She grinned at the thought, then started off again, hurrying now to be past the hall as quickly and as unobtrusively as possible.

CHAPTER 18

NUNCIO

The basket straps were cutting into her back - and now she'd stopped, she needed to pee. There was no-one on the path, so she stepped a few paces into the wood, eased the straps over her shoulders, and squatted down.

She hadn't yet finished when she heard the men's voices - many of them, singing a marching song, and approaching rapidly. She cursed her stupidity in not going further into the woods. It was an eternity before she could move...

She glanced once at the basket and abandoned it - the voices were very near. Crouching low, she scuttled to the side, towards a good thick holly bush. Immediately a harsh voice rang out, challenging her. Or at least that was what she assumed the shout was, she didn't understand the language...

A powerfully stocky figure appeared in front of her, and she let out a little shriek. He smiled and licked his lips, and she whirled round - straight into another of them. This one surrounded her in a bear hug and carried her towards the road. Her arms were pinioned. No point in screaming, but maybe…

She kicked out as high and hard as she could, and was rewarded with a grunt. She kicked again, and the brute dropped her, almost falling against her. She scrambled away and crashed through the undergrowth as fast as she could. She got about three steps away before the shorter one grabbed her. This one twisted her arm behind her back and lifted; it was so painful that she had no thought of attacking him. He forced her on tiptoe back to where his companion was still rubbing his groin.

"Poutain!" he spat, and backhanded her across the face. She cried out as her shoulder was wrenched, and a man on the path called something. Her captor steered her back to the sound and pushed her to her knees in the middle of the path. Her wimple and cap had become lost in the struggle somewhere.

The roadway was absolutely full of men. She had never seen so many people in so small a space! There were still men marching in to what was fast becoming a camp, taking off back packs and sitting down in small groups. The ones nearest were beginning to take some notice of her. Very soon she was surrounded by a jeering mob of men - making it very clear what they wanted with her, despite the language barrier. There was no point trying to run, and she would not give them the satisfaction of crying… it was a relief when an officious little man elbowed his way through the crowd and started yelling at the men. They began to move away, still calling things to her.

The little man turned to her and barked something.

She shook her head in incomprehension. He frowned and tried again.

"Who are you? Where you go?"

Thank heavens for that! Someone I can talk to - and is he in charge? She straightened her back.

"I am going to Ipswich to market, Sir."

"Eepswich? No! Bad you go!" He shook his head rapidly. She stared at him - then noticed that behind him the furthest men were jumping up and putting their packs back on. A pair of horses appeared, coming at a canter. The men were scrambling out of the way and lining up along the path. *What is happening?*

The riders were almost upon them. She was directly in their track! Suddenly the little man looked behind him and realised the danger. He and her captor pulled her aside just in time, snapping to attention themselves. *Is this a chance to run, whilst they're distracted?* The ground was shaking with galloping horses. She froze as they juddered to a halt right next to her.

"What have we here, then?"

The voice was light, a little disinterested. *English! Thank the Lord!* She raised her head to look at the speaker. The horse in front of her was a beautiful well-muscled bay, at the head of a small group of riders. She had only time to get the vaguest impression of the rider - a slight man in fine red woollen hose - before the little officer pushed her head down. A voice behind the rider barked what was probably the same question at him.

She could feel him trembling through his grip on her skull. He answered crisply, presumably an account of how they'd come across her. From the way the horsemen laughed and the man on her other side stiffened, he'd included the tale of her resistance. The sleepy voice spoke again.

"A spirited wench indeed! Let's see her face."

Again her arm was grabbed and used to lift and twist her to her feet. This time her captor caught her hair with his other hand, locking her into position facing the riders.

"Not an unpleasant sight... where are you going, wench?"

"N-nowhere, Sir! Only to Ipswich, to market!"

"A bad day for you to be on the road, I fear. Well, luckily for you, my men don't have time to enjoy you; we have a surprise planned for the Earl of Norfolk that it wouldn't do to be late for. A shame." He gestured to the man beside her. "Strip her to the waist. They can enjoy the sight, at least."

"Sire!"

The brute reached for her. She started to struggle, but her shoulder was yanked hard. She whimpered and froze as her bodice was ripped open.

"Lovely!" The sleepy voice was back. He turned and said something to his companions, then turned back to her. "My apologies, fair wench; but I have lost patience with this entire countryside. All of it seems to be in league against me - be thankful that we are in a hurry."

He bowed mockingly to her, then touched spurs to his horse and was gone. The men were lined up in marching formation and started to move rapidly. The line of them was endless - men leering at her, smacking their lips and making lewd gestures, the nearest reaching out for a quick squeeze. She tried to think only of the pain in her arm…

An eternity later the last of them were past. The oaf behind her goosed her then pushed her away. She fell heavily and was stunned for a moment. When she scrambled to her feet, clutching her torn bodice to her, she was as alone on the path as she had been just a scant hour before. She stumbled back into the woods to retrieve her basket. The shock only began to break when the turnips resisted her one-handed attempts to gather them up, then waves of tears overwhelmed her. It wasn't until the shadows were dark and lengthening that she was able to sort herself out and start the walk home.

A few yards down the road, she stopped dead. *Sire! The soldier called him Sire! The man on the horse must have been the King!* She started to tremble again. *What a terrible, terrible man!*

***

The weather had changed, and so had his costume. For the visit to the Papal Nuncio, Jean was relegated to bag-carrier. Father Lawrence had taken back the lead role, now that the queues of people demanding back-dated services from the Priory had died down a bit, and the diocese as a whole was running more normally. As a result, Father Lawrence was looking warm and comfortable in the Priory's best black wool gown, whilst Jean was shivering a little in a much thinner one.

They were kicking their heels in the cloisters of the

Holy Trinity. Jean looked longingly over to the sunny side, where a group of boys were learning their catechism. *It would help if this gown covered my ankles. I must've grown again...*

The Nuncio was clearly conducting as much business as possible whilst he was in Ipswich - and little Dodnash Priory was not anywhere near the top of the list.

Jean nodded to a group of merchants as they sorted themselves into order and went in to the hall. *I wonder why they need the Pope's man?* He leaned against the wall, closed his eyes, and daydreamed an answer. *They want to trade with the Russ, in the far North - to get coal-black furs, soft as baby's breath, to line the cloaks of royalty - and they need a letter from the Pope to say they're not spies.* He opened his eyes for a moment and frowned. *Or maybe a letter saying that you're not a spy would make people sure that you actually were one?* He thought about the puzzle for a bit then shook his head. *I wonder if they're going to Egypt instead, looking for spotted camelopards in the desert! If I went with them I'd be warm again! Standing still isn't helping...* He levered himself off the wall with his elbows.

"Can I fetch you some mulled ale, Brother?"

"Oh, be still, boy! And don't wander off. You can guarantee that the minute you do we'll be called in."

Father Lawrence swivelled round on the bench and examined him.

"Turn around? - yes, I thought so, you've been leaning against the wall - you have whitewash all over you!"

Jean submitted as Father Lawrence took out his

frustration on his back. The whacking stopped as the merchants filed out.

"...Patriarch in Kiev, then go up-country..." *Oh! Marvellous! They are going to Russia after all! Please can we be soon? Before Father Lawrence felts me?*

One of the Holy Trinity monks popped his head around the doorway.

"Dodnash? - you're next."

Jean crossed himself. *Thank you, Lord!* He bent to pick up the satchel of charters.

"Remember to bow!" Father Lawrence hissed, waving Jean behind him. They processed solemnly into the room and bowed to the man sat at the table. Jean stared at him. *Don't suppose I'll often be in a room with a Prince of the Church... He looks - I don't know - smooth, somehow.* He bent in his turn to kiss the man's ring. *Even if you put Father Lawrence in that same black gown and purple cap, he'd never look half so sophisticated. Me either!* As he stood up again, he saw Prior Gilbert of Holy Trinity standing to one side. *Him, on the other hand, looks as slick as you like... He looks like a cat that's got the cream!*

The Nuncio started speaking, and Jean had to concentrate to make out his rapid, almost whispered, Latin.

"My understanding is that this - Dodnash Priory, is that correct? - barbarous name - owes tithes to the mother house here in Ipswich and has consistently failed to pay them, is that the case?"

Father Lawrence and Prior Gilbert spoke at one.

"Yes, Your Eminence." "No, Your Eminence, that's not the case at all!"

They glared at each other. The Nuncio pointed a finger at the Prior, who bowed.

"Thank you, Your Eminence. All know that the land that Dodnash own in East Bergholt is tithed to Holy Trinity - and to the best of my knowledge, they have never once paid it! More, their servants worship in the church at Dodnash, instead of coming to Ipswich and making their offerings there. This state of affairs is simply wrong, against the natural order of things, and we beg you to right it!"

Jean glanced across at Father Lawrence. He was standing with his arms crossed, looking scornful.

The Nuncio turned and raised one eyebrow at him.

"None of that is true, Your Eminence! Dodnash Priory owns no land in East Bergholt at all and owes no tithes to the Holy Trinity! Our founder, Wimer the Chaplain, gifted us the land in its entirety free of all ties. The land was, in any case, originally tithed to Battle Abbey, not to Ipswich." He nodded once, decisively.

There was a sinking feeling in the pit of Jean's stomach. *The original land gift might have been free... What about subsequent gifts? And I suppose we might own land in all three parishes, being right in the middle as we are!* All of a sudden, he knew what the Holy Trinity prior was going to say.

"Dodnash Priory does indeed own land in East Bergholt, Eminence. Indeed, this young fellow here proved the case in court only very recently." He stopped to smile at Jean. "And Battle Abbey controlled Dodnash land, not East Bergholt."

Oh! You - you scumbag! You set us up all along! Father

Lawrence made a sound like he'd been slapped. It jerked Jean back to the present. He swallowed a lump in his throat.

"Your Eminence, may I speak?" An elegant eyebrow lifted, but the hand gesture was an invitation.

"Thank you, Your Eminence. Prior Gilbert speaks truth, he lost a case in our local court recently concerning the ownership of a piece of meadow that our founder - my adopted father - gifted to me, not to Dodnash Priory. I am not farming it, it is being grazed by my adopted father's nephew, so I have nothing to tithe; and I have no servants to send to Ipswich to church. Prior Gilbert here tried to lay claim to some fields in East Bergholt, but the charter was proved to be a forgery."

He bowed and took a half-step back. Gilbert was still smirking. *What have I missed?*

"Well, Your Eminence, setting aside the tithe on that field for the moment - as well as the question of personal ownership of land by a postulant - let us consider the judgement of that court on the fields in East Bergholt. I'm sure my young friend will agree that the court ruled that Wimer the Chaplain inherited his father's lands by right?"

He paused. Jean frowned, but nodded.

"And so when he gifted his land to Dodnash as a foundation gift, it included both his lands in Dodnash and his lands further afield. He made no distinction between them in the charter, did he?"

Father Lawrence's mouth was open. Prior Gilbert ploughed on regardless.

"Therefore I think we must conclude that Dodnash

Priory as a whole was tied to the Holy Trinity from its inception, and that this is still the case today."

Gilbert bowed to the Nuncio and smiled sweetly at Jean and Father Lawrence.

"Well, Father?" the Nuncio asked.

Father Lawrence looked badly shaken. "Even if the gift included land from both parishes, it was not his intent! He gifted us the land free of all obligation, I'm sure - do we have the charter here, Jean?"

Jean winced. *I'm not sure the gift was free of ALL obligation...* but he had no choice but to dig it out of the satchel. The Nuncio's hand gesture this time meant "give it to me"...

The Nuncio's lips moved as he read the opening phrases, then he read aloud. "I, Wimer, grant in pure and perpetual alms to the church of St Mary de Alneto at Dodnash... all my lands of whatsoever fee... free from all secular obligation. "

He looked up at them and repeated "free from all secular obligation. Not its obligation to the Church, as is entirely proper; this does not exclude any obligation to pay tithes, and it does not alter existing feudal fees." He looked at the parchment again and frowned. "And all his lands of whatsoever fee - not only his lands at Dodnash. This all sounds very clear-cut to me; but I will pray for guidance. I will write and let you know my decision." He held out his ring to be kissed in dismissal.

Father Lawrence slumped back onto the bench outside the door, head in his hands. "Oh dear Lord, we've lost it. We've lost the Priory."

His shoulders began to shake. Jean put a hand on his arm, then crouched down in front of him.

"Surely not, Father!" He made the sign of the Cross, then crossed his fingers. "I expect he'll just decide that we have to pay tithes on the East Bergholt land and that's it. We could cope with that, couldn't we?"

Father Lawrence gazed up at him. He looked like he'd aged twenty years.

"You don't understand, Jean. He's the Pope's voice; whatever he decides, we must do without question. And that misbegotten toad of a Prior was still smiling…"

***

The monks' faces were almost identical masks of dismay. Father Lawrence was giving the Chapter gathering a blow-by-blow account of the meeting with the Nuncio, leaving Jean nothing to do but stand there feeling more and more miserable.

"…and then Jean spoke up and told the Nuncio about how the Holy Trinity's charter was proven to be false, so our ownership of the land was undisputed. That just made it worse; it's so clear that the Holy Trinity has been plotting this for some time, and had set up the timing of the case in the Hundred court so that we'd win the field but risk the Priory."

Everyone turned to look at Jean. Most of them looked sympathetic, but not all…

Father Lawrence continued. "Even when we told him that part of our land had been linked to Battle Abbey, and never to the Holy Trinity, it made no difference." He stopped to rub his face. "I am most terribly sorry, brothers, but I'm almost certain that the Nuncio will decide that we must submit to the Holy Trinity and become a daughter house of theirs. I suspect the fact that I'm not a Prior didn't help, either. I've failed you."

He sat down suddenly. Jean sat too. There was an uncomfortably long silence before the monks all started talking at once.

They all think that we've let them down. And they're right - although I don't see how we could have done better. Distrust the Holy Trinity more, maybe...

The hubbub died down. The monks were talking quietly amongst themselves, just one or two remaining silent. Brother Michael was clearly thinking it all through. He slowly stood up and waited for people to be ready to listen to him.

"Brothers, I think we should thank Father Lawrence and Jean for their efforts. I doubt any of us would have done as well, faced with a Prince of the church, and a sister priory who clearly only have their own interests at heart!"

He paused for a low rumble of assent.

"It's clear to me that we have had the wool pulled over our eyes by the Holy Trinity - although I don't think we could have done anything differently. But I'm wondering if there's one channel we haven't explored."

Father Lawrence sat upright. "Oh? Please continue, Brother?"

"It's the link with Battle Abbey. Jean, you've studied the charter records - what exactly do they say about Battle?"

Jean leaped to his feet. "There's only one charter that talks about it, Brother - I'll go and fetch it."

Has he seen a loophole I've missed? He trotted there and back as quickly as possible, so as not to let Brother Michael's thought processes go off the boil.

"Here it is, Brother. Shall I read it aloud?... It's one of our very earliest charters, the one where the Bishop of Norwich gives us the right to bury our dead here, and the bit about Battle is 'The canons have sworn upon the Gospels that they will not infringe upon the rights of the Parish Church, which pertains to the Abbot and Convent of Battle'. And a bit more: 'Any dispute will be settled by the common council of the churches of the Aldergrove and Battle and the incumbent of East Bergholt, and if this should fail, by the arbitration of the Bishop of Norwich, without recourse to any superior judge'. It was signed by Alan, the Prior of Holy Trinity in those days - so they KNEW about it!"

Brother Michael nodded. "Thank you, Jean. That's very clear; what should have happened is that Battle Abbey should have been invited to speak - as of course should the priest at East Bergholt, but as there isn't one right now, that's not possible. I wonder if the Nuncio knew about this at all? He's only recently been made Bishop, he can't be expected to know all the little wrinkles of the parishes yet. So we need to get Battle Abbey to come in on our side."

Oh, that's brilliant! But is it too late? What if the Nuncio has made his mind up already?

Father Lawrence voiced the same concern. "That's an excellent idea! But how? And if the Nuncio has committed himself to a decision, it won't be easy to get him to consider new evidence."

"You haven't had his letter yet, have you?" Brother Michael asked. Father Lawrence shook his head. "Then we have a window of opportunity! We could ask the Abbot to write to the Nuncio and point out this link to them. But we'd need to move fast! What do you think, brothers - is it worth trying?"

Jean added his own voice to the chorus of Ayes and Yes!

Father Lawrence stood up. "Thank you, Brother Michael, for giving us hope back! I think you're right, that we need to seize the chance, slim though it is. Are we all agreed?"

He looked around. Everyone was nodding.

"Then there's only one man for the job - Jean, please will you go to Battle for us?"

Jean blurted out without thinking, in an embarrassingly squeaky voice. "But I don't even know where Battle is!"

The whole room burst out laughing. Father Lawrence slapped him on the shoulder.

"Don't worry, lad - we'll put you on a ship to Winchelsea; once you're there, the whole countryside can point you in the right direction."

***

"What is the meaning of this?"

Lawrence drew himself up to his full height and glared at the servant who had interrupted Chapter, looking so anguished at the doorway to the chapter house that Lawrence had eventually given up trying not to make eye contact with the man. He handed over proceedings to Brother Michael and stalked to the door.

"Beg pardon, Father - but there's a letter come for Father Wimer! The courier says he has to wait for an answer, too!"

"Well, given how long Father Wimer's been dead, it can hardly be urgent, can it!" Lawrence glanced back into Chapter, then curiosity won over duty. "Give it to me, then!"

There were no particular clues on the packet, with the heavy, good-quality creamy parchment folded and sealed, just two lines on the outside:

To: Father Wimer, Dodnash Priory - or the Prior of same if Fr. Wimer is deceased

From: Guillaume de Petit-Andely, Factor

Lawrence pulled up the cord on his belt-knife and cut the seal, walking towards his office as he did so. The first few words brought him up short, and he perched on the low cloister wall to read instead.

Concerning Jean, son of Jean of Rouen:

Révérend Père Wimer (or the Prior of Dodnash Priory in the unhappy event that Father Wimer is no longer with us),

Please accept my apologies for writing you directly, but I am increasingly concerned at the fate of my employer, Jean de Rouen. I assume you know that he took the vows of a lay brother for a fixed term of 10 years immediately before the siege of Constantinople? He survived that campaign and lived as a Templar servant at one of their hospitals there; I received occasional letters from him inquiring after his estate, and instructing me to send regular sums of money to the Knights.

I believe that he had achieved a kind of peace out in those far lands, and I thought I detected signs that he was planning to come home when his period of service came to an end.

However, I have not heard from him directly for a little over a year and a half. For some time I hoped that he was merely suffering from the delays and difficulties that are inevitable when such long journeys are undertaken; but as time went on, I became more and more worried, and when I realised that the Templar treasury had not made any claims on his estate since the 10-year anniversary of his vow, I wrote to them. It took a further six months for a reply to come back, and when it did, it confirmed my worst fears. Monsieur Jean left Constantinople on a ship bound for the Dardanelles as soon as he was released, and the Templars have had no further communication from him.

I think we must assume that some accident has befallen him on the journey and prepare for the worst. In the event that Jean senior is dead, the estate passes to his son, or if Jean junior is also dead, to a nephew of his mother's. The law states that without a body or witness to a death, a term of seven years must pass before the heir can inherit; I have started that process with the local Abbey.

By my reckoning, Jean junior must now be a young man, and may well no longer be at the Priory. I am most keen to discover what has happened to the boy, and to hand over control of the estate to him or to his named factor - I am feeling the weight of my own years growing, and would like to discharge my duties here to a younger man. I would be most grateful if you would write back to me giving all you know of his status, and forgive my ignorance, whether your order allows him to own property in the event he has taken holy orders. I have given the courier sufficient funds and instructions to send your reply to me immediately, and to follow any information you have as to Jean's whereabouts if he has left you.

Go with God,

Guillaume de Petit-Andely, Factor to Jean de Rouen

Dated this feast day of Saint Agatha in the year of our Lord 1215.

Lawrence refolded the parchment and let it rest on his lap. *Poor boy! We thought his father was possibly dead, of course; but not to know how, or even where - it'll be very hard on him. And what terrible luck that the letter comes when he's travelling!*

He stood, brushed the back of his robe off, and walked towards his office, trying to imagine the kind of life that Jean senior might have led, in the dust and heat of fabled Constantinople. He pulled out his chair and sat, shaking his head, then reached for pen and ink to write to the factor. *Jean made this ink! God works in such marvellous ways. To think that I've been this close to encouraging him to take his vows... Strange that he might be a man of substance now.* He shook his head again, and bent to the task.

***

He ran his already sodden kerchief over his forehead, and grinned at his inconstancy. *I don't know, never satisfied - too hot now, and too cold on board ship...* The hill was punishingly steep, though, especially to legs that had finally learned to enjoy the rolling of the ship, despite the North wind.

He looked up-slope and realised that the line of dark stone at the top of the hill must be the Abbey wall - he was nearly there! He wiped his face again and took a drink from his leather bottle. Below him a cart was toiling up the hill, clouds of dust in its wake. Jean started walking again, hoping to beat it up the hill.

He came upon the gate by surprise. Battle town stretched away at the top of the hill, with the Abbey wall curling round to his left; the gatehouse was tucked away in the turn. Imposing enough to impress, once he'd walked a little way away and looked back; four towers, flags flying - *Good, the Abbot is at home...* and a larger central tower surmounted by some glorious carved arches. The cart clattered through the open doorway, and Jean stopped gaping and followed it.

The courtyard was seething - men, horses, and carts everywhere. Jean flattened himself against the inner wall and tried to make sense of the chaos. There looked to be at least two or three separate markets, each supervised by a harassed-looking monk - the carts were going down the hill a little way, there were sheep and shepherds milling under the trees, and whole wheels of cheese were being unloaded into a building a little to his left. His stomach rumbled, and he tried to remember his last meal. No time for breakfast, as he had helped to load and launch the little river-boat that had brought him up from Rye; and he'd missed supper at the Priory in Rye the day before. It must have been the noon-day meal on the merchant's cog that had stopped at every vill between Margate and Rye. He sucked his tummy in. *I hope the monks keep a good visitor's table - even that cat looks appetising! Where do I go to find the Abbot in all this crush, I wonder?*

That puzzle was solved as the bells began to chime for Terce, and he joined the flood of people heading past the kitchens to the sound. The church was enormous! He could see the whole length of it as he walked to the service - it was easily seven bays long, more than twice as long as little Dodnash. *But then, we only have an elderly chaplain in our graveyard, not the last Saxon King of England! I hope we're not completely beneath their notice...*

He realised that the wide ridge he was walking along must have been the English position in the great battle, at least according to old Oslac, who was ever so proud of his grandfather's having fought here, and who would tell the tale at the drop of a hat if you let him. He edged to his right for a closer look down the slope and whistled soundlessly. *I wouldn't like to attack up that! Terrifying.*

He turned into the great West doors and found a place amongst the crowd. As the priests processed down the nave, the goodwife next to him nudged her neighbour and hissed,

"Look - the new Abbot!"

"Shh! And he's not exactly new, is he?!"

Jean craned his neck, but couldn't be sure which of the sumptuously gowned priests they were talking about.

Everything about the service was glorious; from the faultless singing of the choir - the boys' high trebles and the men's sonorous tones filling every inch of the cathedral-like building - to the mellow tones of the deacon. After days of not being able to attend a service, he should have been lost in the rhythm of it - but once or twice he had to think about a response, rather than it just flowing from him. The atmosphere was all so perfect, it was offputting...

At the end he leaned down and whispered to the goodwife,

"Which is the Abbot, Goody?"

"Abbot Richard, on the left. He's been acting as Abbot for ages, but he only got elected a few weeks ago."

He studied the man as the clergy processed away. Tall, lean, with a noble forehead and an almost ascetic look, he was looking straight ahead as he passed. Jean puffed his cheeks out in a sigh. *Why would a great man like that bother with us? I hope I haven't come all this way for nothing!* He shook his head and followed the goodwife out. *Well, I might as well try to see him, anyway.* He grinned at a memory of Wimer describing the great Ranulph de Glanville - *"He's a man... He pees standing up like the rest of us..."* and went to find a monk to take a message to the Abbot.

Thoughts of the old battle kept forcing themselves on him whilst he waited. He was standing looking over the brow of the hill, lost in imagining the screams of men and horses, when a light touch on his shoulder made him turn round.

"Father Abbot!" He bowed low. When he straightened up the Abbot was looking quizzically at him.

"I'm really not used to people doing that yet! I wonder how long it'll take me?"

He looked out over the slope himself.

"I could do with a walk to clear my head, away from the bustle. Why don't we walk over the battlefield, and you can tell me what your problem is as we go?"

He turned and led the way, long strides making Jean scramble to catch up. He tried not to sound puffed as he told the Abbot all about Wimer, and the Holy Trinity, and the Nuncio. The Abbot asked a question or two as he spoke, and Jean finished the tale as they reached a stream at the bottom of the meadows and stopped. The Abbot was looking up the slope to the church, his eyes dreamy. He spoke slowly...

"They were brave men, attacking up such a hill. God was with them... I often wonder what England would be like had not He guided the hands that slew Harold the Oathbreaker." He shook his head and focused his attention back on Jean. "I had a quick look in our cartulary before coming out to meet you. Nuncio Verraccio should indeed consult with us before making a judgement. To be fair, keeping the King and his barons still talking to each other is probably taking a lot of his attention. I will write to him and remind him that you are tied to this house, not to that land-hungry bunch of Augustinians in Ipswich - there will be a meeting in a place called Runnymede not far from London next week; you could go over there and wait for him with the letter. I'm sending a small group of witnesses, you can travel together."

Just then the bells started to ring for Sext. The Abbot sighed.

"I must go and put on my robes of office again. See the buildings under the church, on the right? - it's the novices' workroom. Wait there for the letter - you may find the company congenial, and they will take you to the refectory for the noon meal."

Jean bowed low; by the time he straightened, the Abbot was a small, fast-moving figure almost at the church. Jean smiled after him, following more slowly to do as he was bid.

CHAPTER 19

RUNNYMEDE

The meadows and the gentle slopes behind them were seething. As they rode nearer Jean began to pick out a pattern - each group of soldiers was centred on one or more tents; some of them rich and colourful, others old and patched. In the very centre the river ran, wide and untroubled. In its midst was an island, its grass the only thing of nature clearly visible.

Hard-eyed men turned to watch the Battle Abbey party pass, hands never far from weapons, and Jean shivered under their gaze. *I pray none of the guards does something stupid, or we'll be spitted! I thought the monks were on the same side as the barons - are these the King's soldiers?* The next tent carried the unmistakable red-on-gold flag of the de Claire arms. *No, these are the barons' men - expecting trouble!*

The head of their little cavalcade stopped and called over to a monk standing outside the tent.

"God give you a good day, Brother - where may we find the Papal Nuncio?"

The monk's accent was strange, but his Latin clear

enough. "I believe he lodges at Windsor Castle, Brother; see the tower yonder? God give you good speed."

He made the sign of the cross in blessing, and they moved on. It felt like every eye in the place was watching them, and the silence was unnerving. *They are waiting for the storm...*

The atmosphere was a little easier behind the curtain wall of Windsor Castle. They found the Nuncio ensconced in a hall in the Upper Court, dealing with a steady stream of people. The name of Battle Abbey got them bumped up the queue a bit. When they were called, Jean attached himself to the back of the group, mouth suddenly dry. *What if he ignores the Abbot's letter? What would we do then?*

The monks finished presenting themselves and parted to let Jean through. *Here we go!*

The Nuncio frowned at him a moment, then his eyes narrowed in recognition.

"You are a long way from Suffolk, young man! What is your business with me?"

Jean swallowed and went down on one knee.

"Your Excellency, I bring you a letter from Abbot Richard of Battle Abbey, concerning the case you heard a short while ago between Dodnash Priory and the Holy Trinity Priory in Ipswich."

He held out the scroll. The Nuncio took it, broke the seal, and read the short note. He raised an eyebrow and looked at Jean.

"The Abbot is very concise. Do you know what it says?"

Jean shook his head. "No, Excellency, only that it is about the land that the Priory was gifted by my adoptive father."

"Indeed." The Nuncio studied him. "Do I not recall that you have a personal land interest in this too? Is it separate from the Priory's founding grant?"

"Yes, Excellency, it…"

A secretary-monk was whispering urgently in the Nuncio's ear.

"My apologies, young man, but I am wanted by the King. Thank you for bringing the letter; rest assured that I will bear it in mind when I have an opportunity to write my judgement on the case. As you can imagine, I'm a little short of time to do that right now."

The Nuncio bustled off. Jean stood and brushed his knee off. *Well, I suppose that's that. Now what?* He turned and thanked his escort, then wandered disconsolately over to the ale table. It all seemed so much of an anticlimax - and still no definitive ruling from the Nuncio. He gulped a cup of small beer. *Go home, I suppose. I'd like to pray first, though.*

He nearly bumped into Roger Bigod, who was leaving the chapel. Jean apologised and tried to dance backwards, stopped as the Earl gripped his shoulder.

"Jean! Whatever are you doing here, lad!"

"I've just delivered a letter from Abbot Richard of Battle to the Nuncio, Lord - about the Priory's land. Now I'm thinking about going home."

The Earl studied him for a moment, then seemed to make his mind up.

"Would you take a letter back to Framlingham for me, lad? For my wife's eyes only - and assure her that you saw he hale and hearty? You could take the opportunity to ask her whether Wimer mentioned his land to her yourself."

"Yes, of course, my Lord - with pleasure!"

So it was that Jean found himself mounted on one of the Earl's horses and going back to East Anglia at the Earl's bidding, with a small purse of silver for his trouble; and very glad to be riding away from the poisoned atmosphere at Runnymede.

***

Jean banged on the side of the waggon as it came perilously close to squashing him against the wall.

"Hey! Watch out there!"

The waggoner waved an apologetic hand back at him and steadied his team.

Jean resettled his basket of butchers' hooks and pots of honey on his arm and walked up the market road - carefully - beside the cart. *Not much for me to sell. And that's a good long list that Brother Cellarer has asked for with the profits...* He ran over it again in his head. *Salt. Most important. If I can't get anything else, I must get salt. A cockerel, if there's a good one, now that poor old Chanticleer isn't up to the job any more. Although getting a live cockerel home in one piece isn't going to be any fun... Rope. Enough for 3 or 4 headstalls. And if I can, a treat for the monks' supper tonight. I wonder if that cheese-maker who was here last autumn is back? I really liked his hard, crumbly cheese. It'd be good to know how...*

"You there! Get out of the way!"

His musings were rudely interrupted by a pair of rough-looking fellows wearing the Sheriff's badge, using their horses to shove a path through the crowd of people heading to market. Jean frowned and gave way, then turned in behind them and followed them into the square. A few stallholders had set up already, and were frantically trying to keep people from treading on their wares as the horsemen turned round and round to make themselves some space. *The King's new Sheriff doesn't seem to care how unpopular he is - at least the Earl's men had better manners!*

Finally one of the riders stood in his stirrups, unrolled a short scroll, and bellowed:

"Hear ye! Hear ye! Let all here present know that our Holy Father the Pope, blessed be his name, has declared that the so-called Magna Carta is null, and void of all validity for ever. It is illegal, unjust, harmful to royal rights and shameful to the English people, and should never have been forced onto our Good King John; it was done so by such violence and fear as might affect the most courageous of men." He let the scroll roll up and pumped his free hand in the air. The crowd was silent. "Further, the Earl of Norfolk, Roger Bigod, has been excommunicated for his part in the vile mummery of the Magna Carta, and must be shunned by all God-fearing Christians!" He left his fist raised for a few heartbeats, then they moved out of the square as roughly as they'd rode in.

The crowd was muttering, mostly in support of the Earl. Jean's first thought was not for Roger Bigod himself, but for the pleasant family he'd visited just before the Magna Carta was signed, the Lady Ida - still beautiful despite her years - presiding over a happy melee of grandchildren, and graciously finding time to talk to him - even though she couldn't help. After their chat he'd been invited to a service in the private chapel at Framlingham, and had been impressed by the children's instant conversion to perfect behaviour as they entered the holy space. The glare from the family's formidable chaplain might have had something to do with that, of course... How would that close-knit family react to this terrible punishment imposed on their paterfamilias? He thought back to what the Sheriff's man had said about the Pope's pronouncement. *I saw no sign of violence in Runnymede - and what fear there was, was fear of the King's treachery! I don't believe that the Earl did anything to deserve being excommunicated. How terrible if he should fall ill! I will add my prayers to the Countess', that he gets through this ordeal safely. And pray for her too, poor lady!*

"Are you selling that honey, or waiting until the bees find it and take it back? What are you asking for it? I've no coin, but I could offer you some eggs?"

Around him, the market had reformed. He flushed and attended to his business. At the back of his mind was a growing disgust at the difference between what he'd seen with his own eyes, and what the King's men were saying. Underlying it was a simmering anger at the way the Earl had been treated. *He was the one working for peace! It's the King who's spreading fear...*

***

Jean picked one last stem of mallow then moved

down the clearing, stripping the flower petals as he walked; leaves and stem on one side of the basket, ready to be made into a syrup to ease the last of the winter's coughs, and flowers to the other to add to a salad for tonight's meal. There wasn't much mallow around yet, after the long wet spring, and he was being careful not to pick too much from each clump.

Better get something else for the salad... There was chickweed, of course, but even the hens got bored with that. He picked a handful of hawthorn leaves for the basket and a couple more for himself, and munched as he searched. *Ah! Lime! Excellent.* He leaned across a ditch to pick some of the small, succulent leaves - and froze.

What was that? It sounded big enough to be a boar! The noise had come from a little further up the ditch. Without moving his body, he slowly turned his head. *There! Something brown! If it smells me, I'm a goner!* He looked around for a stout stick. Not that it would do any good against a boar, but he'd feel much better with something in his hands. He spotted one a few steps away and oh! so slowly began to move in that direction, placing each foot with exquisite care so as not to snap a twig. He was almost there when there was another sound.

Hang on! That wasn't a boar!

"H-hello? Is anyone there?"

The groan came again. Quickly he retraced his steps. What he'd mistaken for a boar turned out to be the back of a man lying curled in the ditch.

"Are you all right?" *What a stupid thing to say. Of course he's not all right!*

Jean climbed down into the hollow. The reason for the man's injuries was clear to see - lying half across him was a heavy branch, and there was a nasty-looking bruise on the side of his head. As Jean watched, he groaned once more, raised one hand to his head, and slitted open his eyes. He caught sight of Jean and tried to scramble backwards, crying out as his foot knocked the side of the ditch.

"Hey! It's all right, I won't hurt you! Look, no-one here but me, you're safe." Jean put his back into the job and rolled the branch away. "There. Let me see your head? Ow that looks sore! Can you sit up? Slow, now…"

The man rested his weight on Jean's shoulder and pushed himself upright. As he straightened his leg he cried out again, one hand going to his head, the other reaching for his ankle.

"Whoah! You are in a bad way! Hold on, let's get a compress for your head, then I'll see what's going on at the other end! Stay still… I thought I saw…"

Jean gathered a big handful of comfrey leaves from the bottom of the ditch and folded them into a pad, bruising them a little to make them lie flat.

"Here, hold this to your head. That's it… Now, let's see your ankle?"

The ankle was obviously swollen, and the man winced when Jean very gently rotated it; but it didn't look broken.

"Hmm, not too bad. I think if I bind this up, you could hobble on it. I know where there's a big strong stick you can lean on! Let's get you back to the Priory and have Brother Andrew have a proper look at you."

The man started to shake his head, then moaned. It took him a little while to be able to talk again.

"No! I have to get home! Before the King's men find me!" He pursed his lips and stared at Jean, clearly frightened at his slip.

"Don't worry. We have as little to do with the King and his men as possible! We have to get you back to the Priory; you need more help than I can give you on the road - and if they're looking for you, the sooner we get you there the better!"

The man shut his eyes again and pressed the comfrey to his head.

"Where am I? What priory are you talking about?"

"You're in Dodnash, and I'm talking you to St Mary de Alneto."

"Who's your patron?"

"The Earl of Norfolk."

The man's whole body relaxed. "Praise the Lord! The Earl is my liege too. It's an omen. Yes, I'll come with you. I have a tale your monks will want to hear, in exchange for some food and shelter, then I must be on the move again as soon as possible."

Jean raised his eyebrows, but concentrated on getting the man up and able to walk. *I'll be happier when I have him home safe, and out of sight, if he's one of the Earl's men - and I can't wait to hear his story!*

"What's your name, friend? I am Jean."

The man gasped as his bad foot touched the ground and tightened his grip on the stick.

"Humphrey le Curt." And as Jean looked up at him, wide-eyed - "Yes, yes, it's a bad joke, I know. Come on, where's this priory of yours, before my head splits in two?"

A couple of hours later, Humphrey was looking a lot better. Brother Andrew's willow tea had eased the pain-lines from his face, his foot was propped on a stool under the trestle, and the lump on his head was swathed in a linen bandage. He was well into his tale - and Jean was being kept busy refilling his ale mug.

"...and they just kept coming and coming. There must've been a good couple of thousand of them - ordinary troops, and archers, and even some crossbowmen. We had a few of those ourselves, the Earl wanting to protect his family despite the cost, and we were very glad of them; without them, that flood of men would have simply overwhelmed us. There was only a few of us, anyway - 55 if you count the ladies' chaplain, which you should, Father Ricardo not being someone to cross, if you take my meaning!"

Jean grinned and poured more ale. He'd met the chaplain...

"So there we were, penned in like a stag encircled by hounds, but ready to fight; then a little before Evensong we saw a party of horsemen gallop in to the enemy camp, pennants flying. My lady Mahelt sent her son up to the battlements to see who it was, as having the sharpest eyesight; and I well remember the shiver that went down my spine when the boy called down that there were three gold pards on a red field - it was the King!

Well, that put the cat amongst the pigeons, I can tell you. Everyone had heard about how the King had taken Rochester castle over the winter, and how all its knights were imprisoned and half its fighting men had their hands and feet chopped off when they eventually had to surrender. If mighty Rochester and its huge garrison couldn't hold out, what chance had we? I tell you, it was a long, long night, seeing those hundreds of watch fires burning all around, and imagining the bloodshed that was to come."

He shook his head and reached for a capon leg. The whole room waited breathlessly whilst he chewed…

"So the sun rose, and we could see people stirring amongst the King's tents, out of crossbow range on Pageant Field. Just as the cocks were crowing a herald rode round to the edge of the drawbridge and shouted that the King was mindful to be merciful, knowing that there were only Bigod women and children in the castle, the Earl being known to be with the false pretender in London. If we surrendered, all would be allowed to go free, and the women would be treated with the dignity of their station. But we only had until Prime to make up our minds."

He stopped waving the capon leg and took another bite. Father Lawrence seized the opportunity to ask,

"The false pretender? - that's the French Prince Louis, then?"

Humphrey washed his chicken down with another gulp of ale and nodded.

"Yes. It seems that he's been proclaimed King in London! - but not consecrated. I suppose they have to get him and the Archbishop of Canterbury in the same place before they can do that - and the King, the real King I mean, King John, isn't making it easy; there's plenty who support him still."

Father Lawrence shook his head in amazement.

"What times we live in! Thank you; please carry on telling us what happened in Framlingham."

"So there we were up on the walls, being careful to march past an embrasure as often as we dared to make it seem as though our numbers were more, whilst our betters made their minds up what to do. The ladies and the Constable were shut up in the hall for what seemed like an eternity... At last the Constable stepped out and called us all down into the bailey. Well, men, he said - we're not going to fight the King. There was both cheers and boos at that, but he waved it down until we were all listening to him again. Then he made us line up along the wall opposite the entrance with our arms, take two steps forward, lay all our weapons down, and step back against the wall. Just as the bells began to peal he had us go to both knees, our hands on our heads. The women and children came out of the hall and stood facing the entrance, then the Constable himself cranked the great doors open and lowered the drawbridge to surrender to the King. It was all over without hardly a shot."

He shook his head and buried his face in his hands. Jean shifted from one foot to the other until he could bear it no longer.

"And what happened next? What's happened to the Lady Ida and her family?"

"Ay, sorry. Got lost there for a moment. Well, the King's riders came in first, fast and furious, to be sure we had really given up, I suppose. Then the King himself rode in at the head of a column of knights. The ladies curtsied to him and stayed bent all the while the knights were gathering up our weapons - only when there was a great pile, well guarded, did the King let them up. We were marched past them and sent on our way, but I did overhear the King a little. I think he was telling the ladies that they would be escorted to one of their northern estates - and I do know that little Roger wasn't to go with them, he's being held as a hostage."

There was a murmur in the room. Jean sat heavily on the end of a bench for a moment, remembering the bright hair and quick laughter of the Earl's young grandson. *Pray God he comes to no harm!*

"And so that's the end of my tale, pretty much - I need to get over to my family in Castle Hedingham as soon as possible. I have a nasty feeling that's where the King is going next, and if the Earl of Oxford is stupid enough to try to defend it, it may go badly for the people living around it. If it wasn't for that wayward branch, I might have been there now - I'm very grateful to young Jean here for pulling me out of a ditch, and for your care and hospitality!"

He looked hopefully into the depths of his ale mug, and Jean moved to fill it again. Father Lawrence was on his feet:

"Thank you, Humphrey de Curt, for bringing us this news, sad though it is. Brethren, we may not say Mass for the Earl whilst he is excommunicate; but there's nothing to stop us holding a Service of Intercession to pray for the safety of his family, and especially for young Roger. We will add it to Vespers tonight - so let us now go and complete our daily tasks so that we can convene early in the church."

In turn the monks stood and filed out. Jean placed

the ale jug on the table in front of Humphrey and followed them. His task this day was to check the candles on the altar; he was pleased to have some time alone there to make his own prayers.

***

Everything was the same in the crowded court room - and yet everything was WRONG. Instead of old Roger de Cressey, there was this new Sheriff, dispensing justice in the name of King Louis - even though he still hadn't been consecrated. *I suppose that it's better now that Louis controls all of this part of the country, at least we have some stability. But I wish he wasn't allowing everyone to have their cases retried...*

He glared across at Prior Gilbert of the Holy Trinity, who was looking alarmingly confident. *He's got nothing to lose, I suppose - if the court overturns the original judgement and finds in his favour, he'll be delighted - and if it upholds it, he'll be no worse off. We, on the other hand, have it all to lose - again! It's not fair...*

Father Lawrence was making his way back from the latrine. There was something odd about the way he was walking... Jean tilted his head to watch. Finally he spotted it - Father Lawrence was holding his habit away from his back. *What's happened?* As he drew closer, there was a nasty smell growing too...

"I slipped." He said, curtly, as soon as he got in range.

"Oh no! Are you all right?" The smell was really very bad.

"Yes. Thankyou. But my habit is soaked - I can't

argue the case like this! I'm going to have to leave you to it. Just remember to stick to the arguments that we made last time. Can you manage?"

Jean bowed, not wanting to open his mouth and get more of the stench than was strictly necessary, or giggle. Father Lawrence snorted, shook his head, and left without saying another word. The crowd parted for him like the walls of the Red Sea. Jean swallowed a smile, leaned back against a pillar, and settled in to wait his turn.

The new Sheriff was a man of few words. He seemed to be letting the court officials do all the talking that was necessary, whilst he lolled in his chair looking half asleep. He spoke only once, to contradict a judgement that the clerk had made - and he spoke in French.

Aha! He might understand some English, or he wouldn't have known what to say just then - but he is happier in French! I wonder how comfortable the Prior is in it? Mine is a bit rusty too... He grinned to himself. Probably the last person he'd spent any time talking French to was Maurice, helping him with his pronunciation - and here he was disputing ownership of some of his land. He stopped reminiscing and concentrated, trying to dredge up words from his memory...

The clerk called them up all too soon. Prior Gilbert was asked to put his case first, as Jean knew he would be - the court would follow strict rules of precedence. Jean listened carefully and kept one eye on the Sheriff - who looked like he was following at least some of the argument. Then it was his turn. He took a deep breath and began, his French becoming more fluid with each sentence. The effect on the Sheriff was electrifying - for the first time he was sitting upright, fully engaged.

"Sir, the Prior has represented the case fairly, but he has omitted a fact that you might not be aware of. The custom in these parts - dating back to the time of the Conqueror and beyond - is that the youngest son inherits the land - which changes the complexion of the case somewhat."

The Sheriff held up his hand to stop him, and asked - in French;

"Did I understand you correctly - you practice ultimogeniture? But doesn't that mean that this Wimer was the rightful heir, and so there should be no case to answer?"

"Yes, Sir - exactly so."

The Sheriff turned to the Prior and said, in only slightly broken English -

"Your case is dismissed. And think yourself lucky that I do not fine you for bringing a false claim. In fact - no, I change my mind - for wasting the court's time, I fine you half a mark. See the clerk on your way out."

Jean bowed to the Sheriff, who nodded gravely back before slumping back in his chair for the next case. Jean smiled sweetly at the Prior and left, biting his cheek so as not to laugh at the expression on his face. *Serves him right! Thank you, Wimer, for keeping my French alive!*

Chapter 20

HIS OWN MAN

Jean did a double-take as Father Lawrence walked into the chapter house. He looked... younger, somehow - pink-cheeked, and with his mouth set in a little O of surprise. He was walking as though his feet were barely touching the ground. *He looks happy! What's happened, I wonder?*

Father Lawrence floated to the centre of the room and stood smiling as the monks noticed his demeanour and began to take their seats expectantly. Sooner than Jean would have believed possible, everyone was settled. Still Father Lawrence beamed at them for a while longer, until Jean was ready to scream. Finally he spoke;

"Brethren. A wonderful thing has happened - at least, I hope you think it's wonderful." He looked down modestly. "I've received the letter from the Papal Nuncio..." he carried on talking, but Jean heard nothing more.

We won! Dear Lord in Heaven, we won! How utterly amazing! He beamed around the room himself. Everyone was crowding around Father Lawrence, clapping him on the back and congratulating him. *Hey!*

What about me? I had something to do with it too? No-one was even looking at Jean. He felt about ten years old - it was that same feeling of being outside the community as when he'd first come to the Priory, all those years ago. He swallowed.

Brother Andrew glanced round and saw him standing apart.

"Isn't that grand news, Jean? Father Lawrence made Prior after all this time?"

It was Jean's turn for his mouth to form an 0, and he could feel his cheeks burning with shame. *It never occurred to me that the Nuncio was here to see whether Father Lawrence was up for the job! Well, of course I'm glad for him!*

Belatedly, he went to add his own congratulations.

"Oh, Jean - I forgot, please forgive me - there was more in the letter, I no more than skimmed it, after his pronouncement on me - here, take a look."

He shoved the scroll into Jean's hands and turned back to the monks. Jean stood where he was for a few heartbeats. *I suppose he's deserved it, he's been waiting so long to be confirmed in post, with no guarantee that he'd ever get formal recognition - he could well have had someone imposed over his head.* Jean smiled at his back, then took the scroll to the light.

The first paragraphs were the usual formal salutations. Then there was Father Lawrence's appointment. Finally he got to the interesting bit...

"I have heard depositions from both sides in this dispute, and Battle Abbey have also contributed. It is clear to me that the initial core of Priory lands, as originally constituted by the Founder, Wimer the

Chaplain, is tied to Battle Abbey alone."

Jean closed his eyes and leaned back against the stonework. *Thank heavens for that!* He savoured victory for a moment, then went back to finish the scroll.

"However," *Oh no! He's put a rider on it!* "However, I find that subsequent lands granted to the Priory in the parish of Bentley are subject to the tithe of the Priory of the Holy Trinity in Ipswich. As it is not possible to split the Priory into its original and accreted parts, on account of the small amounts of land involved - neither parcel would be viable alone - I decree that Dodnash Priory must relocate its buildings to the meadow land pertaining to Bentley, so that the tithe from the original farmland may be paid to Battle Abbey, and the souls of the Priory servants can be unambiguously the responsibility of the Holy Trinity Priory. Dated this day…"

Jean re-read it. *Move the Priory? What a mad idea. And to the meadow below the wood! It floods every year. If you had to choose the worst possible place to put a priory, that meadow would be a contender.* He closed his eyes and shook his head. *And we have no choice - this carries the same weight as if the Pope himself had said it! Well. I suppose we'll have to make the best of it.* He looked over at the new Prior. *Now might be the best possible time to tell him. When he's still glowing from his elevation…*

It took the monks three or four days to reach consensus on the judgement. It was pretty much the only conversation during that time, but eventually they reached the same conclusion that Jean had - that they had no choice. The worry turned to how on earth they were going to manage it. Through it all, Prior Lawrence remained serene. Finally he pointed out that there was no hurry; the Nuncio had failed to set a deadline for the work...

***

She left the slop abandoned on the table where Maurice had slammed his cup and went to the door. She drew her shawl tight against her breasts and leaned her head against the frame. Her stomach felt so twisted that it was difficult to get her breathing... *He was really insistent this time. I'm running out of options!* She stared at the greens and browns of the forest, unseeing. It was the pain in her forefinger where she'd been twisting the same piece of tassel over and over again that brought her back to herself. She angrily shook the finger to get some blood into it and pushed herself upright.

The ale had left a dark stain on the table, and she scrubbed and scrubbed until even the memory of it was gone. Finally she threw the cloth into the wash bucket and stood upright, hugging herself. *What am I going to do? Maurice is getting more and more pushy. I don't think he'll force me out of the house until he has a bride himself, whatever he said earlier, but that can't be long - and if he can find a priest who will marry me without my consent, or if he pays the fee to petition m'lord Bigod to find me a husband, I'm done for anyway...*

She moved over to the door and leaned against the post again, this time allowing the sounds of the trees to soothe her. *I don't know if I'll ever want a man to bed me again…* she shuddered. *All those soldiers… And the King! I'm glad he died of the flux. I hope it was a most bloody and painful death!* Her fingers were wound up in her shawl again. Carefully, she loosened them and bellied the shawl out and around her. Her fingers tightened into a fist. *I don't want anyone to touch me ever again without me saying they can. Ever!* She thumped the door frame for emphasis.

The barn owl floated across the foot of the clearing, wings starkly white against the shadows. *And I don't want to be locked up like a nun, either. I want to be free - I want to choose my own path! I think. I'd be safe from men in a nunnery? - but what if someone nice does come along, and I've shut myself up behind a wall?*

She turned inside and started preparing her evening meal.

Besides, my little nest-egg wouldn't buy me a place of ease in any nunnery, I'd have to go in as a servant - so why bother? I could do what Brother Anthony suggested and buy a corrody from the Priory with it, live in a little shack belonging to the Priory somewhere… although they're none too safe themselves, with the Holy Trinity still circling like buzzards, even after all Jean has won for them.

The turnips were softened and beginning to colour, so she absent-mindedly took the handful of washed greens and began to cut fine slices against her thumb, letting them fall into the pan.

What I should do, of course - what everybody thinks I should do - is to find some nice man who'll look after me. Just like William, who beat me whenever he could. The slices were getting bigger. *Or that slime-ball from the court, with his hands all over me…* She nicked her thumb and sucked it, before the blood fell in the pot. *Maurice thinks I should go for Abel from Brantham, with his one black tooth, and breath like a foetid blow* - her knife was moving dangerously fast again - *or Elfnoth from Bluestones farm, with his hands and face always covered in pustules. If he touched me, I'd die - or kill him!* She ripped the last bits of leaves in two and threw them in the pan. *No. Just no.*

She stirred absent-mindedly for a minute or two, then took a cloth and lifted the pan off the fire. She dolloped a spoonful of pease pottage from the cauldron into a bowl and topped it with the turnip mix, then went to sit in the doorway to eat. Some of the chickens were already in the coop, the rest murmuring to themselves and catching the last of the sun's warmth.

"So, chicks - we're decided, then! All my choices are bad. I don't want to marry anyone that Maurice has picked out - and I have to be out of this house soon. I don't want to be a nun. I could buy a corrody, but then I might be turned out on my ear if the Holy Trinity gets its way; then I'd lose everything. I tried buying my freedom, and I didn't have enough money - although I did hear that the Earl got rid of the last steward for taking bribes. I've got to do something, chicks, or you and I both will be out of a home! Well, not you, maybe, but it wouldn't be me giving you a handful of grain at bedtime! Come on, girls, in you go…"

She secured the coop door and stood enjoying the soft chirrups coming from within. *Living on Priory land wouldn't be too bad - if it was on my terms, and I wasn't going to be married off at someone else's will! Maybe I should have one more go at buying the freedom to choose my own husband, if there's a more honest man at the Earl's court now; and I could go and talk to Brother Anthony tomorrow about what jobs the Priory might need doing in exchange for renting somewhere. Perhaps I could make some simples for them, or all their ale, or something. At least I'd be trying to help myself, not just waiting for the axe to fall!*

***

Jean was in Brantham, checking the Priory's salt workings. The last of the salt had been gathered up some weeks ago, and Brother Cellarer had asked him to check that the lead pans and brine pits were sound enough to withstand the winter's storms. He had soldered a couple of repairs to the huge pans, but now the early dusk had driven him away. His pony was laden with one pan that was beyond repair, slung over the saddle to be melted down at the Priory, so he trudged wearily up the hill beside it.

He had seen the barge earlier, flying the Earl's colours, but had thought nothing of it. Here, though, coming up the hill behind him were riders bearing the same pennant. Sure enough, as they cantered up to him the Earl was at their head.

"God give you a good evening, my Lord!" he called after them.

A little to his surprise, the leaders wheeled round and rode back to him.

"Who's there?" called the Earl, then as he got closer, "Ah! Jean! Well met. I'm on my way to the priory, to pay my respects to the new Prior. Are you committed to getting that nag home yourself, or would you like one of my men to take it, and borrow a horse?"

So it was that Jean found himself sweeping down the broad pasture to the Priory in the midst of half a dozen of the Earl's retainers. He dismounted first and was busy helping the new stable boy with the mounts when the Earl pulled him away.

"Come down with me, Jean - in truth, it's partially because I want to talk to you that I'm here."

Jean's voice squeaked, even in his head. *Me?! He wants to talk to me?* He said nothing, in case it sounded like that out loud.

The monks were boiling out of the main buildings as they drew near, apprehensive at first then relaxing as they recognised the Earl. Brother - no, Prior - Lawrence made his way through them.

"Ah, there's the man of the moment!" called the Earl. "Congratulations at last - it's about time!"

"Thank you, my Lord - I'm aware that it couldn't have happened without your sponsorship, and I'm very grateful."

"Aye, well. You can thank young Jean here for that." The Earl clapped him on the shoulder, laughing aloud at his expression. "Don't look so surprised, man - you reminded me of my duty to the Priory when you turned up at Runnymede last summer. I had the opportunity to talk to the Nuncio one day at dinner. Without your presence, the Prior here might have had to wait a lot longer to be confirmed in office. But talking of dinner - may my men and I join you at prayer and the evening meal, Prior? Once the moon has risen, there should be enough light to pick our way over to Ipswich, we won't impose on your hospitality further."

"But of course! Our pleasure..." and the Prior led the way inside.

Again to his surprise, the Earl had pulled Jean into the conversation as soon as he had served the first round of ale to the top table.

"Stay, Jean - tell me, Prior; the Nuncio led me to believe that he had reached a conclusion on the matter of your dispute with the Holy Trinity - have you heard his judgement there, too?"

"Yes indeed." The Prior frowned. "It's a little puzzling, but we will of course comply. He instructs us to move the Priory buildings in their entirety over to a rather wet meadow below Dodnash Wood, in order that we are properly in Bentley parish. One of the Holy Trinity's issues was that the Priory servants should go to Ipswich on the four holy festivals, as the Bentley people do, but the East Bergholt people do not. I must admit, I'm in no hurry to begin building - the work can only be carried out in the driest of summers, in any case."

The Earl turned to Jean. "Ah, this is the land you've now twice defended against the Holy Trinity? Good job you can hold your own in a courtroom - if you were being forced to move onto land owned by the Holy Trinity, there's no doubt that they would force you into becoming a daughter house. As it is, you've preserved your independence."

Jean smiled his thanks at the Earl, and rose to fill his

ale cup. The Earl waved his hand for him to keep his seat.

"It was your clear head under pressure - and your ability to read and write - that made me decide to divert here this evening - as well, of course, as taking the opportunity to congratulate the Prior here."

He raised his mug in a toast, noticed it empty, and reached for the jug himself.

"Are you under any vows here, Jean?"

Jean shook his head wonderingly. *What does he have in mind for me?*

"No, Lord."

"Good." He turned to the Prior. "I don't know how fast news gets to you here - you must have heard that Sir William Marshal has come out of retirement to be Regent until young King Henry reaches his majority?"

The Prior nodded.

"But you may not know of his plans to reissue the Magna Carta?"

The Prior raised his eyebrows.

"I had assumed that document was dead and buried - the late Pope was certainly very much against it! Wasn't that the cause of your excommunication?"

The Earl frowned in remembrance.

"Indeed. But now both King John and His Holiness Innocent are dead, and the barons have united behind King Henry to repel the French threat, Pope Honorius has been persuaded to withdraw the Papal opposition. And the Regent recognises the Charter's use as a curb on any future overreaching King."

He paused for a gulp of ale.

"The Marshal is a very old man, although praise

God, hale and hearty. But he is keenly aware of the long years before King Henry can rule in his own right, and wants to reissue the Magna Carta as a defence against any possible abuse by a regent who might be more interested in his purse than the Kingdom's best interests."

He drained his mug and turned again to Jean.

"And that's where you come in, if you're minded, Jean. I have a personal stake in several of the Charter's clauses - and both my son and I are charged with implementing the Charter. I need someone who can argue my corner as the Marshal's men redraw the terms of it. The job would require you to travel frequently around, from the Marshal's court to mine, wherever I may be. You'd need to leave the Priory - what say you? Does that appeal?"

His words fell into one of those odd silences that can suddenly occur in a room full of people. Jean fixed his eyes on the table and wished the earth would swallow him, sure that every eye in the room was waiting for his response. Still Prior Lawrence had said nothing, although the noise levels around them were back to normal. Finally Jean could bear it no longer and glanced up at him.

To his surprise, the Prior was staring at the table too, looking sad and older, somehow. He might have felt Jean's gaze, because he looked up and met his eyes - then to Jean's utter astonishment, leaned over and put his hand on top of Jean's.

"I am afraid that I've failed you, my son - allowed my own problems and insecurities to overcome my duty of care to you."

He shook his head and turned to the Earl.

"I beg your indulgence, my Lord, whilst I pass on some news to Jean, here - it has a bearing on your question to him. Indeed, I ask that you give him some time to answer you?"

The Earl looked intrigued and waved his hand for Prior Lawrence to continue. Lawrence turned back to Jean.

"I see now that I've been over-harsh, and made your postulancy more of a trial that it needed to be. I may have soured your view of the church by an excess of zeal. Father Adam warned me of it, and I didn't listen. If your service to the Church is lost, I will regret it all my days. And there's one more sin to add to my tally; I got a letter concerning your father more than a week ago, and I have been delaying telling you of it."

His voice cracked a little, and he reached for his ale mug.

My father! Has he been found?

The Prior put his mug down and Jean automatically reached for the jug to fill it. Lawrence put out his hand to stop him and turned to face him fully.

"Nay, lad. You need to know the contents of this letter, and then I counsel you to go and pray. Your father has been found, Jean - but too late to save him. Your father's factor writes that a man from your village came across him in Sicily many months ago, sick unto death from a fever, and could do nothing for him other than to see that he had a Christian burial. The factor had a premonition that something had happened and wrote to the Priory as your last known address some time ago, begging me to send the letter on if you had left our care, so that you could make proper arrangement for your father's lands. I wrote back at the time and confirmed that you were a postulant here, under no vows. Your father's lands are of course yours now, and you will need to make some provision for them, even if only to confirm your father's factor in his post."

Jean must have looked as dazed as he felt, because the Prior leaned over to grasp his shoulder.

"Go, lad - you need make no decisions now. Go to church and pray for guidance. You are relieved of all other duties."

Jean frowned at him, and looked across to the Earl. He was nodding vigorously.

"Aye, Jean - go and ponder on it! And my condolences for the loss of your father; I know you've been apart from him these many years, but still it is a loss."

Somehow that last command got him on his feet and stumbling backward over the bench. Hardly knowing what he was doing, he left the refectory, only remembering to turn and bow at the door. Both the Prior and the Earl were looking after him, identical worried expressions on their faces; he thought that in any other circumstance he would have laughed.

He started off in the church, but the bright colours on the walls and the strong scent of incense were just too much. He made for the place he loved most, the old oak stump on the ridge line. For a long time he simply sat there, clutching his knees, looking out over the green peace. Finally something like coherent thought returned to him.

I want to travel. I've seen so little of the world… what's beyond that hill, and the one behind that? And now I can. He shook his head in bemusement. *Two ways! I could work for the Earl, and play a part in his great undertaking; or I can go to France and take over my father's concerns.* He tried to remember anything about his father's business and came up with a complete blank. *Something about soap?* Even his father's face was unclear in his mind. He could remember the house quite well, warm brown stone with a view over green slopes down to a river. He got to his feet and started to pace. *This morning my biggest worry was whether I could get fish out from the main pond without getting mud on my habit! I'll be glad to be back in hose and tunic…*

He stopped abruptly in the act of standing up, and instead leaned back against the stump again. *Huh! I seem to have decided to leave!*

He remembered the letter and reached over to where he'd dropped it. He scanned it; the contents were just as the Prior had described. Then he got to almost the last sentence and blinked. He frowned at it, and read it again.

"I have been reinvesting the moneys from the estate over the years into buying land and a few mills, and renting them out; the income from these rentals, and from the sale of produce from the home farm, is around 80 marks per annum. A full accounting is ready for Jean's perusal…"

He let the parchment fall into his lap again and whistled softly. *Good Lord, I'm rich!*

The view beneath him was lovely as ever, the small whitewashed church set against the vivid green meadows, with woodland behind. The dormitory block was screening the cloister, so he couldn't see Wimer's resting place. *Ah, old friend - more father to me than my real father ever was - I shall miss you! But I can always come and visit.* He stood and started to walk slowly down the hill. *So - France, or England? The Earl, or my duty to my father's tenants? Wow. I could even get married...* An image of Edeva flashed into his mind, and he shook his head. *I wish... but no chance.* The bell was ringing for a service, and he watched as a monk walked rapidly from the beehives to the church. Without feeling the slightest guilt at missing the service, he bypassed the church and went to sit on the cloister wall near Wimer's grave.

What do you think, Wimer? I like the Earl, and trust him - and I don't know a single soul in France. I'm not even sure who my overlord is. And what an opportunity the Earl is offering me, to travel, to see the land - to be trusted with a part in such a great undertaking! I might be able to meet the great William Marshall, perhaps even the new boy-King! He leaped off the wall and smacked his fist into his hand. *I choose to serve the Earl! France will always be there. I'll write to - my! - factor in the morning.*

Behind him he could hear the monks leaving the church. Some would come to the cloister, to enjoy the last warmth of the sun... He ran to the far wall and leaped over it, then trotted round the long way to the church to avoid them all. Now at last he needed to pray - to offer to God the upswelling of joy in his heart.

***

Edeva was so relieved to get out of the courtroom, for all that it meant more delay. It was terribly stuffy and hot in there, bodies crammed together... *Perhaps I should have risked leaving it a month or two more - given the Earl's sheriff a bit more time to sort things out after the French had taken themselves of English soil.* She certainly hadn't been expecting the Earl to be here himself, and with him a whole slew of people trying to petition him directly.

She walked over to the well. Someone had left a bit of water in the bucket, and she scooped it up gratefully, thankful not to have to draw up a new bucketful herself. She turned and leaned against the well coping to watch the bustle. There were almost no other women visible - the crowd seemed to be all younger men. Certainly that had been true of the court cases she'd listened to. They had all been men who had come into an inheritance during the last years of King John's reign, and were eager to reassert their fealty to the Earl now the King was safely dead and couldn't impose the kind of punitive taxes he'd been making everyone pay before he met his end. It helped of course that the Earl's place was assured even though he'd supported the French, thanks to his relationship with the Regent.

She supposed that in some ways it was fair to make her wait. Every one of these gentlemen outranked her socially, and their estates provided livelihoods for many souls. Her own bid for the ability to choose her own husband, or none at all, was simply not important to the smooth running of the countryside. *Only important for my own peace of mind - once I've paid the fine, I'll be safe from the lot of them...*

And suitors were circling round, like mangy old buzzards. However useful she was around the house and on the land, Maurice wouldn't turn down any more offers for her. He'd made that clear. *I HAVE to buy my freedom - either that or give in and take one of his choices...* Her stomach turned over at the idea.

People were turning and going back inside. The court must be restarting. She took a last sip from the dipper. *Whatever it takes, I must keep going until I have my freedom!*

Jean heard the bell begin to chime for Vespers from two fields away and squeezed his new palfrey into a trot, enjoying the mare's smooth gait. Sir Roger would likely have timed the court to finish just before the bell. *I can hear the service, settle in my mind exactly what I want to say, and give him a precise briefing on the two competing clauses. Then I can stay on for the evening meal. Perfect timing!*

The bell stopped as he dismounted and handed his reins to a stable boy. He walked briskly to the church, reaching it just as the doors were closing.

As ever, the perfume of the censer comforted him, and he closed his eyes - blind from the sunshine outside anyway - to pray. When he had finished, he glanced around. The small church was crowded. Clearly the court had only just ended, or perhaps was still running. The air was close, uncomfortably so after his ride, and he was hot in his shirt and jerkin.

The bell rang for the elevation of the host. As though it was a signal, the woman in front of him collapsed. He caught her awkwardly under the arms. Unseen hands helped him drag her backwards the short distance outside, then closed the door behind him. She was beginning to stir, and he manoeuvred her until she was sat on a stone trough in the courtyard, head bent over her knees.

He was glad enough to get out of the church himself and drew in great lungfuls of air unsullied by packed humanity, hovering in case the woman needed more assistance. Finally she raised her head a little and he got a glimpse of her face.

"Edeva!"

"Jean! I'm so sorry to be a trouble, but I haven't eaten anything since…" she waved her hand, unable to remember.

"No, no - no trouble at all. Are you feeling better now? Stay there, don't get up."

He took her hand and sat himself, tugging her back down next to him. She looked into his eyes, startled - and he forgot to breathe, deafened to all around him, all his boyish yearning for her now transformed into something much deeper and stronger. She gazed back, eyes dark and wide, for an eternity… With an effort he looked away.

"Well, hunger is a problem I can do something about."

He became aware that he was still holding her hand, and leaped to his feet without releasing her. He bowed low and kissed the back of her hand.

"Madam. Be so kind as to accompany me to a shady

bower I know of and allow me to test my influence over the kitchen." *Shut up, you fool, stop babbling…*

She stood without repossessing her hand. She heard nothing of his speech as he half walked, half danced in front of her, the skin-to-skin contact from their hands sending thrills all through her. She was very much aware of the play of muscles in his back, the curl of his hair, the length of his calf. *Why have I never looked at him properly before? When did he become so handsome? …and he's kind…* He led her to a shady seat on a tree-trunk, and once again kissed the back of her hand before solemnly depositing her hand in her lap.

He walked backward for a few steps, then turned to complete his kitchen-raiding mission. As soon as his eye contact broke she lifted her hand to her lips and pressed where his lips had rested. *Would he want me? He's no money, of course, except what the Earl gives him, but that doesn't matter - my own little nest-egg would be enough to set us up in a little cottage somewhere. And he's in favour with the Earl. I could ask Maurice to go and talk to him - he'd be pleased, at least! Oh Jean. Come and hold my hand again.*

Suddenly the failure of the court to hear her case - mattered not a jot.

The End

AUTHOR'S NOTE

If you look up Dodnash Priory on the map, you'll find it marked as an Ancient Monument in a meadow below Dodnash Wood. The Ancient Monuments website shows the map:

https://ancientmonuments.uk/104204-dodnash-priory-site-of-bentley#.Xd6lbuj7RqQ

What the map view doesn't give you a good idea of is the feel of the land – how the stream valley floods with the first rain of the winter and stays waterlogged or frozen all winter long. It's too wet even for the sheep who inhabit it during the summer; they're moved to higher ground, leaving the ducks undisturbed.

It is without doubt the site of the priory – today there's only one chunk of flint aggregate, fallen on its side; but I've seen aerial photographs from an exceptionally dry summer that showed very clearly the layout of cloisters, a dormitory wing, and the church.

Why on earth you'd want to build a priory there has been a puzzle that has occupied me for years – and once I had discovered the first site of Dodnash Priory – described in the predecessor to this book, Sheriff and Priest – the mystery only deepened. What could possibly have made the prior and canons move from the perfect spot that Wimer had chosen for them?

My frown got worse as I did some reading in the

Suffolk Record Office; they'd been ordered to do so by the Pope! Why did the Pope even know about this tiny little priory in the heart of the Suffolk countryside, let alone bother to make them move?

The research took about three years, and I still hadn't figured it all out. Then one of the local landowners banged on my door and asked if I'd like to read some of his early manorial records? The implications of a pencilled note inside the cover – "Ultimogeniture practiced here" – was the final piece of the puzzle…

I've taken some small liberties with the historical timeline; I've conflated news of Pope Innocent's rejection of the Magna Carta in August 1215 (news reached England in September) with Roger Bigod's excommunication in December.

The Holy Trinity prior - Gilbert - was actually the Ipswich Peter & Paul Priory's prior. The Holy Trinity's Prior at the time was probably another William, too many Williams around already!

Jean, Edeva, and Goda are imaginary; Wimer, Maurice, William, and Prior Adam are all real, as of course are Roger Bigod and the other local barons, as well as King John, the Papal Nuncio, the various Sheriffs, and others of the great and good.

The bulla from Pope Innocent lll telling Dodnash Priory to move over to Bentley was dated 21st March

1215. The Magna Carta was signed on 15th June that year. Clearly the negotiations were a bit boring...

If you've enjoyed this book, please leave a review on Amazon – just a sentence or two is fine. They help a lot!

If you'd like to have a copy of the timeline of the early years of Dodnash Priory, and the momentous events happening around them, I'm giving one away if you sign up to my newsletter. You'll also get a bonus 12th century steampunk short story, in which Bad King John features again – as well, of course, as being the first to know news of the next book!

More details at nickymoxey.com

Thank you for reading,
Nicky.